COLUMBO:
THE HOFFA CONNECTION

WILLIAM HARRINGTON

A TOM DOHERTY ASSOCIATES BOOK
NEW YORK

COLUMBO: THE HOFFA CONNECTION

Copyright © 1995 by MCA Publishing Rights, a Division of MCA, Inc.
A novel by William Harrington
Based on the Universal Television series COLUMBO
Created by Richard Levinson & William Link

Cover art by Dan Gonzalez

A Forge Book
Published by Tom Doherty Associates, Inc.
175 Fifth Avenue
New York, N.Y. 10010

Forge® is a registered trademark of Tom Doherty Associates, Inc.

ISBN: 0-812-55078-1

First edition: July 1995
First mass market edition: August 1996

Printed in the United States of America

0 9 8 7 6 5 4 3 2 1

Note to Reader

PART ONE

ONE

An exuberant crowd filled the Hollywood Bowl early, a whole hour before the show was scheduled to begin. The promoters had sold every seat. All day the rumor had circulated that someone had counterfeited thousands of tickets and that some holders of genuine tickets would arrive to find their seats taken. The counterfeit tickets didn't appear, but four thousand people showed up without tickets, naïvely supposing they could buy them at the door. They milled around outside, grumbling. Some of them accosted people approaching the gates with tickets in their hands, offering fifty dollars—even a hundred—for a ticket. A few people with tickets called for bids.

A hundred uniformed police officers were on special duty outside and inside. Sergeant Ed Dugan, LAPD, working inside, spotted a fistfight and rushed in to break it up. He separated two young men, one with a bloody nose, and ordered them to sit down and be quiet.

"Hey, Sarge, how come you didn't make a collar there?" an officer asked him.

"Are you kiddin'?" Dugan replied. "If I made a collar, I'd have to take those guys to the station. Hell, man, whatta ya think? I'd miss the concert!"

The officer looked up at the sky. "Well, we got Regina weather," he remarked.

The legend was that rain never fell on a Regina concert. Actually, it had rained on the night of a Miami concert—and the night after, too—compelling the promoters to cancel and refund the ticket money because they had booked their megastar for a performance in London the following night. But rain had never postponed a Regina concert in Los Angeles, and never in New York.

The sun set. The sky darkened. Then suddenly at 7:30 it was alight again with scores of red, white, and blue laser beams crisscrossing above the Bowl. Instantly a crashing sound filled the Bowl: a computer-generated mélange of rhythms and tones such as no musical instruments had ever made.

Six dancers pranced onto the stage: three male, three female, three black, three white, each with a beautiful physique and a handsome face. The white dancers wore sheer black body stockings, the black dancers white ones. Every feature of their bodies was dimly visible in the low stage lighting and distinctly visible when hit by the brilliant flashes of strobe lights. They danced barefoot, an athletic and acrobatic performance.

After two or three minutes the dancers slowed and danced a sinuous and erotic ballet routine. Then the three young women jumped on the men's backs and rode piggyback and giggling as the men trotted offstage.

The crowd stood and roared.

"AND NOW . . . LADIES . . . AND . . . GENTLE-MEN! *REGINA*!"

A thick curtain of smoke rose in front of the stage. A wall of crisscrossed red laser beams formed a backdrop. Strobes flashed on the smoke. The computer-generated cacophony rose to an ear-blasting crescendo, and abruptly the curtain of smoke disappeared, sucked away by powerful fans.

Regina stood in the center of the stage. The audience, on its feet, howled, stamped, screeched, whooped, clapped. She smiled and bowed.

Regina was a young woman in her late twenties, of medium stature, busty, long-legged, and with a bit of a belly that swelled slightly over the waistband of the black bikini panties that were part of her costume. She wore also a strapless bra, a garter belt that supported fishnet stockings, and shoes with stiletto heels. Her shoulder-length hair was straw blond, bleached to the point of brittleness—it was in fact a wig. Her thin, plucked eyebrows were dark brown, as were her eyes. She wore an overall makeup that lightened her skin to almost white, but her lipstick was flaming red.

She clutched a wireless microphone in her right hand and belted out her signature opening line:

> You wouldn't call your crotch va-jeena.
> So don't call me Ra-jeena.
> I'm . . . RAY-GINE-A!
> An' we're gonna have a *hell* of a time!
> Ho-ho!
> One hell of a, hell of a time!

The music erupted into a frenzy, and so did she. She strutted around the stage, singing a song about dancing. The lyrics clearly had two meanings—and the second meaning was not dance, but copulation. Her voice was shrill. She threw her head back and forth, and the hair of her wig swung wildly.

The main stage lights dimmed gradually, and more and more Regina was visible only in the sharp bursts of the strobes, which flashed twice a second now. She turned her back, pulled down her bikini panties, and strutted around showing her bare bottom.

Her six dancers came onstage again, now in identical bright red leotards cut high on their hips, and backed up her frenetic dancing and singing with a vigorous routine.

Regina stalked across the stage, ran across the stage, stalked across the stage, all the while clutching the microphone close to her mouth and muttering, murmuring, or shrieking the lyrics that ranged from risqué to crude—but remained carefully on the edge of obscene and never crossed that line.

She tossed the microphone aside and danced. The backup dancers left her alone on the stage. With the main lights out, she danced in the light of one red strobe. The duration of its flashes diminished. Their frequency increased. It gave her performance the character of a flickering silent movie. Then the intensity diminished. Staring at Regina in the quick, short bursts of strobe light, the audience could not tell for sure whether or not she had lowered her bikini panties and was dancing with her crotch exposed. Most chose to believe she was, and they stood and yelled.

They were already happy, and what they had seen was not even half the show. They knew there would be no intermission. A Regina show was nonstop, for two hours and fifteen minutes. Her shows built to a climax, then slacked off a little, then built to another peak. All of them.

2

At 10:00 a silvery Rolls-Royce entered the driveway of Regina's estate in Beverly Hills. Although cars crowded the narrow lane bumper-to-bumper, space had carefully been left for the Rolls to glide through unimpeded; and it stopped only at the front door to the sprawling Spanish-style mansion. Before the chauffeur could come around to open the door, Regina opened it and flung herself impatiently from the car, stark naked.

Without the blond wig, she exposed her hair: dark brown and brush cut. Her skin gleamed with sweat. Speaking to no one, she strode through the house and out the back door to the swimming pool, where she threw herself off the edge and into the water. She floundered. People gathered around the pool as she thrashed and struggled and gradually made her way across the pool to the opposite side. Breathless and sputtering, she reached up and accepted a glass from Johnny, her houseboy, a handsome dark-visaged young man. She drank. Straight gin, no ice.

Her guests gathered around her, none of them surprised to see her naked, most of them anxious to have a look at her—or, as it was for many of them, another look.

The guests were mostly young people. Only two or three of the men wore jackets. The others wore bright-colored slacks and golf shirts. Two wore shorts. Most of the women were determinedly young—that is, afraid to age, afraid to lose whatever it was they prized. A few of them wore chic minidresses. The rest were in slacks or jeans, mostly with T-shirts—three wore skimpy halters.

The pool was kidney-shaped, forty feet long from end

to end. At its widest point, it was some twenty-five feet from side to side. A diving board was mounted at the wide end. Three palm trees stood in the pool area, which was embraced by the two wings of the house. Other subtropical shrubbery shielded the pool from curious fans who might approach the fence.

Regina climbed out of the pool. Johnny handed her a terry robe. She pulled it on. He handed her a cigarette and snapped a lighter for her.

"Oh, Maude, for God's sake!" she exclaimed to a middle-aged woman who stood a little back, smiling faintly and watching. "You got any idea how tough it is being me?" Off the stage, the famous star spoke slightly accented English. She walked over to the woman. "You know?" she repeated.

Maude Ahern nodded. "I do know, dear," she said. "You may believe I do."

Maude Ahern was a free-lance writer, a stout woman who should have eschewed the tight designer jeans she was wearing. She had done a sketch of Regina in *Rolling Stone,* another in *New York Magazine,* and was working on one for *Vanity Fair.* She was a self-proclaimed lesbian, and rumors had circulated that her respectful—even affectionate—treatment of Regina in her writing was in part because at one time they had been lovers.

"Oh, God, Mickey," Regina said to a gaunt, ugly young man who came up to her and Maude. "Pronounce judgment."

Mickey Newcastle grinned at her. "First-rate," he said. "Tomorrow we'll go over it, and I'll give you some ideas to make it top-notch."

"Wherever do you collect your clichés, Mickey?" asked Maude.

Regina kissed Mickey. "Thank you, lover," she said. "I can always depend on you."

He walked away, and Maude said to Regina, "I'll never understand how you can plant a kiss on that unkempt, unwashed, pimply wretch."

"He was a big star in his day," said Regina.

"Yes. In the days when unkempt, unwashed, pimply wretches with crooked yellow teeth were the idols of British rock."

"Meow, Maude!"

Maude laughed. She lifted an eyebrow. "You didn't show it tonight, did you? Not really. *I* saw the little black G-string under the panties."

Regina laughed louder. "Leave a girl *some* secrets."

"A girl who walks through her party in her altogethers hardly has any secrets," said Maude.

Regina stuck out her tongue at Maude, dropped her robe, and trotted over to the pool to jump in again.

A few feet away, Christie Monroe watched angrily. She had been close enough to overhear most of the conversation between Regina and Maude; and as she watched Regina splash in the pool, she was unable to conceal her contempt entirely.

"A real class act," she murmured to Bob Douglas, nodding at the naked Regina thrashing around in the pool.

"Watch it," Douglas cautioned her. "She's still the source of our bread." He took Christie's hand and squeezed it.

Christie Monroe was a far more beautiful young woman than Regina: genuinely blond, with fine, smooth hair to her shoulders, soft features, wide blue eyes. The tiny flared skirt of her white minidress displayed her long, shapely legs; and its bold décolletage showed off her high, firm breasts. She was one of the six dancers who worked behind Regina.

Bob Douglas was a handsome man. He bore a distinct resemblance to the late Rock Hudson. He wore soft stone-washed jeans and a white golf shirt. A gold chain hung around his neck, suspending something inside his shirt. Everyone who knew him knew what it was: a smaller-size replica of his Olympic gold medal, won for ski jumping. He was almost never without it.

Mickey Newcastle approached them. "What time can you be over to the Bowl tomorrow?" he asked Bob.

"I don't know. Whatcha have in mind?"

"I think there are two or three places where we ought to go over the sound," said Newcastle. "It's first-rate now, but I'd like it to be top-notch."

"You want me to reprogram some?"

"Maybe a little. Can we experiment a bit?"

"Sure," said Bob.

Newcastle started to turn away, but he paused and grinned at Christie. He pointed at her half-empty glass of Scotch. "Take it a little easy on that, dear," he said. "You're looking a little wobbly, and I wouldn't want you to fall in the pool."

"Or jump in," she said.

When Newcastle had moved away, Christie snorted. "*He's* going to monitor my drinking? That cokehead! Did you catch his eyes? Already dilated. He's been out and copped some speedball. He'll be blind before the night's over."

"But she still listens to him," said Bob. "Don't get on his bad side."

"I don't know how long I wanta work behind the bitch."

"Well, I know how long *I* want to work for her," Bob said. "As long as possible. I couldn't make this kind of money anywhere else. And neither could you."

"Don't you resent what she did to you, even a little bit?" Christie asked.

"Of course I resent her. But you should understand how much the money soothes my hurt feelings."

Christie tipped her glass and finished her Scotch. "You know, she really flashed it tonight. She wasn't wearing the little black patch under her panties."

Bob shrugged. "She could appear starkers and get away with it," he said. "The place was swarming with cops. If they'd wanted to raise hell about her, they could have done it." He grinned. "They enjoyed it just as much as anybody."

Regina climbed out of the pool again, where Joshua and Barbara Gwynne were standing. Johnny did not appear with her robe, but she didn't care. She accepted a cigarette from Barbara and a light from Joshua.

The Gwynnes were owners of Joshua Records, the company that recorded and sold discs of Regina performances. In their fifties, they were probably the oldest people at the party. Joshua was a nondescript, balding man who kept his remaining hair dark with Grecian Formula. Barbara was a polished, elegant woman— made so by the careful attentions of cosmeticians and coiffeurs.

"Couple of good tracks in the new show," Joshua said.

Regina nodded. "Hey, is that a nice fresh martini you've got there? Would you mind letting me drink that one?"

"Gonna cut those tracks with us?" Barbara asked as her husband handed the star his drink.

Regina smiled and slapped Barbara's arm. "Sure," she said airily. She shrugged. "I'm not sure how well that new sound of Bob's will play on discs, are you? I guess that's a problem for Joshua Records, huh?" She turned. "Hey, Johnny. Thought you'd never catch up with me." She reached for the white terry robe.

"It isn't easy," said Johnny.

Regina laughed. She took Johnny by the arm and walked off. Over her shoulder, she said, "Hey, thanks for the drink." Then she spoke to Johnny, but the Gwynnes could hear it—"Hell, I'm thanking Josh for my own gin!"

"Whatta you wanta bet he's something more than a houseboy?" Barbara said to Joshua.

"Never mind," Joshua said grimly. "What I'd like to know is if she really means she'll cut those new tracks with us."

"You can't trust her. You know that."

"I will never understand what the public sees in her," said Joshua quietly. "She can't sing. She can't dance. She's a no-talent vulgar whore."

"And how many millions of discs have we sold?" asked Barbara. "Look at this crowd. How many people are here who don't live off her? No talent? She's possessed of a *hell* of a talent: the greatest talent for self-promotion that either of us has ever seen. And something else. Name me somebody with a greater talent for manipulating people. What Regina wants, Regina gets—from everybody."

"Yeah. Poor Maude Ahern—"

"Are you kidding? 'Poor' Maude? She got a million-dollar advance for an 'authorized' biography of Regina."

"If it's 'authorized,' it will conceal every goddamn fact about her." Barbara shrugged. "Hell, what *are* the facts? What do we know about her? Even you and me? What do we know?"

"We know her real name," said Joshua. "Regina Celestiele Savona."

3

"Who's staying? Who's staying?" Regina mumbled. " 'S after mi'night, and I want—"

Johnny put an arm around her waist. "Easy, babe, easy," he said. "Nobody if you don't want 'em."

Regina was unsteady. She had a glass of gin in hand and continued to sip, but she staggered.

Johnny wore the white shirt and black bow tie of a houseboy. A well-put-together young man, the features of his face were so fine as to give him a charm verging on the effeminate. His brown eyes could have been the eyes of a pretty girl, but the bulge in the crotch of his tight black pants dissipated any suspicion he was anything but male.

"Who wants to stay?" Regina asked.

"Well—Mickey does. He's a little . . . you know. Couldn't find his way home."

"Shit. Never could."

"The Gwynnes asked if they could. They're in no shape to drive. Same thing with Bob and Christie. I told them it would be okay, and Christie *crawled* up the stairs."

"My bes' frien's, huh? Gonna stay for breakfas'. Tell 'em I want them to come for a swim with me, 'fore they check out."

"I'm afraid they've checked out already, babe," said Johnny. "The Gwynnes might, but—"

"Chickenshit. Can't hold their liquor. That's 'cause they're *Americans*. No Americans can . . . drink."

"True."

"Johnny . . . Light me a cigarette. I'm gonna sit here and look at my swimmin' pool. Get me some more gin."

She threw off the white terry robe and sat on a wheeled wood-and-vinyl chaise longue, smoking and staring at her pool. The estate was suddenly silent—suddenly for her; she hadn't noticed the departure of her guests, few of which had sought her out to thank her for her hospitality.

Johnny came back from the poolside bar, carrying a water glass full of gin.

"Siddown," she said to him.

He pulled up a chair and sat beside her.

She swallowed gin. "Who could figure a li'l girl named Regina Celestiele Savona would ever live in a place like this an' have her own swimming pool?" Speaking with her accent, she did not pronounce "Regina" in the English way, to rhyme with "vagina;" she pronounced it as an Italian speaking to an Italian, and she was Ray-*jee*-na Chay-*less*-ti-*ay*-la Sah-*voe*-nah.

Johnny glanced up at a window on the second floor, where a light had burned all evening and burned yet. Regina saw the glance and looked up at that window.

"You're indebted to him," said Johnny.

Regina raised her glass. "To the man upstairs," she said.

Johnny nodded. "Why don't I close the house? Mickey has gone to bed. The Gwynnes have gone. Christie crawled up the stairs, and I don't think Bob was in much better shape. I don't think there's anybody left. I'll check to see that nobody's left, lock the gate, lock the door, and turn off the outside lights in front. Okay?"

"Okay."

"Then I'll come back, and I'll watch you swim. Okay?"

"Won' let me drown?"

He grinned and shook his head. "Never. But don't go in the water till I get back."

4

When he returned, Regina was dozing.

"Hey! You were gonna swim for me!"

She shook her head. "Worn out. Pooped. Gonna go sleep."

"Wanna feel better in the morning?" he asked. "One last swim. Damned good for you, babe. Cool water. A little exercise."

She shook her head. "Don' swim too good, y' know. You'll jump in if I start to drown?"

"Absolutely."

She yawned. "Well . . . does make you feel better. Cool water. Like you said."

She looked around, found her glass, and swallowed the last of the gin he had brought her a few minutes ago. She rolled off the chaise longue and staggered to the edge of the pool. She dropped awkwardly into the water and began to flounder, as before.

Johnny stayed close and watched her thrash and splash. She grinned at him and slapped at the surface, trying to propel herself toward him. She reached him, coughing and laughing. She grabbed the edge of the pool.

Johnny thrust a knife forward and held it to her right eye.

"*Johnny!* What the hell!"

He did not cut her. He held the point of the knife to her eye and waited calmly.

"Johnny . . . ?"

Regina threw herself back from the edge of the pool. She turned, and with smooth, powerful strokes, propelled herself rapidly to the other side.

There she encountered Mickey Newcastle, kneeling on the edge and threatening her with a knife.

She lunged backward, submerged, and swam underwater to the base of the diving board. When she threw herself upward, Johnny was waiting.

Regina screamed. As she fell back into the pool, her wrists struck the edge. She moaned at the pain and grabbed each wrist with the opposite hand.

They wouldn't let her come out. She retreated to the center of the pool and treaded water. She tried one side of the pool, then the other. Each time she found a knife pressed to her eye.

It was the way terriers sometimes killed rats: by chasing them into the water and not letting them come back to land, chasing them along the edge of the water, yapping and snapping, until they drowned.

Regina screamed again. "Guys! What the hell? Why . . . ?"

Judging Mickey the weaker of the two, and the less resolute, she swam to his side of the pool and lunged up, flailing with her arms to knock him aside. Trying to hold the knife to her eye as she flailed and jerked, he cut a wide gash along her cheekbone. She dropped back into the water.

"You goddamn hophead idiot!" Johnny screamed at Mickey.

Slowly Regina lost strength. She was in excellent physical condition—she had to be to do her shows—but she was exhausted and dehydrated from her performance and weakened by all the gin she had poured down her throat. She couldn't stay afloat. She sank, then spluttered to the surface, then sank again, then struggled up.

"Why . . . ? Oh, Jesus, why?" she spluttered. "Wha'd I ever do to you, but good?"

She swam to Johnny, to plead, but he touched his blade once more to her eye. "I *knew* you could swim like a fish, babe," he muttered. He pressed the knife against her eye, and she retreated into the pool.

She fought for her life, but her arms and legs failed. Weeping and screaming weakly as she choked and coughed, the megastar sank for the last time.

Johnny stood. He looked up at the lighted window on the second floor. The old man was watching. Johnny did not dare to lift an arm, to wave, as if to say, there, by God, it's done. The old man shook his head angrily. They had botched it. The cut on her cheek would bring a homicide investigation.

The curtains closed and the window went dark. Johnny stood staring for a moment, wondering what the old man would do. Suddenly his eye caught movement at another window. It was a hallway window on the second floor. Someone was watching, for God knew how long, and now that someone backed away and disappeared inside the house.

Christ! There was a witness!

TWO

1

You'd think somebody had shot the Pope, DiRosario thought. Or the President of the United States. Here he was, Sergeant Tony DiRosario, in command of a unit that had nothing to do but keep reporters and screaming fans and the morbidly curious away from this estate—a hell of a job for an eighteen-year veteran and twenty young officers—and, Jesus, he might have to call for backup!

They had all kinds of excuses why he should let them in. They represented ABC, CBS, CNN, and NBC. They came from AP, Reuters, or UPI. They loved her. They were her closest friends. Never a day went by that she didn't call them. They had exactly the same astrological sign. They didn't believe she was dead. They wanted to prove it was a fake. She wasn't dead. She couldn't be! They—

"Sergeant. My name is Maude Ahern. I'm writing the authorized biography of—"

"Ma'am, I'm sorry. You may well be doing just that, but you can't get in here. Not now."

"Credentials? I—"

DiRosario shook his head. "Ma'am, if you showed me credentials proving you were President of the United States, I couldn't let you in here."

"I was here last night. I was one of the last people who saw her, I imagine."

"Let me have your name and phone number. When the detectives come and take over the investigation, I'll give that to them."

"Sergeant, I don't mean to be aggressive or obnoxious—"

"I don't want you to be one of those either, ma'am. But I can't let you in. Positive and final."

"Christ! I walked a mile. The streets are—"

"Crazy. I know. She did a concert just last night. How many were there? A hundred thousand? I guess the Bowl doesn't hold that many, but—"

"I was there, too."

"Yes, ma'am. You say your name is . . . ?"

"Maude Ahern. Here's my card. I'm sure the detectives will want me to—"

"Yes, ma'am. So you'll be where they can get you on this phone line?"

She shrugged and walked away.

One after another. And here came another one.

"Hiya, Sarge. Ain't this a mess? You know, I had to walk a mile to get up here. So. Well, anyway, I'm here."

"Right," said Sergeant DiRosario. "You're here."

The man who stood before him had tousled graying hair and a knowing smile that wrinkled the corners of his eyes. The smile was almost enough to make the sergeant let him pass. But he also had a frayed raincoat, a rumpled suit, and a necktie knotted so the narrow end hung below the wide end. He held the stub of a cigar in his left hand.

"Gotta match?" he asked.

"Sir, I don't carry matches."

"Most people don't anymore. I can't ever seem to find one when I need it. Well—" He dropped the unlighted stub into a pocket of his raincoat. "So, it's up the drive there?"

"Sir, you can't go up there," the sergeant said firmly. "I'm sorry, but nobody can—"

"How come I can't? Oh . . . I guess I— Didn't realize you didn't know me. Me, I, uh . . . I'm Lieutenant Columbo. Homicide. My case, y' understand. Here's my, uh, badge and ID."

Sergeant DiRosario stared at the disheveled man standing before him. Columbo. He'd heard the lieutenant was an eccentric, but this was more than he could have guessed.

"Sorry, Lieutenant, I just didn't recognize you." He shook his head apologetically.

Columbo nodded. "Time was when everybody on the force knew everybody else, just about. Department's got too big for that, hasn't it? So, anyway—"

"Right up the driveway, sir," said the sergeant. "I understand they've taken the body out of the pool, but of course it's still here—that is, until you get here."

"I was walkin' my dog on the beach," said Columbo. "Supposed to be a day off for me." He shook his head. "I guess I must be wicked."

"Sir?"

"What they say. Y'know. 'No rest for the wicked.'"

2

Columbo walked past six black-and-whites and past the emergency-squad ambulance. He wondered how come the paramedics always left the emergency lights flashing, even when they had parked in a driveway like this.

The front door was not locked. He opened it and walked into the house. All the activity would be out

behind, by the swimming pool, and he walked through
the house toward a back door. Glancing into the living
room, he saw a group of unhappy people sitting on the
couches and in chairs. He didn't stop to ask who they
were.

"Columbo!"

The friendly greeting came from Detective Sergeant
Martha Zimmer. "Martha!" He was glad she was on the
case. He had worked with her before, several times, and
knew her as an intelligent, effective officer. She was short
and a little too heavy—so chubby, in fact, that the
department might have insisted she lose weight if the
powers that be had not understood that she had gained
weight during each of her three pregnancies and had
difficulty getting rid of it. She had dark hair cut short,
and plump apple cheeks. She wore a navy blazer, her
badge displayed on its pocket. Her 9mm Beretta hung in
a shoulder holster under her left arm, not much con-
cealed.

Columbo shook Martha's hand. "Hell of a mess,
huh?" he said, glancing past her at the pool deck, where
the body of the megastar lay under a white sheet.

Martha nodded. "It's not for sure that she was murdered. But it looks like she was."

Columbo spotted the medical examiner sitting at a
glass-topped table writing notes.

"Dr. Culp, huh? I'm glad to see him. He'll do a good
job. You talked to him yet?"

"Sure. But you should, too."

Columbo walked over to the doctor. "Hiya, Doc," he
said.

Dr. Harold Culp looked up and grinned. "Hey, Columbo. You ever get that stomach of yours fortified?"

Columbo grinned and shook his head. "Nah. I'm still
goin' to wanta throw up every time you make me look at
another corpse you've cut open. Maybe I better look at
this one before you go to work on her."

The doctor was forty or forty-five years old, but

already turning gray and bald. He wore horn-rimmed bifocals. Like Martha, he wore a navy blazer with brass buttons, and gray slacks. "It's a goddamn *tragedy,* Columbo," he said grimly, nodding toward the corpse. "So young . . ."

"So famous," Columbo added. "So rich."

Dr. Harold Culp got up and walked over to the body. He pulled off the sheet. Regina had turned pale and bluish. Columbo nodded, and the doctor covered her up again.

"How long's she been dead?"

"Eight hours or so."

"Cause of death?"

"I'll tell you more about that after the autopsy," Dr. Culp said. "She'd been under water a long time. Of course, it looks like she drowned. But it may not be that simple. Both her arms are bruised. Also, there's an abrasion on her right wrist. The bruises and abrasion suggest a struggle. But she may have got the bruises and abrasion earlier—say, during the course of a very energetic performance. And it's possible that she died of something else—say, an overdose—and somebody threw her body in the pool to make it look like she drowned."

"What about that cut on her cheek?" Columbo asked.

"She didn't die of that."

"I didn't figure she did."

"It's six centimeters long. I didn't probe it much, but I'd judge it's not even a centimeter deep. The knife hit her cheekbone. That's not a stab wound, incidentally. That's a slice."

"I'll be checkin' in with ya, Doc," said Columbo.

3

"You've already figured out, I expect, who found her and how and when," Columbo said to Martha.

"The maid found her, about nine-thirty this morning. The maid's name is Rita Plata. She arrived about eight-thirty. The house was a colossal mess, from a party here last night. She worked inside the house for an hour before she came outside to see what she had to clean up around the pool. She saw the victim at the bottom of the pool."

"Eight hours . . . That means she died around one-thirty. Was anybody else in the house?"

Martha smiled. "Oh, yes. Quite a collection. In the first place, Regina had a full-time houseboy. His name is Johnny Corleone."

"Corleone?"

"Right. You know, there really is a town in Sicily named Corleone. Anyway, he's twenty-eight, and he's the live-in houseboy. Besides that, there were at least six other people in the house overnight. Regina's aged grandfather lives in a suite of rooms on the second floor. His name is Vittorio Savona. I haven't tried to talk to him. Johnny and Rita agree that he's feeble and does not speak English."

"Can Johnny speak Italian?"

"Sort of, he says. Okay. Regina, Johnny, and the old man make up the household. But there were five other people here overnight. It seems that certain people stay overnight with some regularity. She had issued a standing invitation to certain people. It seems to have been, 'If you've got so drunk or high you can't drive home safely, stay.'"

"Thoughtful," said Columbo. "So, who stayed?"

Martha consulted her notes to get the names exact. "First, there's a superannuated British rock star named Mickey Newhouse. Apparently he had a great deal to do with teaching Regina the basics of the business, and she hired him as a sort of artistic manager—if 'art' is a word we ought to apply to her exhibitions. They were lovers for a while, Johnny thinks."

"'Kay. Who else?"

"Mr. and Mrs. Joshua Gwynne. They own a company called Joshua Records and did her recordings. Then, a couple named Bob Douglas and Christie Monroe. Douglas is the computer programmer who creates those nauseating raucous sounds that substituted for music in her 'concerts.' Monroe was one of her backup dancers. They shared a room last night."

Columbo smiled. "I guess you didn't like Regina much. That is, you weren't a fan."

"I think she represented everything that's wrong with our country," Martha said.

"I'll invite ya to expand on that idea sometime. Meanwhile—"

"We made them all come down and wait in the living room. I checked out their rooms while they were downstairs."

"You didn't grab any evidence?"

"No, of course not. But—C'mon and take a look."

The house consisted of a main block and a wing that slanted off at an angle to the east. Martha pointed to the open door into Regina's suite, which occupied the entire west end of the house. The next suite, occupying about half as much space, was where her grandfather lived, behind a closed door. A hallway divided the rest of the second floor in half, and the houseboy's rooms were on the northeast corner. The hall turned and ran the length of the east wing, with two guest rooms on either side. The guest rooms were also separated by a short perpendicular hall that afforded all the guests access to the balconies on the north and south sides of the wing.

"Save the best for last." Martha nodded toward the door to Regina's suite. "Let me show you something interesting first. Down the hall."

She led him to a room she identified as Mickey Newcastle's. Martha told him to look in the bathroom. Lying beside the basin was a hypodermic needle, a vial of white powder, and a bottle of distilled water.

The next room was the one where Joshua and Barbara

Gwynne had slept. It was notable for the complete lack of anything personal: no nightclothes, no cosmetics, toothbrushes, or razors in the bathroom. They had not expected to stay all night.

Bob Douglas and Christie Monroe had. Their shared overnight bag was open on a small table. In the bathroom were their toothbrushes, his razor, her cosmetics, combs and brushes, and a set of contact-lens fluids: cleaner, saline solution, and lubricating drops.

"I guess they had high times." Martha, pointed at the rumpled bed. A sheer black nightgown was half-stuffed under one of the pillows. A spot in the center of the bottom sheet bore a yellowish stain that looked like dried semen.

Johnny Corleone had a small suite at the front of the house, not overlooking the pool. It consisted of a little sitting room, a bedroom, and a bath. It looked very ordinary and suggested nothing.

"Hey Martha, take a look at this," said Columbo from the bathroom. "Looka."

He was pointing at a tiny round frosted bottle of perfume, capped with a gilded butterfly. It sat in a mount in the bottom of a little box. Script on the top half, which lay to one side, labeled the perfume "Annick Goutal—Paris—Gardenia Passion."

"So," she said.

"Would Johnny be using that himself? I mean, is that something a man would use or—"

Martha grinned. "Definitely a woman's scent," she said. "And not available on a houseboy's wages, either."

Columbo grinned. "I wonder if we can find any more of that in the house."

They did, in Regina's personal suite. In her own rooms she had lived like a queen. Her sitting room and bedroom were lavish and, some would have said, tasteless. Everything was white: carpets, drapes, walls, bedclothes, upholstery. No pictures hung from the walls, only mirrors in white frames. One whole wall of each room was a mirror. When she saw herself in these mirrors, she must have seen the only touch of color in these determinedly white rooms.

The sheets on her king-size bed exuded a subtle but distinctive scent. Columbo had not opened the perfume bottle and did not recognize the scent as the same, but it was the same: Gardenia Passion.

"There's an odd thing, don't ya think?" said Columbo. He pointed to a small steel safe sitting to the right of the bed. "It's the only thing in the room that's not white. Make a note to get it opened, Martha. Gotta know what's in it."

Regina's huge, tiled bathroom was all white, too, and equipped with a whirlpool tub almost large enough to swim in, a marble shower stall that included a needle spray and bidet, a toilet with armrests and a slanting padded back, and another bidet. White towels hung on white racks. The only touch of color in the bathroom was the pale-gold wrappings on extra bars of soap— *Savon Fin, Gardenia Passion, aux sucs de laitue 2%.*

"The lady must have favored the smell," Columbo said. He picked up a bar of the soap—there could be no fingerprints on that—and he sniffed it. "Well . . . if that's what ya like. What's *'sucs de laitue'* mean? Y'know?"

"My menu French tells me *laitue* is lettuce. What *sucs* is, I don't know. Probably extract or something like that."

"Gardenia and lettuce. Odd combination, don't ya think? On the other hand, what is it the French say? 'Everybody to his own taste.' Right?"

"I'm going to make a guess," Martha said. "That bar of soap is worth fifteen dollars."

"Y' don't say? My, some people do live well."

"She didn't die well," said Martha.

3

Columbo walked into the living room, where the house-guests waited with various degrees of impatience and apprehension. Regina's obsession with white had not prevailed here, and Columbo guessed the room was very much as it had been when she moved in. It would have been difficult to believe the furnishings, though conspicuously luxurious and expensive, were in her taste; they were the dark-wood-and-leather appointments of a Southern California Spanish-style mansion and had a somewhat gloomy aspect. It wasn't Regina's room for sure, and he guessed she hadn't spent much time there.

"Hey, folks," he said. "I apologize for keepin' you all waiting like this. I know it's a big inconvenience. But I do thank ya for cooperating with the Los Angeles Police Department. Uh . . . Do you mind if I smoke? I've got a certain fondness for cigars. If it's okay, anybody gotta match?"

Martha handed him a cigarette lighter. She didn't smoke, but she'd picked up a lighter and put it in her jacket pocket when she heard she'd be working with Lieutenant Columbo.

He fished his half-smoked cigar out of his raincoat pocket and sucked fire into it. That gave him a moment for a quick study of the six subjects in the room. Subjects. That was what he would call them now. Suspects? Maybe later.

He identified Johnny Corleone readily enough. Yeah, the good-looking fellow in black slacks, white shirt, black bow tie. Sure. The houseboy.

The grungy man had to be Newcastle. He might be anxious for a fix by now.

That left the two couples. Okay, the older pair had to be Mr. and Mrs. Gwynne, and the younger pair were Bob Douglas and Christie Monroe.

"Well," he said. He sat down on the piano bench at the Steinway grand. "What a beautiful room this is. What a beautiful home. And what an awful tragedy here. Uh—I guess I should tell you I'm Lieutenant Columbo, LAPD Homicide. I gotta ask a lot of questions. I'm sorry, but we don't have any alternatives, you or me. I got no grounds to hold you here, and you're all free to leave if that's what you wanta do. But I'll have to ask my questions sooner or later, so—"

"A homicide detective," said Joshua Gwynne. "Are we to understand that you think Regina was . . . *murdered*?"

Columbo nodded. "For the moment, that's the theory the evidence most supports." He shrugged. "Could be it was an accident, but right now it looks like somethin' else entirely."

"Well, Lieutenant," said Joshua, "you know how to do your job. But the last time I saw Regina, she was staggering drunk, reeling around, and jumping in the pool. She couldn't swim. I mean, she could just barely. The party broke up. Most people went home. The rest of us went to bed. If she drank some more and—"

"And jumped in again, she might have drowned

accidentally," Columbo interrupted. He nodded.
"That's true. But there are other facts that don't square
with that. Like, she had a knife wound on her face."

"*Knife* . . . wound?"

"Yes, sir. So, y' see, that's why I've gotta investigate.
And I've gotta do that the only way I know how, which is
by accumulating all the facts I can and trying to put
them together. Which means I have to ask a lot of
questions. I'm sorry to have to take your time."

"Lieutenant," said Christie Monroe. "I'm half-blind
without my contact lenses. And half-blind with a hangover headache. I wonder if I could go back upstairs, put
in my lenses, and take some Advil?"

"Of *course,* ma'am," said Columbo. "You go right up
and do that."

She stood. The cocktail dress with the flared miniskirt
that she had worn last night was not appropriate for a
morning meeting of this kind. "I wish I had other
clothes, too," she said almost tearfully, her glance suggesting that she somehow blamed Columbo that she
didn't.

"You look very pretty, ma'am," Columbo said.

She hurried from the room.

2

"The first thing I'd like to know," said Columbo, "is
what was the last time each one of you saw Miss Savona
alive?"

"*Please,* Lieutenant," said Mickey Newcastle, "don't
call her 'Miss Savona.' No one ever did. It sounds hokey.
She was 'Regina' to everybody. She didn't like anybody
calling her anything else."

"Okay. When did you last see her?"

"I don't know," Newcastle said. "It had to be sometime around midnight. I was pretty well out of it by then.

I'd had a lot to drink. And you're going to find out, so I might as well tell you, that I use controlled substances. Maybe you'll want to arrest me for that. I really don't much care. With Regina gone, I don't have much left in life. I devoted my whole being to making her a great star, and now—"

"Spare us, Mickey," Bob Douglas interrupted. "We all know that without Regina around to pay you an exorbitant salary and support your habit—"

"You bastard!"

"—you'll be hard put to keep yourself out of cold-turkey withdrawal. But don't tell us you made her a star. She was a star without you—and without me, too, I admit. Without any of us. She had *talent,* Mickey. You wouldn't know anything about that."

"Uh . . . gentlemen," said Columbo. He looked at Newcastle. "You last saw her about midnight, the best you remember. How about you, Mr. Douglas?"

"I've gotta make the same confession he's made. I was schnocked last night, out of my skull. I remember her doing the pool bit. She'd jump in and pretend she was drowning, whooping and giggling. Frankly, Lieutenant, Regina liked to show herself off naked. That's why she liked to have parties here. It was her place, and she could do it."

"But when?" Columbo said. "When'd you last see her?"

"I can't say it was any time much after midnight. About midnight is when Christie and I went upstairs. We were—Whoo! If you know what I mean."

Columbo turned to Joshua and Barbara Gwynne, who sat together on a couch, looking hung over and unhappy. "When'd you last see her?"

"Lieutenant," said Joshua, "the death of Regina is going to cost my wife and me millions. I don't know if we can keep Joshua Records afloat without her. If that doesn't exonerate us, I don't know what would."

"Mr. Gwynne . . . You don't have to exonerate yourself. Nobody suspects you of anything, that I know about. All I'm asking is, when did you last see her?"

Joshua glanced at Barbara. "Maybe a little later than midnight," he said.

Rita Plata, the maid, came in carrying a tray laden with a coffeepot and cups. The others had had coffee before, and she presented the tray first to Columbo. He took coffee, as did Martha.

"That brings us to you, Mr. Corleone." Columbo turned to the houseboy. *"Parla italiano?"*

"Non parlo bene," Johnny answered.

"Va bene," said Columbo. "That's alright. When did you last see her?"

Johnny shook his head. "She asked me to bring her a drink. I don't know just when that was, exactly. People were leaving. There was a lot of traffic in the house: party breaking up, people looking for her to say thanks, and so on. I got her a gin. But I don't know what time that was. I think the last time I saw her was when I brought her the gin."

"Where was she then?"

"Sitting at a table by the pool. She was talking with somebody, a man. I don't think I knew him."

"What's the earliest time she could have been at the pool alone?" Columbo asked.

"The earliest time? I don't know, really. I guess it must have been after two o'clock."

"What time did you go to bed?"

"It must have been two-thirty. I took a bottle of Scotch and went up to my rooms. That had to have been about two. I watched television while I put down a couple of drinks, and then I went to bed."

"Your rooms are . . . where?"

"At the front of the house. I have a view of the driveway. Her rooms have a view of the pool. So do her grandfather's rooms. The guest rooms are in the east wing. Mickey's room has a view of the pool. So does the room the Gwynnes were using. The one Bob and Christie were in overlooks the front lawn."

"In other words," said Columbo, "if she was in the pool at, say, two o'clock in the morning, you couldn't have seen her from your windows, and Mr. Douglas and Miss Monroe couldn't have seen her, but Mr. Newcastle and Mr. and Mrs. Gwynne could have."

"Not really," Joshua Gwynne said. "The balcony outside our rooms is not private. Anyone in the house can go out on that balcony by coming through a little hall. So you don't undress and go to bed in any of the guest rooms until you pull the drapes."

"Okay," said Columbo. He looked around for an ashtray, spotted one on a coffee table, and walked over to deposit his cigar butt. "Ah, here's Miss Monroe. Just in time. I hope your headache's better. I was just about finished with asking when each person last saw Regina. When did you see her last, Miss Monroe?"

Christie sat down beside Bob Douglas. She frowned deeply. "Lieutenant, I . . . I don't remember how I got up to our bedroom. I'm told I got down on my hands and knees and *crawled* up the stairs. I don't remember . . . *anything.*"

Columbo ran a hand over his rumpled hair as if he supposed that might substitute for brushing it. "Uh, I wanta change the subject a little," he said. "There must have been some kind of struggle. I mean, even if she drowned accidentally, she must have screamed for help. Didn't anybody hear anything?"

"The idea that she would scream is an *assumption,*" said Joshua Gwynne. "Maybe she struck her head on the edge of the pool and knocked herself unconscious."

"But she didn't," Columbo said. "The medical examiner looked for a bruise and didn't find any. What he did find was a knife cut on her face."

"She *did* scream," said Mickey Newcastle. "I heard her. I'd got up in the night to go to the bathroom. I heard a scream. I went to the bedroom window, pulled the drapes apart, and looked. I didn't see Regina. There was a man standing beside the pool. He had light hair, cut very short, and he was wearing a red nylon jacket. His back was to me. He was just standing there. Then suddenly he broke into a run, running as fast as he could go. He looked back, and he ran into the diving board and fell. But he scrambled up and ran again. He ran out of the light, and I couldn't see where he went."

"You didn't see Regina?"

"No. From that window some palm fronds partly block my view of the pool. If she was in the pool, I didn't see her."

"Well, why the hell didn't you go down to see what was happening?" Joshua asked. "If you heard her scream—"

"Seeing the man suddenly take off and run, I supposed somebody—maybe Johnny—had come out of the house. Or maybe she'd gone inside and got a kitchen knife or a gun. Or maybe he saw her using the phone. Anyway, I didn't see her. And . . . And she didn't scream again."

"Besides, you weren't in very good shape," Joshua sneered.

"Besides, I wasn't in very good shape."

"Mr. Newcastle, what time was this?" Columbo asked.

Mickey shook his head. "I don't know. There's no clock in the room, and I don't wear a watch."

"Did anybody else hear anything?" Columbo asked.

No one answered.

Columbo reached into his raincoat pocket and pulled out a steno pad. "I oughta be makin' some notes," he said. He patted his jacket pockets. "Pencil . . . I don't know where my pencils go. Mrs. Columbo always makes sure every morning before I leave the house that I've got a nice yellow pencil."

"I'm taking notes, Lieutenant," said Martha.

He glanced at her. "So y' are. I appreciate it. Y'know, I always wonder about those Sherlock Holmes TV shows. *He* never takes any notes. I can't see how he remembers everything. Anyway—"

"How much more of our time are you going to need, Lieutenant?" Joshua asked.

"Not much, not much. One other thing I need to ask about. The medical examiner found bruises on Regina's wrists and arms. Also an abrasion, like the skin scraped off. I wonder if anybody noticed those bruises or that abrasion? I mean, when she was alive."

They all shook their heads.

"Well, then. We've got your names and addresses, don't we? We may have to talk again, a little. But for now, thank you all very much."

The group rose and left the room, and went upstairs to get their things from their rooms. Martha went back outside to supervise a photographer who had just arrived.

"Mr. Corleone," said Columbo. "I do need to ask you another question. Has the grandfather been notified?"

Johnny nodded. "I went in and told him before the police arrived."

"Aahh. How'd he take it?"

"He cried."

"Poor old fella. I wonder what he'll do. Go back to Italy? I'm going to have to talk to him."

"He's not easy to talk to," said Johnny. "He's a grumpy old man."

Columbo smiled. "I'll talk Italian with him."

Johnny frowned. "I'm not sure you can. Regina told me he speaks an odd dialect of some kind. Actually, he can speak a little English."

"He must be worried about what will happen to him. I mean, she was providing him with a home."

"I think he's got a little money."

"Hope so. What about you?"

Johnny shrugged. "A job's a job. I'll be around here for a while, I expect. Her business manager will want somebody to look after the house. Then I'll have to find something else."

Columbo rubbed his cheek. "Odd," he said. "Except for the old man upstairs, nobody's shedding any tears. It's gonna cost all the rest of you money, I guess. Is anybody gonna weep over her?"

"Yeah," said Johnny. "Millions of fans."

"Strangers," said Columbo. "Her friends—"

"Lieutenant Columbo," Johnny Corleone interrupted. "As you investigate this case, you're going to find out that Regina didn't *have* any friends. She didn't give a damn about anybody, and nobody gives a damn about her. Except for the money it's going to cost a lot of people."

Columbo nodded. "Too bad. Well, here're two of the people comin' down. Oh, Miss Monroe, I need to speak with you just a moment. Alone, if you two gentlemen don't mind."

Christie sat down on a couch facing Columbo, who sat on another one, leaning forward. That flared little skirt showed off a pair of gorgeous legs, for sure, and maintaining a professional demeanor did not forbid him from taking notice.

"Uh . . . just one little thing, Miss Monroe. I find a little discrepancy in your statement. Nothing big. Just one of those things I gotta clear up in my mind. I'm peculiar, I guess, but when I hear an inconsistency, I just have to clear it up."

"What is the inconsistency, Lieutenant?" she asked, a little impatiently.

"Well . . . y' see, you said you'd drunk so much last night you had to crawl up the stairs."

"They tell me I did. I don't even remember. I'm ashamed, but that's what I did, apparently."

"Maybe you can explain somethin'. You took out your contact lenses. You couldn't see very well this morning and wanted to go back upstairs and put them in. And you *did* put them in, right?"

"Yes, they're in now."

"Right. Well, I never needed glasses, so I don't wear contact lenses. Always thought if I ever needed glasses, I'd rather have contacts. But I've got some friends who wear them. I've watched them take them out and put them in again. And it looks to me like that takes a good deal of what y' might call manual dexterity. If you were so drunk you couldn't stand on your feet, how in the world did you take your lenses out?"

Christie smiled. "I've worn contact lenses for eleven years. The routines of putting them in and taking them out become instinctive. You don't have to think about it, you just *do* it, the exact same way every time. In eleven years, I suppose I've put them in and taken them out four thousand times. I've done it sloshed many times. Sometimes I've gone in the bathroom in the morning with a roaring hangover and seen my lenses neatly stored in the case, all cleaned and disinfected and ready to wear."

"That's amazin'," Columbo said.

"Besides, Lieutenant, you know how it can sometimes be when you've poured too much into your stomach. Some things you can't do, some things you can."

"I've never been that drunk," said Columbo. Then he grinned and added, "Well . . . not for many years. When I was young, I— Yeah, I can understand."

"I hope that explains away your inconsistency," she said pleasantly.

"It sure does. And thank ya, ma'am. Thank ya. That puts my mind at rest on that little detail."

3

Johnny Corleone knocked respectfully on the door to the grandfather's suite.

The old man opened the door.

"Signor Savona, this is Lieutenant Columbo of the Los Angeles Police Department. He's investigating Regina's death."

The old man nodded curtly and gestured to Columbo and Johnny to come in. He was a little man, not much more than five feet tall, and somewhat stooped in his posture. Columbo guessed he had once been stocky and probably athletic. His gray hair was bristly short. He wore a houndstooth-checked jacket of dark brown and cream wool, a black polo shirt, and black slacks. He sat down and pointed at a chair for Columbo.

"La mia condoglianza, signor," Columbo began.

The old man waved his hand. "Speak In-liss," he said. "Better . . . understand."

Columbo nodded. "I am sorry about the death of your granddaughter."

"Much money . . . bad girl," Signor Savona said. "'Regina Celestiele,'" he sneered. *"Putana!"*

"She, uh, drowned right under your window, sir. They say she screamed. Did you hear her?"

The old man shook his head firmly. "Sleep," he said. "Pills. Sleep. T'under . . ." He put his index fingers to his ears and shook his head. "Not hear."

"So, you couldn't know anything about what happened?"

"No. No thing. Dead . . . Bad girl. But dead? Not good. Sorry . . ."

Columbo stood. "I'm sorry too, sir. I wish I didn't have to bother you."

4

Johnny Corleone stood in the doorway to the mansion and watched Columbo walk down the driveway and through the police line that guarded the estate from the horde of reporters and cameramen who continued to insist on access. He saw many of them charge after Columbo. It was as if the detective were running a gauntlet.

Too damn bad, but not his problem. He closed the door and trotted up the steps.

He reached Mickey's room just in time. Mickey sat on the toilet, his arm constricted by a knotted length of rubber tubing, about to inject himself.

Johnny snatched the needle away from him. "No, by God! For once in your cokehead life you've gotta keep a cool head."

"Johnny. Just a—"

"You get locked up, they'll make you go cold turkey. And that's *your* problem, but I don't wanta get locked up with ya. The old man wants to talk to us."

Mickey drooled. "Well, a drink, anyway," he said.

Johnny poured two fingers of Scotch and handed it to him. "You fucked it up last night," he said in cold anger. "And what's this shit story about a guy in a red nylon jacket? You think that cop bought that?"

Mickey nodded. "He bought it. He'll buy anything. He's a dummy."

Johnny smiled. "Yeah. I guess if I gotta have a homicide dick on my tail, I couldn't pick a better one than that idiot Columbo. C'mon. The old man wants us."

In his suite, the old man sat down in his reclining chair that overlooked the pool. He regarded the two younger men with scorn. He was still entirely capable of hardness and scorn.

"In my life," he said, "I've had to deal with incompetence, with fuckin' *idiots*! But never two like you."

"I can't help it if she threw herself at me when I had the knife in my hand," Mickey pleaded. "I didn't cut her. She cut herself. I didn't—"

"Shut up!" the old man yelled. "You need a fix, don't

you? Well, go to your room and have it. But don't you leave that room, or you'll be the next one at the bottom of the pool."

Johnny led Mickey to the door and stepped out into the hall with him for a moment. "Cool it, man," he said. "Take your shot and stay in your room, like he says."

"You promised me money. I'm runnin' outta—"

"I won't let you run out. I don't know if the old man's gonna pay me, all things considered. But I won't let you go cold turkey. Now, go take care of your problem. We'll talk later."

Back inside, with the door closed and locked, Johnny sat down and faced the old man.

"That one's no good," the old man said. "Got to go."

"That was the deal, wasn't it? Cokeheads sometimes get strange things in their fixes. That was the deal. Mickey gets a little something fatal in his shot. But not today. Not so quick. We got enough trouble."

The old man drove his fist into his palm. "Why couldn't a couple of guys handle drowning the broad? Don't think *you* look so good. You let her bang her arms on the edge of the pool. The coroner will probably find bruises."

"He already did," Johnny admitted. "But that's easy enough to explain. She fell in the pool. But the cut on her face is somethin' else again."

"You picked your helper. I still think you could have done it alone."

"Not with a woman that swam like a goddamn fish!" Johnny argued. "It's a damned good thing you told me she could. I'd bought her story that she couldn't swim."

"Now we got this homicide cop on our hands," the old man said sullenly.

"He's not too bright."

"You don't think so? It's an act. He's too *goddamn* bright."

"You suppose he saw through *your* act?"

"Of all the homicide detectives in L.A., we get one who speaks Italian," the old man complained.

"What about my money?" Johnny asked.

"Why should I pay you when you screwed it up? But I will. Look at the couch. The red-and-orange cushion. First payment."

"A cushion?"

"Take it to your room and open it up. Some more in a week or so. And some more after. I said you'd get money, so you get money. Now send that maid up here with some lunch. And pour me a bourbon before you go."

5

In his sitting room, Johnny cut open the cushion and sat down to count the money stuffed inside it—$227,500. Okay. And more to come.

He picked up the telephone and punched in a number. The line rang. It was answered.

"Pronto."

"Carlo? Johnny. Shit's in the fan up here."

"What?"

"An L.A. homicide detective was here, named Columbo."

"I heard of him."

"He insisted on talking to the old man. I don't think the old boy's act went over."

"You don't *think* so? It went over or it didn't go over. Which is it, Johnny?"

"I'd have to say it didn't go over. Columbo didn't say anything, but I don't think he bought it. I got a feeling he's gonna be looking around."

"You mean he's gonna find out?"

"Not impossible. Even the old man thinks he's smarter than he acts."

"Okay, Johnny. What time's the maid leave? What time will you be there alone with the old man?"

"She leaves at four-thirty, but Mickey Newcastle will still be here."

"You know what to do about him. Put him to sleep."

"Carlo, what are you going to do?"

"Just open the door when I get there, Johnny." Carlo hung up the telephone.

FOUR

"Lieutenant! Lieutenant Columbo! What's happened? What's the word?"

"Hey! Millions of people have a right to know!"

"C'mon, Lieutenant! You can't hold out on us!"

Trying to walk back to his Peugeot, Columbo had managed to work his way through a gauntlet of yelling reporters, starting just outside the gate and continuing down the street, not the mile he'd told Sergeant DiRosario he'd had to walk, but several hundred yards. They yelled questions. Some of them even grabbed at his raincoat. A few had been smart enough to identify his car and hang around it, waiting for him. They had him blocked.

The cameras were rolling tape. Whether or not he said anything, he was going to be on every television news broadcast for the rest of the day and night. "Hey, look, guys. You should talk to the chief. I'm sure there'll be a statement from Regina's office. I don't know much more than you do."

"Will you at least confirm that she's dead?" a camera-man shouted.

Columbo sighed and nodded. "Yeah, she's dead."

"And you're a homicide detective," another one yelled. "You wouldn't be here if it was just an accident."

"Not correct." Columbo pointed a finger at the man who had just spoken. "We look into any death where there's a *possibility* of homicide. We do that because if we don't, the evidence gets mixed up. The fact that you see me here doesn't mean she was murdered. We don't *know* that."

"You suspect it?"

"It's a possibility," Columbo conceded.

"What was the cause of death, Lieutenant?" a woman shouted.

"Since the bottom of her swimming pool is where they found her, we have to figure she drowned," Columbo said wryly. "The medical examiner will fix the cause of death."

"The cops escorted two cars out of here," said another reporter. "Who were those people?"

"I'm not gonna say right now. She had several over-night guests in the house. None of them are suspects."

"If you're talking about suspects, you're talking about murder," the woman reporter said.

Columbo flipped his hands around. "Figure of speech, ma'am. There's just a *possibility* of something besides accidental drowning. No point in embarrassing her house-guests, who satisfied me they were all upstairs asleep when she drowned."

"Was she drunk?"

"What about drugs?"

Columbo shook his head. "The medical examiner will—"

"Some of the neighbors say there was a wild party here last night. Raucous. Yelling, screaming."

"Nobody said that to me. They told me there was a party. Okay, guys? Can I get in my car now?"

"Lieutenant! Was Mickey Newcastle one of her overnight guests?"

Columbo looked up the hill. A black-and-white, lights flashing, rolled slowly down the street, sounding its siren now and again to clear the crowd out of its way. It stopped by the Peugeot, and Sergeant DiRosario got out.

"Need a little help, Lieutenant?" he asked.

"A little *polite* help," Columbo said. He glanced around him at the growing, pressing crowd. "Guys doing their jobs."

The sergeant spoke to the crowd. "Okay, folks," he said firmly. "You heard what the lieutenant said. We know you're just doing your jobs. Now I'm gonna have to do mine. You've gotta let the lieutenant drive on. I don't want to have to radio for backup and have officers start shoving."

The media people backed away from the Peugeot.

"Is that car gonna start?" the woman reporter asked.

"Oh, yes, ma'am," Columbo said. "You take care of a car, it'll take care of you. I don't even *know* how many miles it's got on it. I mean, the speedometer is on its second go-round, y' know. Y' see, my car's a *French* car. The French, they really knew how to build them in those years. I can tell you stories about how this car has—"

"How come there's newspaper over the window?" she asked.

"Don't want the sunshine to fade the upholstery," he told her. "Like I said, you gotta take good care of a car. I try to park it in the shade, but you can't always do that."

The woman laughed and shook her head. She and the others gave up on Columbo and turned to Sergeant Di Rosario. "Hey, Sarge! Whatta *you* know about what happened up there last night?"

Columbo opened the door and rolled down the window to let air into the car. The newspaper fell away, and only then did he discover that a woman was sitting on the passenger side, smiling broadly and looking pleased with herself.

She was an exceptionally attractive woman with green eyes and red hair, wearing a green polo shirt and a pair of cream-white stretch pants, stretched to their limit by stirrups. "Hello. I'm Adrienne Boswell," she said.

"Ma'am—Miss Boswell . . . You gotta get out of my car."

"All I want is a ride down the hill," she said. "I walked all the way up here, and . . . well, it's hot. Surely you wouldn't deny me a ride down to my car."

Columbo scratched his head. "I bet you're a reporter," he said.

She smiled and nodded. "A girl has to make a living."

"I can't talk to you," he said. "Not after just refusing to talk to any of the others."

"All I asked you for is a ride."

"Well— Kinda scrootch down, will ya? It's better they don't see you with me."

He started the Peugeot, listened alertly for a moment to the sound of its engine, then put it in gear and moved down the hill.

"If you can tell me anything at all, I'll protect the source," she said. "I won't quote you. I won't acknowledge having talked with you. I won't use your name."

Columbo drew a deep breath. "She was murdered. Is that what you wanted to know?"

"How?"

"She was drowned."

"Suspects?"

"When a person like that is killed, there's a whole world of suspects. Anybody could've killed her."

"Maybe somebody who thought she was a bad influence on American youth," Adrienne Boswell suggested dryly.

Columbo shrugged.

"Let me give you my card," she said. "You might want to call me. Believe it or not, I've been known to be helpful to investigators. I can use methods you can't."

"I'll keep it in mind, ma'am."

"I won't help a man who calls me 'ma'am,'" she said, only half-facetiously. "I'm Adrienne. And there's my car. I'm grateful to you, Columbo."

"My pleasure . . . Adrienne," he said.

2

"Looka you! Looka you, Columbo!"

Columbo glanced up from the pool table to the television set mounted on a bracket on the wall of Burt's.

"Turn that off, will ya, Burt? How can a man concentrate on a pool shot when he has to look at his own ugly mug on TV?"

Burt accommodated him and switched off the television set. "Hey, you got a big job on your hands," he said. "How you got time to play pool?"

"I get a lunch break, don't I? I come in here, get my bowl of the best chili in L.A. and shoot a couple racks of nine-ball. Time to think—or would be, if I didn't have to look at TV."

He shot pool in his raincoat. That explained the blue stains: cue chalk. And the red ones: chili.

"Hey," said Burt. "Off the record. Way off the record. You saw the body, didn't ya? What'd she look like?"

"Like a woman that had drowned and been underwater all night," said Columbo. "Whatever you got in mind, Burt, I recommend you don't think about drowned corpses."

"She was *somethin'*, wasn't she, though? I mean, she showed *it all* on stage!"

"I wouldn't know." Columbo lined up a shot on the seven. "I never saw her on stage. Not my sort of thing. Mrs. Columbo and I, we take in shows now and again—but none like that. We're just not interested in that kind of thing. I got nothin' against it, y' understand, or

against people who like it; but it's just not my kind of
show. If I wanted to see naked, I'd just go to a strip show.
Not nearly as loud, and not nearly the price for a ticket.
Seven, eight, and nine. You gonna owe me a dollar,
Burt."

Burt put his dollar on the rail without waiting to see if
Columbo sank the last two balls. He knew he would.
"Hey," he said. "Look who's here! Can't resist Burt's
chili, can ya, darlin'?"

"Last week I had my stomach lined with lead," said
Martha Zimmer. "Which your chili will corrode. Yeah,
Burt. A bowl of chili. And a Pepsi."

Martha mounted a stool and watched Columbo sink
the eight and nine balls. He climbed on a stool beside her
and reached for his bowl of chili, which stood on the
shelf behind the stools.

"Got it lined up yet?" Columbo asked. "Who killed
her?"

"The water," said Martha. "She tried to breathe
water."

Columbo crushed crackers between his hands and
dropped them into his chili. "Hey. You got any more
specific ideas?" he asked Martha.

"Two." She pulled a steno pad from her jacket pocket
and tore out a page. "There. That's the name, address,
and phone number of a Mr. Steinberg, who lives next
door. He called in to say he heard a commotion last
night and is willing to give a statement. In fact, I gather
he's anxious to give a statement."

Columbo stuffed the note into his raincoat pocket. He
took a spoonful of Burt's fiery chili. "Mmm!" he said.
"You can't get chili like this—"

"I know," she said. "Outside Mexico, which is not
where Burt comes from."

"You notice how those people this morning weren't
telling the truth, exactly?" he asked. "Oh . . . Sorry. You
said you had *two* specifics."

"Right. The other one is interesting. I had all the usual stuff done: photos, fingerprints . . . Just on impulse, I had the kitchen knives checked for prints. You know, she was cut with a knife, and—"

"And?"

"So I had the knives checked. On the kitchen counter there's a wooden block with slots in it for seven knives and a sharpening steel. Sabatier knives. You know the name?"

Columbo shrugged.

"Expensive kitchen knives. About the most expensive you can buy. Made in France."

"In France! Y' don't say."

"All those knives are sharp as razors," Martha continued. "I'm serious. You could shave with any one of them. Five of them are covered with prints. The boys lifted those prints, and we're having them run. But get this: two of the knives are absolutely clean. *Wiped* clean. A five-inch boning knife and an eight-inch slicer."

"*Two* knives," said Columbo, frowning. "Two . . ."

Burt brought Martha a deep bowl of meaty chili, crackers, and a Pepsi.

"Right." She shook salt onto the chili.

"You didn't find a smear of blood, Regina's type?"

"C'mon, Columbo."

"Sorry, Martha. It's good work. But two . . . Huh. That brings up all kinds of ideas, doesn't it?"

She took a spoonful of chili and grimaced. "What I figured," she said.

3

Columbo stood for a moment outside the door of the offices of Wilcoxen, Josephson & Steinberg, Attorneys & Counsellors at Law. The building and the elevator foyer on the twenty-sixth floor were formidable. He looked around for someplace to deposit the butt of the cigar he had been smoking in the car; and, seeing no place, he pinched it to be sure the fire was out absolutely and deposited it in his raincoat pocket.

He opened the door and went in.

"Sir?"

The receptionist was haughty.

"Uh . . . ma'am, my name is Columbo. Lieutenant, homicide, Los Angeles police. I'd like to talk to Mr. Steinberg. He called and said he'd like to see somebody from homicide."

The tall, spare woman wore spectacles hanging from a chain around her neck. She peered at him with the skeptical air of a clerk taking a welfare application. "I shall see if Mr. Steinberg is available." She picked up the telephone.

"Mr. Steinberg will be available in a few minutes," she told him. "You will have to wait."

"Waitin' is a large part of my business, ma'am." He sat down. "You don't get any special police training for it. You just have to learn to do it, on your own."

Steinberg was indeed available in a few minutes. His secretary, a short and plump young woman with a friendlier air than the receptionist, led Columbo through a maze of halls.

The lawyer stepped out of his office to extend a hand to the detective. "Mort Steinberg. I understand your name is Columbo. I'm pleased to meet you."

"The pleasure is mine, sir," said Columbo. "My, you've got beautiful offices. And . . . Well, if you lived next door to Regina, you've gotta have a beautiful home."

"To be altogether brutally frank, Lieutenant, it *was* beautiful and will *be* beautiful, now that the woman is dead. Is that a despicable attitude?"

"I don't make judgments like that, Mr. Steinberg. I can imagine why you feel that way."

"Have a seat on the couch," said Steinberg. "I'm about ready to call for afternoon coffee. Will you join me? I'm about to light a cigar, too. Are you interested in one of those?"

"I love a cigar now and then. I have to admit, I do favor them."

He would love this one. It came from a wooden box and was encased in an aluminum tube. Two dollars and a half, he figured. Maybe more. Steinberg was young, he thought, for a man who lived in the neighborhood he had seen this morning, practicing law with his name on the door in offices like these. He was small, though solid, maybe athletic, with curly dark hair, liquid brown eyes, and an imperfect complexion.

"Let me explain my brutal attitude toward the death of Regina," he said. "Before she moved in, we had a lovely neighborhood. The people who live along the street are . . . well, you know, a *nice* sort of people. Quiet. Take good care of their properties. And so on."

"I understand."

"Well," Steinberg continued, "from the time she moved in, nothing was the same. Noise. Intrusion. You know, Lieutenant, she wanted to buy my place, made an offer. What'd she want to do, turn it into a *kennel* for the kind of people she associated with? Anyway— You saw what it was like this morning. I had to have police assistance to get away from my house. It has been almost that bad many times before, when her devotees mobbed the neighborhood after one of her whorish, vulgar performances."

"I get your point, sir," said Columbo. " 'Course, Regina Savona is *dead*. . . ."

"Yes, of course," Steinberg said. "No one deserves to die by murder. Except maybe Hitler or Stalin, and certainly I don't suggest she was in their category. You know something? She was worth so much money that I could have sold out and let her have the neighborhood.

Maybe I would have, if she'd lived." He stopped, shook his head. "What kind of society have we built, Lieutenant, where a woman doing what she did can earn enough money to buy *my home* out of her petty cash?"

"Millions of people are mourning her," said Columbo. "But between you and me, and off the record, I haven't come across anybody who mourns her that *knew* her."

"You're in charge of the investigation, Lieutenant?"

"Yes, sir. Sergeant Zimmer was the first detective on the scene and took charge. The captain called me next. I was out on the beach, walkin' my dog, and Mrs. Columbo drives up and says— Well, it was supposed to be my day off. Which makes no difference. You had somethin' to tell us?"

"Yes, I do. Really. Apart from venting my spleen. Forgive me for that."

Columbo grinned. "I'd forgive you for murdering her yourself, for a cigar like this one. I'd have to arrest you, ya understand . . . but I'd *forgive* you."

"I'll have my secretary wrap up half a dozen of them for you."

"Well, sir, I'm not supposed to accept gifts."

"From suspects." Steinberg chuckled. "From me? Why not? And it's off the record, like the comments we've made to each other about Regina."

"I thank ya, sir."

"Well— Ah, here's our coffee."

They suspended the conversation while the secretary poured coffee.

"What I have to tell you," said Steinberg, "is that I may have heard the murder being committed."

"I wanta hear about that."

"She had another one of her rowdy parties last night. Our children couldn't sleep. My wife and I couldn't sleep. You know, it's a good fifty yards between that house and mine, but— Anyway, this time we were spared what often happened—that the party went on until dawn. I guess the woman was tired after one of her so-called concerts and let the postconcert party wind down early. Around midnight it started to get quiet, and by one o'clock it was absolutely silent over there."

"Yes, sir."

Except— Except that after a while, I heard a woman screaming. She screamed several times; I'd say four or five times. Then it was quiet again. Finding out this morning that Regina was dead, and hearing on the radio that possibly someone had murdered her, I thought I ought to call and offer this information."

"What time did you hear this screaming?" Columbo asked.

"One twenty-three," Steinberg said. "I looked at the clock. I suppose I should have called the police, but . . . Well, hearing screaming over there was nothing unusual. Besides, there were people in the house. There were always people in the house. She was never there alone. And to be perfectly frank about it, Lieutenant, I really didn't give a damn."

4

In the offices of the coroner, Columbo sat down across the desk from Dr. Culp. "Can you spare me from another look at the corpse?" he asked.

Dr. Culp nodded. "I can spare you that privilege," he said.

"Don't tell me the cause of death was somethin' besides drowning."

"I won't tell you that. She drowned, alright. Between one and two A.M. Apart from the cut on her cheek and the bruises and abrasion on her arm, she had suffered no injury. In other words, she didn't bang her head on the edge of the pool."

Columbo scratched his jaw. "Any possibility it was accidental?" he asked.

Dr. Culp shrugged. "That's *your* department. Do you think it was accidental?"

"It would be easier to think so if she didn't have that cut on her cheek."

"The alcohol content of her blood was point one eight percent. Drunk as a skunk. Also, she'd had a sniff of cocaine during the evening. Not more than one, I'd think, but one for sure." The doctor paused and smiled slyly. "And guess what else we found. In her stomach."

"What?"

"Semen. Sometime during the evening she gave somebody oral sex."

"Any idea when?"

"Normally, I'd say that would clear out of the stomach in an hour or so. In her case, the amount of gin in her stomach and intestines had slowed down the digestive process. Could have been two hours: within the last two hours before she died."

"I'd give a lot to know who the man was," said Columbo. "Could have somethin' to do with the motive."

"There's a way to find out," said Dr. Culp. "We can run a DNA test."

"You got a big enough sample to do that?"

"It doesn't take much. Of course it's all mixed up with alcohol and other substances, but I got a sample good enough for the test. Under the microscope, I can see the poor little dead sperm cells in it."

"Deoxy— Deox— Finish it for me, Doc."

"Deoxyribonucleic acid. Every cell in every living creature on earth contains DNA. It's the genetic code. When a frog impregnates a frog, the DNA in the chromosomes of both male and female ensure that the offspring will be frogs. Other elements of the DNA cause the offspring to inherit specific traits of the parents. Your own DNA makes you *Homo sapiens* and makes you something like your parents, yet different, so that your children will be like you and your parents and your wife and her parents but not clones of any of you."

"Some tough cases have been cracked with DNA tests," said Columbo.

"Actually, Columbo, it works out the other way a lot of times. The FBI reports that twenty-five percent of the DNA in semen taken from rape victims doesn't match the DNA from the accused. It's won a lot of acquittals, too."

"But it's a matching process," said Columbo. "How we gonna match the DNA from what you found with some guy's semen? I mean, I can't ask a bunch of guys to—"

"Blood samples," said the coroner. "Actually, we could find DNA in strands of hair, fingernail cuttings, and so on. But blood samples would be best. Can you think of some way to get your suspects to give blood samples?"

"I haven't got any suspects," said Columbo.

"Any man who was in the house that night."

Columbo ran a hand through his hair, rumpling it even more. "I guess I can try."

"I'll have the sample run," said the doctor. "You understand, I don't run DNA tests. It's one hell of a specialty and takes a special lab to do it. Something new."

"I know the sex-crimes division uses it a lot in rape cases," said Columbo. "Me, only one time. A charred body, burned up with gasoline. But there was enough tissue and blood left to get a sample for a DNA test. The technicians matched that with the DNA in hair left in a hairbrush and made an identification of the body. Science . . ." He laughed wryly. "Someday they'll actually invent a lie detector—which will retire a lot of guys like me."

"Don't count on it," said Dr. Culp. "The polygraph is a scam."

"You know that, and I know that," said Columbo, "but it's one of the great myths loved by the American people."

"It'll take a few days to get the DNA test done. Get us some blood in the meanwhile, okay?"

"Okay."

FIVE

"Mick."

Mickey Newcastle sat on his bed in a vest undershirt and yellowed Jockey shorts, smoking nervously. "I made a mistake," he said disconsolately.

"Your first one?" Johnny said sarcastically.

"C'mere. Look. Look down there. I told that stupid dick Columbo that I saw a guy in a red jacket run into the diving board. Look out there. You can't *see* th' fuckin' diving board from this window. I said I couldn't see Regina in the pool because of the palm fronds. What I couldn't see was the diving board. Christ, I suppose we could climb up and cut—"

Johnny Corleone shook his head. "Don't even think of it. Look, you're worrying too much. She *drowned.* How she got a cut on her face—"

"Johnny, I couldn't help it!"

"Okay. Suppose Columbo decides she was murdered. So who murdered her? There's no way to hang it on us.

To start with, what was our motive? I worked for her, so now I'm out of a job. You worked for her, and you are out of a job."

"What about our money?" Mickey asked.

"The old man's unhappy because of the cut. But he'll pay. He knows very well that if one of us was arrested for murder, we'd finger him in a minute. He's got no choice but to pay."

"You said you wouldn't leave me cold turkey."

"Hell no, Mickey. Hey, I was tough on ya about that this morning. But you gotta right to relax. I know how it is. I brought somethin' for ya."

Johnny pulled a handkerchief from his pocket. He handed it to Mickey, and Mickey unwrapped it. His eyes glittered as he saw a vial of white powder.

"Shoot it and have a good time," Johnny said. "I'll see ya later. Now, listen. Don't leave this room. Just shoot and lay down and dream. Okay?"

"Okay."

As soon as Johnny was gone, Mickey took the plastic pill bottle in the bathroom. He opened it and sniffed the white powder.

Well, maybe . . . he thought.

He sniffed the powder in a vial of his own. He shrugged. No difference.

Even so . . . Wrapped in a handkerchief. No fingerprints. Mickey sighed heavily. He poured the white powder into the toilet and flushed it. Then he used distilled water and mixed a fix from his own diminishing supply. He had to have some money. He had to get out and cop. But for right now— He poured the mixture carefully into his syringe.

Lying on his bed, he tied a length of rubber tubing around his left arm. He stared until he found a vein, then stabbed himself with the needle and pushed down the plunger. In ten seconds he was drifting in misty bliss.

2

The maid, Rita Plata, left at four-thirty, as Johnny had told Carlo she would. At five the doorbell rang.

It was Carlo Lucchese, with two other men. Carlo, the man Johnny had talked to on the telephone a few hours ago, was a tall, thin, swarthy man, wearing a handsome double-breasted suit. The other men wore suits not nearly so well fit or cared for, and they were conspicuously deferential to Carlo.

"Johnny Discount," said Carlo. "Meet Sal and Frank. Nice to see you again, Giovanni. Everything under control?"

Johnny nodded. "Newcastle's out. I gave him a fix with something in it that ought to put him out for good."

"Be sure of that, Johnny," Carlo said. "Let the cops deal with him—just another crackhead that shot up some bad stuff."

"Gotcha. But, Christ, man! She dies here last night. The old man. Then Newcastle—"

"They might think that's damned odd, but they can't hook *you* onto anything, can they?"

"No. I don't see how they could."

"No. It's one thing that shit happens. It's another to hook it to a guy. Anyway, Johnny, tell me what choices we got."

"I agree with you, Carlo. I don't see we got any."

"You made a mistake in going along with the old man."

"Hell, Carlo, you'd have gone along yourself for the money he offered."

"It was stupid, Johnny. Not as stupid as he was in deciding he had to have her killed, but stupid. Some very big guys don't want the old man identified."

"So, you—"

Carlo nodded. "Hey! Don't think too much. Let's go up and see him."

They went up the stairs, four of them: Johnny, Carlo, Sal, and Frank. In the hallway outside the old man's room, Carlo told Sal and Frank to step back out of sight and wait. Then he knocked on the door.

The old man opened the door. "Carlo," he said. "What brings you here?"

"Was in the neighborhood and just thought I'd stop by. How's tricks?"

"When you get to be eighty-one years old, you got no tricks left in you. Johnny, pour Carlo a drink. Hell, pour one for me. The doctors don't know everything."

The old man picked up the remote and switched off the television set. "So whatta ya know, whatta ya say?" he asked. "What can I do for you? You can't kid me you just stopped by to say hello. I been around longer than that."

"I did, really," said Carlo. "On the other hand, who do you know in Arkansas?"

"Arkansas? Hell, man, I never been in goddamn Arkansas in my life."

Carlo accepted a glass of Scotch from Johnny. Johnny handed a glass to the old man.

"I'm gonna put a little more soda in mine," said Carlo as he rose and walked toward the little bar.

The old man nodded. Carlo walked behind him. He handed his drink to Johnny and pulled a silk scarf from his jacket pocket. With a quick, deft movement he dropped the scarf over the old man's head and jerked it tight around his throat. The old man threw his glass across the room as he thrashed and kicked and struggled for breath. He grabbed feebly at the scarf and tried to pull it away, but Carlo was far too strong for him. He choked loudly. His face turned red. His eyes bulged. He gagged. Strangled, he ceased his weak struggle for his life and he died.

Johnny stared, half sick. "I'll clean the place up," he said. "There won't be a trace of him. No fingerprints, nothing personal that could identify him. I suppose I ought to call the detective and say 'Signor Savona' has disappeared."

"First, you're going with us," said Carlo. "I want you to see what we do with him. It's time for you to get the picture of what we do with guys that screw up."

"I've just seen what you do."

"You think so? You haven't seen it all yet. Don't be a candy-ass. You've gotta know your trade, Johnny. You've got to know the business you're in."

3

They wrapped the limp body of the old man in a blanket and carried it down through the house and out to the garage. Two cars sat side by side: Regina's green Lamborghini and Johnny's red Ferrari.

Carlo shook his head at the Ferrari. "Never get it in there," he said. "Sal, you bring *our* car up to the garage doors."

Johnny pressed the button to open the doors and stepped out on the driveway. Carlo came out. For a full minute he stood, glancing sharply around to be sure no one could see the garage from a nearby house or from the street.

Sal backed a black Ford up to the garage. He opened the trunk, and he and Frank lifted the wrapped body into it.

"You follow us," Carlo said to Johnny.

Johnny followed the Ford to a red brick warehouse on Washington Boulevard. The big doors opened by radio control, and reluctantly Johnny drove his Ferrari inside, uncertain if he would ever again see the outside of this windowless building.

Carlo, Sal, and Frank began to take off their clothes,

piling them on the seats of the Ford. "Hey, whatta think you're gonna be, a man of leisure?" Carlo snapped at Johnny. "We got work to do and need work clothes." He pointed at some coveralls hanging on pegs.

Johnny stripped to his slingshot undershorts and pulled on one of the coveralls. Carlo put on cotton work gloves and tossed a pair to Johnny.

Sal and Frank moved efficiently, shoveling cement and sand into a small electric concrete mixer. Carlo led Johnny toward the rear of the warehouse, where half a dozen fifty-five-gallon oil drums stood in a row. He rocked one back and forth to be sure it was empty.

"Okay, Giovanni. You know how to cut the top off one of these?"

Johnny shook his head.

"You don't know much, do you? Well, watch me. Next time, you'll know how."

There was a special heavy tool for cutting the tops off drums—like an oversized can opener, except that it worked with two long handles. When Carlo finished he nodded at Johnny, and the two of them carried the open drum to the front.

The concrete mixer ran noisily. Frank opened the trunk, and he and Sal lifted the body out. Sal walked to a workbench and picked up a heavy sledgehammer. Frank rolled the body out of the blanket and laid it facedown on the warehouse floor. Then, to Johnny's horror, Sal raised the hammer and brought it down in the middle of the old man's back. The crunch was sickening. Johnny felt his stomach coming up.

"They won't fit in a drum," said Carlo. "You have to be able to fold them over."

Sal and Frank did just that. Having shattered its spine, they could bend the body double and fold it into the drum. The two men pressed it down. They stopped the concrete mixer, rolled it to the drum, and poured wet concrete over the body until concrete covered the corpse and the drum was full.

"Okay," said Carlo. "We change clothes and go to dinner. You know Luigi's in Santa Monica? It's a great place! By the time we have a first-class dinner and get back, that'll have set enough so we can move it."

4

On their way back from dinner, they stopped at a bakery, and Sal and Frank borrowed a bakery truck. They drove it into the warehouse, beside the Ferrari and the Ford.

All four changed into coveralls again.

"Now," said Carlo to Johnny, "you're gonna find out why we *really* brought you along. We need all four of us to lift that son of a bitch."

They strapped the drum to a loading cart, which made it much easier to lift into the bakery truck. They left the warehouse, driving just the truck.

Afraid, his pasta and wine churning in his stomach, Johnny sat in the front seat with Carlo, who chatted about things inconsequential: the weather, the smog, the likelihood of another earthquake. Johnny knew where they were going—out to sea. It was nearly midnight now, and they were going to put the drum aboard a boat, take it out, and dump it.

A fishing boat lay moored at a dock in Long Beach. They lifted the drum aboard. Carlo started the engines. Sal and Frank cast off the lines. The boat moved slowly and quietly. They didn't go out very far—maybe ten miles, as Johnny guessed.

Carlo stopped the engines. The boat rocked in the swells as the four men struggled with the drum, now off the cart, and managed to roll it over the gunwale. It dropped into the Pacific and sank.

"So long, ol' buddy, 'ol buddy," said Carlo. "It was nice knowing you."

On the return run, Carlo called Johnny to stand beside

him at the wheel. "Listen," he said. "You got to clean that room up. You can't leave anything that would identify him, or we've done this for nothing. You can't just wipe the fingerprints off everything. The thing to do is pack up some of his clothes and all his bathroom stuff, make it look like he scrammed. You'll have to wipe the bathroom fixtures, the light switches, the television . . ."

"He didn't have much personal stuff," Johnny said.

Carlo nodded. "It made you sick to see Sal bust his back, didn't it? Well, just remember that. If the cops make the old man, you'll get your back busted the same way."

Johnny did not reply but stared toward the coastline, anxious to get ashore, get back to the warehouse and into his own clothes, his own car. He wondered if it wouldn't be a good idea if he just drove away and tried to disappear. After all, he had the $227,000 the old man had given him, and—

"Incidentally, Johnny," said Carlo, "I bet you find some money in those rooms. Not just a little bit, either. Whatever you find, it's yours. If you don't find any, let me know. We'll take care of you." He slapped Johnny lightly on the shoulder. "We're not such bad guys, you know."

5

It was almost 3:00 A.M. when Johnny finally returned to Regina's mansion. The place was quiet—dead quiet and dark. He hurried upstairs and into the old man's rooms.

He found two suitcases in a closet. That would be helpful. The old man had had three suits, three sport jackets, and half a dozen pairs of slacks. Johnny packed all of those clothes, together with shirts, underwear, socks—not all, but most of what the old man had owned.

The old man had lived simply, with no more than five or six books, a few magazines, the newspapers, for diversion. His daily life had revolved around television. He had sat day after day in a lounge chair in front of a mammoth set, connected to cable, every channel possible, and had switched from channel to channel with a remote-control gadget. He'd had a VCR and a few tapes. *The Godfather. The Longest Day. The Secret of Santa Vittoria.* Also *Deep Throat* and *Debbie Does Dallas.*

He'd kept a bottle of Scotch always on hand, and one of gin. He had not smoked. The story about him, from Regina, was that he had lived for many years with one wife, always faithful to her, and in those years he neither drank nor smoked. He'd lived for his work, she said. She should have known. She had been close to him for some years, when nobody else was.

Johnny looked for money. He found it. His $227,000 had been inside a cushion. He found $142,000 more—in hundred-dollar bills in neat plastic-wrapped packages taped under the bathroom basin and in the springs of the old man's recliner. The old man had promised more for the killing of Regina; but he wouldn't have to share this with Mickey, so it would be enough.

In the top drawer of the old man's bureau he found four hundred dollars more in tens and twenties, and twenty or so dollars in coins, some cuff links, some keys, and a wristwatch. He found an Italian passport in the name Vittorio Savona and dropped it into one of the suitcases.

The watch . . . My God! Vacheron Constantin. It was worth thousands! It wasn't in Johnny's nature to leave so beautiful and expensive a thing for someone else to grab or to lie in a brown manila envelope in a police property room awaiting the return of the owner. He slipped it on his left wrist.

He took the money and suitcases to his own rooms. Returning, he set to work to eliminate fingerprints: his own and the old man's. TV remote, TV set itself, doorknobs, light switches, bathroom fixtures, windows, alarm clock, knobs and pulls on furniture. He went over every smooth surface he could think of, including the bulbs in the lamps.

The sun was up, and Rita was due in less than two hours when he decided he had done all he could.

He put the old man's suitcases in his car. He'd deep-six them as soon as he could.

Even now he could not go to sleep. He took a shower. Standing under the spray of hot water, he focused on a vital question: Who had stood at the hall window last night and witnessed the dispatch of Regina? Why had that person said nothing to Columbo? Was some bastard setting up to blackmail him?

Who was it? Not Mickey. He had been down there at the pool. The Gwynnes? If they had heard Regina screaming, they could have looked down from their bedroom window. In the hall that led to the balcony, it could have been only Bob Douglas or Christie Monroe. Which one of them would be in touch, demanding money?

6

Johnny lay down but could not sleep. Rita would arrive at 8:00. He would have to be up. He would have to "discover" that the old man was gone and Mickey was dead—overdosed—and call the police.

He went down to the kitchen and started a pot of coffee. He put some bacon in a pan and fried it. The stimulating crackle and aroma of frying bacon revived him a little. He cracked two eggs and scrambled them in the bacon grease. He put bread in the toaster.

"God, that smells good, and Jesus Christ, am I hungry!"

Newcastle! Standing in the kitchen door in undershirt

and underpants, the shaggy Mickey was alive and talking!

Johnny fought to control himself. "Hey, man, I'd have banged on your door if I'd known you were awake."

"Oh hell," said Mickey. "You know me. I shot up, enjoyed myself, and slept like the dead for . . . for how many hours?"

"How many hours you been awake, man?" Johnny asked. The question was, had he heard Johnny working in the old man's rooms? Of course, he'd been in the wing, not in the main house—

"Just long enough to take a shower," said Mickey blandly. He yawned. "I guess I'm not one hundred percent awake right now."

"Well, look. I'm sorry I didn't do enough bacon and eggs for two. Why don't you have these, and I'll make some more for myself?"

"Wouldn't want to take your breakfast away from you."

"I wish you would. I ate too much last night. Went out to an Italian restaurant and pigged out on pasta. Here, Mick. You eat this, and I'll make another plate."

Newcastle began to fork the bacon and eggs into his mouth. "I don't know about you," he said, "but I'm thinking we got away with it."

"We got a problem, Mick," Johnny said ominously.

"What?"

"I went out last night. Left about six, six-thirty. I came back close to midnight. I figured the old man would have been long asleep and wouldn't want me coming in to check on him, so I went to bed. I checked in on him first thing this morning. He's gone. Packed his clothes and took off."

Mickey Newcastle frowned. "I never did buy the story he was her grandfather. But—"

"But right. Where does an eighty-one-year-old man go? In a few hours? Who helped him? I'm with you, Mickey. He wasn't her grandfather. So, who was he?"

Mickey slammed down his fork and knife. "Why can't anything be *simple*?" he cried. "And . . . *Hey!* What about the money? What'd he do, skip and leave us hangin'?"

"I'm afraid so."

"But . . . Jesus Christ! He hires us to— Then we do it, and he skips on us? Johnny . . . You know I gotta problem! This was gonna solve my problem, once and for all. Enough money to—"

"Hey, buddy. I told ya I wouldn't leave ya to go cold turkey. I got some friends. I got some resources. You'll get what you need."

"But I was gonna be *independent*!"

Johnny stood behind Mickey and put a hand on his shoulder. "You're a goddamn *talent*, Mickey. You're always gonna be in demand. I can help you. I got friends who can help you. But— Hey! Why you need help from a guy like me and my friends? You were the artist behind Regina! Everybody knows that."

Mickey squeezed tears from his eyes. "But I gotta have cash every week! You know for what. I can't *wait* for people to recognize my talent."

Johnny patted Mickey's shoulder. "You don't have to worry about that, ol' buddy. I'll take care of what you need, until you can handle it yourself. The old man checked out and left us cold. But I know where I can come up with some operating capital. Hey! Maybe we'll make us another Regina! You made that broad. How many cheap whores are there, ready to take her place? Just relax. Take it a day at a time. It's all gonna come out alright."

7

Rita was at work in the kitchen. Mickey had gone back to bed. Johnny tried to count the number of hours that had passed since he'd had any sleep.

At 8:00 he telephoncd LAPD headquarters and asked for Lieutenant Columbo.

"The Lieutenant is out on assignment, sir. Can anyone else help you?"

"Who's in charge of the Regina investigation? This is Johnny Corleone, her houseman."

"I'll connect you with Sergeant Zimmer, sir."

Usually, Sergeant Zimmer knew how to contact Lieutenant Columbo, even though he violated every rule of the Los Angeles Police Department by running around in his personal car, with no radio. About 8:40, both of them came to the door.

Johnny made a point of appearing in his black bow tie, white shirt, and black slacks: his uniform as Regina's houseboy. "I called you, Lieutenant . . . Sergeant . . . because something very odd has happened."

Columbo pulled his cigar—not one of Steinberg's, but one of his own—from between his lips and dropped it in his raincoat pocket. "Somethin' odd?" he asked.

"Yes, sir. Signor Savona has disappeared."

"Disappeared?"

"Yes, sir. I went out to dinner last night. I was . . . upset. You can understand that, can't you? I got back about midnight and went to bed. When I got up this morning, ordinarily I would first have checked in on Miss . . . On Regina. Well, there was no point in knocking on her door. So I went and knocked on her grandfather's. He was usually awake by, say, seven-thirty. He didn't answer. I tried his door. You know, you're always concerned about a man his age. The door was unlocked, so I went in. Not only was he gone, he was *packed* and gone. His clothes, his other things, all gone. I didn't call the police until eight because I figured you wouldn't be on duty much before then. I thought you ought to know before anybody else heard about it."

Columbo reached for his cigar, looked at it for a moment, and dropped it back in his raincoat pocket. "You say his things are gone. What's gone?"

"What do you want to talk about?" Johnny asked. "His clothes. His . . . toiletries. He left a few clothes. But he took most of his things, as if he didn't expect to come back."

"How old is he?" Martha asked.

"In his eighties, I guess," said Johnny. "And he was not very strong. I don't see how he could—"

"You were gone how long?" Columbo asked. "Four hours?"

"Longer than that. I went to a restaurant in Santa Monica where they serve good Italian food. I had a couple of drinks, an antipasto, pasta, wine, dessert, and coffee. Afterwards, I stopped in a bar where there was a show. With the driving, I guess it was close to six hours. When I got in, I took a shower and went to bed. I don't know if he left while I was out or while I was asleep."

Columbo nodded. "So . . . Signor Savona. You figure he couldn't have left by himself? Somebody had to have helped him?"

Johnny nodded. "I don't see how he could possibly have left the house himself, with all his things."

PART TWO

6

Martha and Columbo walked through the house. A surprise: they found Mickey Newcastle still living there. He explained that he would be leaving this morning. He did have a place of his own.

The rooms the old man, Vitorrio Savona, had occupied were as Johnny Corleone had described them: empty of most of his clothes.

Columbo stood in the sitting room. He had reached into his raincoat pocket and taken out a hard-boiled egg, which he frowned over and peeled, then took a bite. "Do you see somethin' odd about this, Martha?" he asked.

"I think the whole damned thing's odd," she said.

"Yeah, but— Look around. Now, the old man lammin' would have packed his clothes, his toothbrush and shaving stuff, and so on, right? But his magazines and newspapers? I know he had some. I saw them here yesterday. But look— Nothin'. Why, you figure, would he pack up and take last week's *Time*, last month's

Playboy? And where's yesterday's *L.A. Times?* I saw them layin' around here."

"It *is* odd," she said.

"Let's get the fingerprint boys in here and check the place over. I'd like to lift a set of prints and run them through the FBI files, just to be sure Vittorio Savona *was* Vittorio Savona.

"This place is too *tidy,*" Columbo said. "It's like the way they clean up a bedroom after somebody dies."

2

Columbo found Johnny in the kitchen.

"Uh, Mr. Corleone—"

"Johnny."

Columbo nodded. "I wonder if you'd mind giving the medical examiner a sample of your blood. I hate to ask, but it's just routine, y' understand. We're gonna ask the same of everybody who was in the house the night Regina died."

"No problem," said Johnny. "Did you find blood-stains on her? After she'd been in the pool all night?"

"On her terry-cloth robe," said Columbo.

"Oh. Well, no problem. How do I give this blood sample?"

"One of two ways. If you wouldn't mind stoppin' by the county medical examiner's office— Or we can send somebody out to get it."

"I'll go in and give it, Lieutenant. No problem."

"Maybe you could bring Mr. Newcastle with you. We'd like a sample from him, too."

"No problem."

"I'd appreciate it. I see two real expensive Italian cars in the garage. Are those—"

"The Lamborghini was hers," Johnny said. "The Ferrari is mine. When you said expensive, you said the right word. She gave it to me. As a gift. Can you believe it?"

"Well, sure. Sure, why not? Well, we'll be on our way. You'll let me know if you hear anything from Signor Savona? I really wanta know what became of him."

"Sure thing."

"Okay. I appreciate it."

"Anything I can do to help, Lieutenant."

"Well . . . Say, that sure is a beautiful watch you got there! Was that a gift, too?"

"As a matter of fact, it was. I imagine you've guessed there was something between Regina and me besides the houseboy-mistress relationship."

"I hadn't guessed. A watch like that . . . Would you mind letting me have a look at it?" He extended his hand.

"Not at all." Johnny pulled off the watch and handed it to Columbo.

He squinted over it. "Vacheron Constantin . . . I wish Mrs. Columbo could see this. It's somethin' special. That was a really generous gift."

"Regina was a generous person," said Johnny. "Demanding but generous."

"Well, thank ya." Columbo handed back the watch. "I didn't notice that yesterday morning when we talked. You weren't wearing it then, huh?"

"As a matter of fact, no. I was sort of rousted out of bed yesterday morning, you remember. I hadn't shaved either."

"Oh, sure. So, see ya later."

3

Standing in the driveway, Columbo talked with Martha.

"I gotta meet with Mr. Fletcher, for lunch. He called

and said he wants to talk to me. Invited me to lunch. Ya know who I mean? Joe Fletcher, Regina's agent. Tell ya what I'd like you to do, Martha. Talk to Immigration and Naturalization. I'd like to see the records on Regina's entry into this country, also her grandfather's. Then talk to the Italian consulate. I'd like to know what the Italian police have on Signor Vittorio Savona. If anything."

Martha grinned. "Great minds run in the same direction," she said.

4

When Joe Fletcher asked what he would have to drink before lunch, Columbo said that technically he shouldn't have a drink, since he was on duty. Then he said he supposed a light Scotch wouldn't hurt anything. He had left his raincoat in the car, rather than check it and take a chance of having someone else handle it roughly and make something fall out of a pocket. He was aware that Fletcher had passed judgment on his wrinkled gray suit—and that the judgment was not favorable.

"I'm glad we encountered each other in the parking lot," said Fletcher. "Your car fascinates me."

"It fascinates everybody that sees it. It fascinates me, sir, to be perfectly frank. It was made in France, y' know. Technically, I'm supposed to drive a city-owned car when I'm on duty, but the City of Los Angeles doesn't own a car that gives as good service as my car has given me. The way I look at it, when you have somethin' that gives good service, reliable and all, you should take good care of it and depend on it."

They had met in the parking lot of a restaurant called Pacific Sun. Fletcher had explained on the telephone that Regina had favored it, and he thought maybe Columbo would like to see it. Its specialty was sashimi and sushi, but teriyaki was also available. Columbo had taken one look around and judged that Pacific Sun was a place for a woman who could afford to give her houseboy a Ferrari automobile and a Vacheron Constantin watch. It was chic and expensive, and it appeared to appeal to men who didn't wear neckties. His own blue-and-green tie was the only one in the place—and he had tied it as usual with the narrow end hanging below the wide end.

Joe Fletcher was a flamboyant man. His polo shirt was fire-engine red, his slacks were fire-engine green, his shoes were sandals worn without socks, and he carried a tooled leather handbag. He was probably forty years old, but his hair was already white. It was also fine and moved in any breeze that touched it. His pale-blue eyes were sharp and penetrating.

"Well, Lieutenant," he said after their drinks had been served, "do you have any idea who killed her?"

"I've got an idea or two, but so far nothing's jelled enough that I'd want to talk about it. Did you know that Signor Savona packed up and left during the night?"

"And went where?" Fletcher asked.

"Nobody seems to know. That is, the houseboy doesn't know. What's your impression? Would anybody tell Johnny Corleone? I mean, would anybody take him in on important secrets?"

"I hope you don't remain of the impression, Lieutenant, that Johnny was just a houseboy."

"No. He told me he wasn't."

"But there's nothing particularly significant about that," said Fletcher. "I wasn't at the party Thursday night, but I'll wager I could have identified half a dozen men she'd had affairs with. She was not monogamous. She had the morals of a tomcat. It was one way she influenced people. Lieutenant, sex was how Regina said 'please,' how she said 'thank you,' and how she said 'I'm sorry.'"

"What I can't figure out," said Columbo, "is the motive. Why would anybody want her dead? Who's better off for it?"

"That's a very good point, Lieutenant. If I were you, I'd be looking among strangers. I'd be looking for an intruder. Everyone who was there last night—I can hardly think of an exception—will lose money or a job or both, because she's dead. I know what it's going to cost me. I hate to think of it."

"What do you mean 'strangers?'" Columbo asked. "What strangers would those be?"

"She was threatened," said Fletcher. "All kinds of people threatened her: men who claimed they were in love with her, men who claimed she'd made love with them and abandoned them, men and women who said she was a threat to the country's morals . . . and so on. I've got file boxes full of threatening letters."

"You take any of that stuff to the police?"

"Three times stalkers plagued us. One of them went to jail. You may remember the case. If I were you, I'd check to see what became of Edgar Bell after he got out of the slammer. He didn't just think he was in love with her. He was sure she was in love with him, too."

Columbo scanned the menu. He assumed Fletcher was picking up the tab. He couldn't put the bill from this kind of place on an expense account.

"Do you like sushi, Lieutenant Columbo?"

Columbo grinned. "I like anything that comes from the ocean. To tell the truth, though, I never tried any of it raw."

"Don't let me push it on you, but I'm going to have a sushi assortment."

"I'll take a chance," said Columbo. "You order."

Fletcher nodded and shoved the menu aside. "Lieutenant, I want the murderer caught. To be perfectly frank with you, I'm hoping it was not an intruder but somebody I can sue for what her death is going to cost me."

"Meaning who?"

"Of the people who stayed overnight, I can tell you that only the Gwynnes have that kind of money. Joshua

Records is a big business, even if the loss of Regina damages it severely. You see ... They were going to suffer that loss anyway. She was negotiating with another company."

"I guess Mr. Newcastle is not well off," said Columbo. "I gather he was dependent on her."

"He was damn well off once. He spent everything he had on his habit. He's addicted to speedball, which is a combination of heroin and cocaine, and the stuff is very expensive. He was on a salary with Regina, Incorporated. I know he sometimes took advances on that salary. If she refused him another advance and he was getting the shakes, there's nothing he wasn't capable of. You know how those people can be. I guess that's a point."

"Mr. Douglas and Miss Monroe stayed overnight," said Columbo.

"Bob is a genius," said Fletcher. "He's got a great future ahead of him, Regina or no Regina. But he's not worth much now. Christie is what we call a wannabe. She wants to be another Regina. She'd like to be another Madonna. She'd even like to be another Bette Midler. None of that's impossible, either. She's got more singing and dancing talent than Regina ever dreamed of. What she lacks is Regina's instinct for self-promotion—plus Regina's cold, calculating ability to use people and abandon them. But a good agent can make up for those deficiencies."

"You can't think of any motive—"

"Bob and Christie? No. Well, I suppose there's one possible motive. For a month or so Regina made Bob her number-one man. She couldn't get enough of him. He supposed she was in love with him, was making a commitment to him. He was about as naïve as a man can get. I'm sure he was terribly disappointed when he found out she'd moved on to somebody else. He should have realized there was *always* somebody else, even when he was with her every night. I guess he thought she'd betrayed him. I'm sure she hurt him. But that wouldn't give him a motive to kill her."

Columbo tipped his head and raised his eyebrows. "Ya never know."

"Bob came out of it on his feet. He's got something better. Christie's a sweet, beautiful girl, and she's genuinely in love with him. What motive could she have for killing Regina? Only that Regina had hurt the man she loves. No motive, in my judgment. None for either of them."

"I can't reach that conclusion so easy," said Columbo. "In a society where kids kill kids for a gold chain or a leather jacket— Anyway, you understand I have to look at the people who were in the house when she was killed. You say you were not there?"

"I was supposed to be, but I wasn't. I"—he looked up at the waiter—"Two of my usual." Then he turned again to Columbo. "I had something better to do that night. When you'd seen Regina naked once, you'd seen all there was." He sighed. "I said an intruder. Actually, there were a lot of people there who might have wanted to do her harm, even if it cost them something. She climbed over people. She used them and tossed them aside. She was not a nice girl, Lieutenant."

"How'd she get to be what she was?" Columbo asked.

"I asked you to meet with me so I could tell you. That's really the point. Let's have another drink."

Columbo had become aware that Joe Fletcher was no inconsequential man. People coming into the restaurant made a point of waving and smiling at him, though no one came near their table. The people who spoke were flamboyant in the same style that he was: men with long hair pulled into ponytails, linen suits, shirts open, gold chains hanging on their bare chests, women with cascading hair or practically no hair at all, in colorful tight pants, some in miniskirts so short their panties showed when they sat down. They were the kind of people who performed at Regina-type concerts, or wanted to. Obviously, Fletcher was a man who had something to do with whether or not they made it.

"I met Regina about eight years ago," he said. "She came into my office and said she wanted me for her agent." Fletcher shook his head. "Lieutenant, that's not the way it works. Hell, she'd never performed in public. Not even once. She was unknown. That kind of kid doesn't come into *my* office and ask *me* to be her agent. She had— You couldn't say she had balls, could you? But she had a lot of nerve, and it took me about five minutes to discover she had gritty determination. The trouble is, so do a lot of kids. That's not enough. They don't make it on no more than that."

"But you did take her on."

"I took her on. Lieutenant, she had connections. She told me there was a casino hotel in Reno that would book a show, with her as lead singer and dancer. C'mon! An Italian broad with no experience and no obvious talent. But she gave me the phone number of a man who would confirm it. I called him, and he turned out to be the manager of the Rancho Toiyabe Casino Hotel. Well—Reno. Las Vegas it ain't. Rancho Toiyabe. Caesar's Palace it ain't. But it was real. She really had a booking. She'd arranged it herself. What she needed me to do was get her the right kind of contract and help her put together a show."

Fletcher paused as the platters of sashimi and sushi were put on the table. He lifted his chopsticks and dipped a bit of raw red tuna in soy sauce.

"Uh, maybe you won't mind if I use a fork," said Columbo. "I never did get the hang of those chopsticks."

"Not at all."

Columbo tried the tuna first. "Say, this is good. My! Ya learn somethin' new every day. Anyway, you were saying—"

"Even if she did have the booking, I didn't want her as a client. In all modesty, Lieutenant Columbo, I do bigger things than what she was at that time. I named another agent I thought would take her on. Then I found out something else about her. Regina was *persuasive*. It's nothing unusual for young women to— You know what I mean. But she 'persuaded' me right there in my office. The girl was an *artist*." He shrugged.

"What kind of show did she do? That first show."

"The same kind of thing she would always do, except on a smaller scale. I tried to keep it on a small scale. After all, nobody was paying her a fortune to do a show. But"—he shook his head grimly—"That was something else about Regina. She didn't care how much she spent, if she got what she wanted. She spent more than she made. She lost money on the show. She came up with the extra money: $40,000. She called it an investment."

"She *had* that much money?"

Fletcher nodded. "And it wasn't the last time she would make up a loss."

"What was she spending all that money *for*?"

"Musicians. Lighting. Sound equipment. Backup dancers. The whole works."

"Isn't it unusual for the performer to be paying for things like that?" Columbo asked.

"Regina offered herself as a packaged show. Clubs and arenas couldn't just hire Regina. They bought the packaged show. As time went on, it got fantastically expensive. When she came to me, her package was too small for me, as I've mentioned. She became the biggest thing I ever did. They're rare, Lieutenant. Regina. Michael Jackson. Madonna."

"Why'd she become such a big success?" Columbo asked.

"Two reasons," said Fletcher. "She used money and . . . and her special power of 'persuasion' to get people to work for her. Mickey Newcastle is a dopehead bum today, but he was a major rock star ten or twenty years ago. Regina couldn't read music. Mickey could and did. He gave up whatever was left of his own career to promote hers. It's not too much to say that Regina was. Mickey Newcastle reincarnated. She paid him, sure. But she 'persuaded' him, too. Bob Douglas is the finest electronic music man in the business. Kurt Deutsch designed the laser light show that went on behind Regina. He's another genius. And so on."

"Talented people were willing to work for her," said Columbo. "Did she pay generously?"

"Very generously. More and more, over the years. But she left bodies scattered over the landscape."

"Uh . . . What do you mean by that, sir?"

"She hired the best she could get. But nobody had any job security. They had to understand there was no such thing as gratitude, no such thing as loyalty. If a man or woman was doing a great job but Regina spotted somebody she thought could do it better . . . good-bye. Severance money, sometimes, but no thanks. Even guys she'd 'persuaded'—just 'goodbye.'"

"So some people hated her?"

"You better believe it. For example— It looked like she was just wearing ordinary underwear on stage. No way. Edith Goldish designed that stuff. Edith designed her stage undies for three years. One day a guy who called himself 'Mister Don' got to her. He showed her a line of scanties, and the next day he was her designer. Edith got the word when she showed up at a production meeting with some things she'd put together, and somebody told her Regina didn't want to see them—or her. She didn't even have the decency to meet with Edith and give her the word."

"We were talking about her first shows," said Columbo, "and you said there were two reasons why she was a success from the first. What was the other reason?"

"She had a finely honed instinct for treading the fine line between raunchy fun and offensively obscene. Hell, Lieutenant, any girl can go on stage, flash her crotch—or pretend to—and tell dirty jokes. Regina didn't get to be a mega-star that way. There was a lot more to a Regina performance than that. I said she had no talent except for self-promotion and so on. Actually, she did. She had a talent for showing a little more skin than most performers would dare show, for snapping out one-liners nobody else would touch, and for singing utterly outrageous lyrics, while making it all seem good clean fun: just naughty, no more. She knew she couldn't sing worth a damn and couldn't dance at all, and she knew audiences knew it, too; but she made them all believe the whole show was just one hell of a good time. And you know something, Lieutenant?" Fletcher's voice broke, and he ran his hand across his face. "It . . . was."

Columbo stared at the raw fish, the fiery horseradish, the ginger, and the pickled rice on his plate. He chose a bit of the rice wrapped in seaweed. He let Fletcher have a minute to collect himself.

"I'm going to miss her," Fletcher said quietly.

"Yes, sir."

"I'm going to tell you something else. I don't think the old man who lived in her house was her grandfather."

"I wondered about that," said Columbo.

"He was always there, in the background, her éminence grise. I wonder if he wasn't the source of the money she used in the early days. When we went to Reno that first time, she couldn't 'persuade' in her suite because he was living there with her. To tell you the honest-to-god truth, Lieutenant, I had the impression she slept with him. He became feeble in the last two or three years, but he wasn't then. He was a presence. I'm not quite sure what that means, but that's what he was."

"Did you ever talk to him?"

Fletcher shook his head. "Never. She told me he didn't speak English."

Columbo nodded, but did not tell Fletcher the old man had spoken English to him.

"So the old boy scrammed," Fletcher said. "I'd like to know what he had to hide. I mean, it's obvious, isn't it, that he didn't want you to find out who he is?"

Columbo nodded. "I have to figure that."

Fletcher was silent for a minute or so, while he savored his lunch. Columbo followed suit.

Then Fletcher spoke. "I'm afraid I haven't given you anything very specific," he said. "I thought it would be helpful if I filled you in on some background information."

"I'm very grateful to you, sir," said Columbo. "Y 'see, *information* is the name of my business. The only possible way I can figure out what's happened in a case is to hook facts together, one and another, and try to make sense of them. I just gotta get together all the facts I can and try to find some pattern in them. We've been talkin' about talent. Me, I don't have any. I mean, I don't get brilliant insights. I just have to do it my way, which is to plod along, collectin' information, until sooner or later some kind of sense starts to come out of it. So any facts you give me are useful."

"I hope so," Fletcher said.

"I have to ask you a question, though. Can you account for your whereabouts Thursday night? Say, from midnight on?"

Fletcher grinned. "I'm glad I'm not the guilty person. At midnight I was at The Body Shop, sitting at the bar. I talked to the bartender. When the last show was over, I picked up a young lady named Dawn Breeze, an 'exotic dancer' whose real name is Shirley Sheldon. We went to my place. *I* have a houseboy. Mine's really a houseboy. He was still downstairs when I came in. He fried some bacon and scrambled some eggs, about one o'clock. Shirley and I ate and then went to bed. I can give you her phone number and address. Okay, Lieutenant?"

"I gotta do my duty, sir." Columbo returned Fletcher's grin.

SEVEN

1

Captain Sczciegel—pronounced "SEE-gul"—stopped by Columbo's desk. "Catching up on your paperwork?" he asked. The captain was tall, thin, and bald. He was in his shirtsleeves, showing his 9mm Beretta which hung in a holster under his left arm. He stared skeptically into Columbo's wastebasket, which was half-full of memoranda and directives. "That's the poop from the group," he said. "Have you read and absorbed all of it?"

Columbo looked up with a sly smile. "Oh, absolutely. Except the directive on how to handle a prostitute in custody—making sure a female officer is called, and all that. In our line of work, you and I, we're never going to arrest a prostitute. If I ever get one, I'll handcuff her to something and call in and ask what to do."

Sczciegel shook his head. "How you going to do that, Columbo? You don't carry any handcuffs."

"I lost 'em, and was embarrassed to ask for another pair."

The captain sighed, but he grinned. "How'd you manage to lose a pair of handcuffs?"

"Well, I put 'em on this guy. He was a murderer. This was years ago. And a corporal took him in custody and drove him off to be booked. I mean, the corporal had my prisoner and my handcuffs. The prisoner copped a plea and went to San Quentin. I never saw him again. Or the handcuffs either."

"The corporal—"

"Yeah, but I didn't get his name. I was kinda busy, y' see. I'd got the one guy, but he was just one of two who'd killed— Anyway, I never did see those handcuffs again, and I never did get around to pickin' up another pair."

"Columbo— Pick up a set of cuffs. Stick 'em in your raincoat pocket. Anyway, I didn't stop by to talk about handcuffs. What I need to know is, how's the Regina case coming along? The media gang is really raising hell."

"Well sir, I suppose I'd have to say slow but sure. Somethin' very odd has happened in the case. An elderly man lived with her. She told everybody he was her grandfather. Well . . . yesterday morning the houseboy called to say the old man was gone, disappeared. Martha Zimmer and I looked over his rooms. He was gone, alright. His stuff was gone."

"He must have left fingerprints, and like."

"That's what's the oddest part of it. Martha got the fingerprint boys in yesterday afternoon, and they went over the rooms looking for prints. And guess what they found? The only fingerprints anywhere were mine, Martha's, the houseboy's, and the maid's."

"Yours?"

"On the doorknobs. I had to get in. But everything had been wiped. Like the flush handle on the toilet. Like the water glass on the basin. Everything. Nothing was left in his rooms to indicate who he was. His rooms were like a hotel suite that's just been vacated by somebody who stayed just one night, leaving nothing behind to say who was there."

"Which means?"

"Which means that Signor Vittorio Savona was not Signor Vittorio Savona," said Columbo. "Which then raises the question, if he wasn't Vittorio Savona, who was he? Also, why was he so anxious we not find out who he was? Also, who helped him? He didn't clear out his rooms and wipe his prints off everything, plus pack his clothes and leave the house in the middle of the night. He was in his eighties. He had to have help. Somebody besides him didn't want us to find out who he was."

"You have to consider the possibility he didn't leave voluntarily," said Sczciegel.

"We have to consider the possibility he was carried out dead."

"Who knows he's missing?"

"Outside department personnel, nobody but Mickey Newcastle, the houseboy, and the maid—plus, of course, whoever moved him. I've been hounded by the news guys, but I haven't told 'em."

"Maybe we can keep this quiet a little while, till you get a chance to work on it some more. I'll have to report it to the chief. But get this part straightened out as fast as you can."

"If we had another day on it, we might be able to be a whole lot more specific."

"You got it."

Columbo stood. "I'm off, then. I've got people to talk to."

"Keep me informed," Captain Sczciegel said.

"I'll do that. See ya later."

Columbo started out of the office, his raincoat flapping around him.

"Uh, Columbo." The captain raised a finger to stop him and caught up with him. "One little thing, Lieutenant. You haven't turned in your revolver. Regulations require it. You've got to turn in that gun and get the new issue, the automatic. You can have either a Beretta like this one or a Smith & Wesson. But you haven't turned in the revolver."

"Well . . . I haven't got around to it yet. I'll—"

"Columbo . . . Don't tell me you can't find your revolver." Sczciegel wore a lugubrious expression.

"Oh, no, sir. I know where it is. It's wrapped in a—"

"Bring it in, then. Immediately. Get the new gun. Take it out to the range, practice with it a little, and qualify with it. That's an order, Lieutenant. I can't have guys in my division running around without standard-issue sidearms."

"Yes, sir. Soon as I get the Regina case cleared up."

"Okay," said the captain. "As soon as you get the Regina case cleared up."

2

"Hey, Columbo! Wait up!"

He turned and saw Martha Zimmer hurrying among the parked cars.

"Hiya, Martha. You workin' on Sunday, too?"

"Oh, no. I just came in to police headquarters to see if I could pick up a bowling partner."

"I'd be happy to go bowling with ya. Mrs. Columbo just loves to bowl. Of course, she bowls better than I do. She bowls in a league. But if you and your husband would like to—"

"Columbo, I've got some news for you. Kind of important, I think."

He leaned against his Peugeot. "'Kay. What ya got?"

"I faxed our request to Immigration and Naturalization, like you said. They came back pronto, a fax that came in while I was in the shower this morning. Regina Celestiele Savona entered the United States on a tourist visa on August 17, 1988. She came in from Milan on an Alitalia flight. Two months later she made application for a work permit, a green card, listing the kind of work she wanted to do as 'entertainer.' She got the green card. Three years later she applied for naturalization. In September 1993 she was sworn in as a United States citizen."

"Vittorio?" Columbo asked.

Martha shook her head. "There is no record of a Vittorio Savona ever entering the United States. The Italian consulate agreed to put in a request for information from the Italian police. I haven't heard from them yet."

Columbo pinched his chin. "So who was the man called Vittorio Savona?" he asked rhetorically.

"'Was.' You think he's dead?"

Columbo shrugged. "It's possible. Where did Regina enter? New York?"

Martha nodded. "Kennedy Airport."

"You don't suppose . . . you don't suppose Immigration and Naturalization could supply us a list of people who came in from Italy through Kennedy on that day?"

"Why not? I'll ask and let you know what I find out."

"I 'preciate it. I really do. Uh . . . see ya for lunch?"

"Not if you're going to Burt's. I've endured that once this week already. The stomach can only stand so much."

"The finest chili in Los Angeles," said Columbo. "Ya gotta learn to appreciate the finer things in life, Martha.

3

Joshua and Barbara Gwynne lived in a penthouse so high that they had a view of the Pacific and on clear days Santa Cruz Island. Columbo had smoked about half of one of Mort Steinberg's fine cigars in the car, and he had stubbed it out carefully and put it in his raincoat pocket before he entered the building, encountered an unfriendly doorman, and took the elevator to the pent-house.

"You live in an elegant place!" he said as Barbara Gwynne showed him the way to the living room.

"Paid for from the earnings of Regina recordings," she said, nodding sadly.

"You suffer a terrible loss, then," said Columbo.

"Oh, yes. I'm afraid we do. Only last Thursday night she had agreed to let us make cuts of the songs from her new show. Now—"

Barbara Gwynne, Columbo observed, was an elegant woman. Late on Sunday morning, she was dressed in a pair of black silk pajamas embroidered with gold thread. She was fully made up, her chemically blond hair carefully brushed. He judged she was . . . maybe fifty, maybe a year or two older. Her complexion suggested her age. Her skin was thick, evidence of a long-time smoking habit.

"Josh will be out in a minute. At this time on Sunday morning, we usually have Bloody Marys. Will you join us?"

"Technically I'm on duty . . . But—"

Barbara Gwynne picked up and tinkled a small silver bell. A maid in black dress and white apron appeared. "The Sunday-morning brunch will be for three," said Barbara. She spoke to Columbo. "Would you like her to hang up your raincoat, Lieutenant?" she asked.

"As a matter of fact, ma'am, I've got stuff in my pockets that I might want. Like my notebook and pencil. You understand."

She nodded. She took a Camel from a box of them lying on a coffee table and touched the flame of a lighter to it.

"Maybe you won't mind if *I* smoke," Columbo said.

"Go right ahead. There are a few places where it's still accepted, and this is one of them."

He could testify to it. The elegant apartment stank of

cigarette smoke. Columbo pulled out the half-smoked stub of the third of Steinberg's excellent cigars. He fumbled in his pockets. "Oh, say. Gotta match?"

She snapped her lighter and offered him fire.

"Thank ya, ma'am. A man gave me six just wonderful cigars. I've been saving them back and smoking one just once in a while. You know. They're something elegant you get not very often, and you don't want to be casual about them."

"I guess there's a difference between expensive cigars and cheap," she said. "Not so with cigarettes. Once you're addicted, you'll smoke anything. Anything. One's the same as another."

"Never smoked cigarettes," said Columbo. "I— Oh. Mr. Gwynne. Nice to see you."

Joshua Gwynne entered the room with the pained air of a man suffering a hangover. He wore a blue silk kimono over white pajamas. "Have you figured out who killed her yet?" he asked.

"No sir, I haven't. Do *you* know?"

"If either of us figures it out, you'll be the first to know," said Joshua Gwynne, dropping heavily into a chair.

"Well, you might be able to give me some help on it," said Columbo. "In the first place, would you folks mind giving the county medical examiner samples of your blood?"

"Why would you ask us for a thing like that, Lieutenant?" Joshua asked.

"Well, sir, ya see we found a small bloodstain on the terry robe Regina was wearing. We'd like to match that against the blood of all the people who stayed overnight—plus maybe some others."

Josh glanced at Barbara. "You aren't going to match either one of us, for sure. We'll give the blood. I think we'd rather have our own doctor take it. Would you mind having an officer pick it up from his office?"

"Glad to do it that way, Mr. Gwynne. Glad to."

The maid arrived carrying a tray. On it were a bottle of Stolichnaya vodka, a bucket of ice, a pitcher of tomato juice, bottles of Worcestershire and Tabasco sauces, glasses, salt, and a small plate of lime quarters.

"I'll officiate, if you don't mind," said Barbara.

While she was mixing their drinks, the maid went out and returned with a tray of bread sticks, crackers, wedges of various cheeses, and a plate of raw vegetables.

Columbo had a hard-boiled egg in his raincoat pocket, and he would have liked to peel it and eat it with his drink; but he thought better of it and didn't take it out.

"Aside from giving blood, how can we help you, Lieutenant?" Joshua asked.

"Well, sir, what I'm worried about most is *motive*. I can't figure out so far why anybody wanted to kill Regina—unless, that is, it was some stranger who came onto the estate in the night and murdered her out of some wild notion of—"

"Not likely," said Joshua. "That whole neighborhood has a private security patrol on duty twenty-four hours a day, reinforced at night. They were especially alert to Regina's house. A young woman in her line of work got threats. Besides, there was an electronic security line just behind the fence."

"It was probably switched off for the party," said Barbara.

"Right," Josh agreed.

"Then somebody could've—"

"No," Josh interrupted Columbo. "They'd have had to *know* the security system was switched off."

"Well . . . they'd have had to know there *was* one. Anyway. Were there people at the party that you didn't know?"

Barbara handed Columbo a Bloody Mary. "How many people do you think were at the party?" she asked.

"I don't know."

"Well, if you have the impression there were hundreds of people there, it was nothing like that. More like twenty-five or thirty. They were all people she was willing to have see her naked and drunk, which might suggest the majority of mankind but really didn't. There was no one there I couldn't identify. Everybody there knew everybody else. A stranger would have been conspicuous."

"I think we could probably write down a list of everyone who was there," said Josh. "You probably already have a list."

"I do, but it'd be helpful to have another one," said Columbo. "And, say, this is a wonderful drink. Very tasty. I thank ya."

"Motive, Lieutenant," said Josh. "I have the same problem you seem to have. She had offended a lot of people. She had hurt a lot of people. But . . . *enough to kill her?*" He shook his head.

"I get varying stories about what kind of person she was," said Columbo.

"Regina was a vicious, scheming, destructive whore," said Barbara.

"Barbara—" Josh cautioned.

"She didn't climb a ladder to success," Barbara continued. "She climbed over the bodies of everyone who ever helped her. Everybody who ever worked with her bears a scar or two."

"But nothing that would cause anyone to want to kill her," Josh insisted.

"Has anyone told you what Regina did to Christie Monroe?" Barbara asked.

"No, ma'am."

"Barbara, this is—"

"I'm going to tell it, Josh. Lieutenant Columbo will draw whatever conclusions he sees fit." Barbara drew a deep breath. "Regina has always worked with a small troupe of backup dancers. They always play a role very subordinate to hers. When she's onstage, the lighting on them is subdued. They are quiet—in motion but quiet. They are interchangeable. If one of them stands out, particularly if it's a woman, Regina gets rid of her immediately. Nobody is to take even a little attention away from the star."

"Those dancers can *dance*," said Josh. "They have dancing talent, which is something Regina didn't have."

"One day, during a rehearsal," Barbara continued, "Regina turned on Christie and started yelling at her. 'You know what's wrong with you, you whore. You're too fuckin' *good*. So get off my stage.' She was jealous of her. Christie broke down in tears. She begged to be allowed to stay. She needed the job. Mickey stepped in. He told Regina they couldn't get another dancer in time for the show, which was that night or the next night. Regina just shrugged. Christie stayed. Regina never said another word about it. But that's not the half—"

"Barbara—"

"The half of what she did to Christie," Barbara went on. "Les McIntyre, who owns the Lido, expressed an interest in featuring Christie in a number in one of his shows. When Regina heard about that, she called Les and told him he'd be on her all-time shit list if he hired away anybody that worked for her. It would have been a big break for Christie, and she didn't get it because Regina killed it."

"Are you suggesting Miss Monroe killed Regina?" Columbo asked.

"No. She couldn't have done it. Anyway, she couldn't have done it by herself."

"As long as you have your claws out, you might as well tell him about Michelle," Josh suggested.

"You never saw a Regina concert, did you, Lieutenant?"

"No, ma'am, I never did."

"Then you never saw the six backup dancers. Christie is one. Another one is Michelle Durand, who is African-American: a stunning beauty with long, gorgeous hair. Regina insisted she shave her head—which I suppose was okay, considering what Michelle was paid and that shaving the head is an attractive style for some African-American women. But Michelle is a sensitive person and was humiliated by it. Then Regina made jokes about it—jokes about something that had already reduced Michelle to tears."

"What Barbara is saying, Lieutenant, is that some people think the world is better off without Regina. But not us. Her death is going to cost us dearly. And not Christie or Michelle, either. They're losing a damned good salary."

Without asking if he wanted another, Barbara mixed a second drink for Columbo.

"I'm gonna tell you something in confidence," Columbo said. "The old man upstairs—he's gone. Disappeared."

"How could he? And why?" Josh asked.

"We haven't figured that out yet. What I'd like to know is, who is he?"

"I can tell you one thing for certain; he wasn't her grandfather," said Barbara.

"How do you know that?"

"I don't *know* it. But I'll tell you who I think he was. He was Regina's Howard Hughes. In the figurative sense. I suppose you know there was something very strange in the way she got her start. She had money behind her. I've always thought the old man was her moneybags, and when the house was quiet, she went to his rooms and slept with him."

"That's not just speculation," said Josh. "One night a year or so ago, Barbara and I stayed overnight. I guess you know that certain friends had a standing invitation to spend the night. That's the way it was Thursday night. Anyway, Regina was having a great time that night. It wasn't a postconcert party, and she wasn't tired and didn't get too drunk; and it was pretty close to three o'clock before she said good night and started up the stairs."

"It was more like two o'clock," said Barbara.

"Anyway, we were ready to call it a night, too, and we followed right behind her. By the time we got to the top of the stairs, Regina had opened the old man's door and was going in. He was angry, Lieutenant. He said something pretty ugly to her."

"What'd he say?" Columbo asked.

Josh glanced at Barbara. "He called her a whore. He said he was too old to stay up all night. He said she'd better start coming up earlier. Before she closed the door and we couldn't hear any more, she said, 'It's only when I party, Gran'dad. Anyway, I know how to wake you up. Wake up is something you can still do.'"

"He was speaking English, I suppose," said Columbo. "With a heavy accent?"

"No accent at all," said Barbara.

"None at all," Josh repeated.

EIGHT

Columbo took half the afternoon off. He needed to get away from people for a couple of hours and take some time to think through all that the witnesses had been telling him. That Sunday afternoon was suitable for walking on the beach—not for swimming or surfing, though a few hardy boys and girls in rubber wet suits were on their boards. The cool wind whipped Columbo's raincoat around him. It swept the smoke off the tip of his cigar. His attention was divided between the surfers and Dog.

The surfers had inspired a happy fascination in the basset hound, and he had apparently decided he wanted one of his own. Each time one of them came ashore, Dog would run to him, barking and wagging his tail.

"Say, mister, he won't bite, huh?" asked a pretty girl who was just uncovering her sun-bleached hair.

"Well, miss, I never tell anybody a dog won't bite. He never did yet, and I don't think he will, but you never know for sure. There's nobody can guarantee a dog won't bite."

"What's his name?" she asked.

"Dog. Just Dog. I rescued him out of the pound, and I spent a lot of time tryin' to think up a good name for him. I thought I'd watch how he acted and that would suggest a name for him. But I couldn't call him Sleep or Drool, which is all he did."

The girl laughed. "That's great!" she said. "Mister, you got a sense of humor!"

"In the meantime, I just called him Dog; and I guess he heard me call him that so much he figured it must be his name. Anyway, it's all he'll answer to."

The girl extended her hand, and Dog licked it.

"Can he swim?" she asked.

"Yes, miss, he sure can. That's somethin' *I* never learned to do, but Dog can do it. One of my neighbors has got a pool, and sometimes Dog goes swimming— sometimes welcome, sometimes not. I'm not sure he likes the water so much. My wife thinks he likes to swim, but I think he goes in to drown his fleas."

"Oh, he has fleas?"

"I s'pose all dogs have fleas. Anyway, he likes drowning his fleas better than getting dusted for them."

"Would he like to go riding on the board?" she asked.

"I bet he would. Try him."

The girl encouraged Dog to center himself on the board and sit down, and then she pushed him out into the surf a few yards. Dog yapped and wagged his tail. She stayed beside him and guided the board.

"Hey, Columbo!"

"Hiya, Martha."

"Mrs. C. told me where to find you. What you trying to do, drown the dog?"

"Just 'cause I can't swim doesn't mean he can't. He can do some other things I can't do, like scratch his ear with his foot."

Martha grinned and nodded. "Investigating the death of Regina gives us a status we never had before," she said. "Worldwide cooperation. The Italian police have already responded to our request for information." She opened her bag and took out two sheets of paper. "In English, yet."

Part of it was in English. The faxed letterhead was not, and Columbo read the name of the agency that was replying: SERVIZIO INFORMAZIONI SICUREZZA DEMO-CRATICO. The letter was signed by Galeazzo Castellano, *principale,* of the Milan office of SISD. It read:

We join millions throughout the world in mourning the tragic and premature death of Regina Celestiele Savona. It is our honor to offer every possible cooperation to our California colleagues in solving the mystery behind this vicious crime.

Our records disclose that Regina Celestiele Savona was born at Marina di Bardineto, in Liguria, on September 14, 1965. Her parents are Lorenzo and Maria Savona, both born in Marina di Bardineto and still living there. She was one of five children, two sons and three daughters, of which she was the eldest daughter. She obtained a passport on June 30, 1988. Our government was informed that she had applied to become a citizen of the United States and that she did become a citizen in 1993.

Marina di Bardineto is a small fishing village on the Golfo di Genova. A few families there make part of their living diving for sponges, as do the Savonas. This industry, once important, is now mostly a tourist attraction. Scuba divers and passengers in glass-bottom boats observe the sponge divers.

You asked about Vittorio Savona. Regina's paternal grandfather, Vittorio Savona, lives in Marina di Bardineto, where he sells fish in a waterfront market. He is illiterate and has never been more than a few kilometers from the town.

There is an element of mystery in Regina Celestiele's departure for America and her immediate success there. The Savonas are not a prosperous family. How, then, did the girl obtain the money to travel to the States? There is no obvious answer on which people in the town agree. If it would be helpful to your inquiry, I will send a man to Marina di Bardineto to make further inquiries.

"That would be helpful," Columbo said. "Wire the man and tell him we'd appreciate it if he'd do that."

"Will do."

"So . . . If her grandfather's still alive in Italy, then who was the old man in the house? Obviously there's some connection between the murder of Regina and the disappearance of the old man. If we're gonna find out who killed her, we've got to find out who he was. Or is."

2

Mickey Newcastle lived in a flat in Santa Monica. Columbo stopped there on his way home from the beach.

"Uh, Mr. Newcastle, would you mind a lot if I brought my dog in with me? He's just been for a run on the beach, but I've knocked all the sand off his paws."

"Bring him in. And welcome. What can I do for you, Lieutenant?"

"Well, I thought maybe you could give me some help with the problem of identifying the old man who lived with Regina and has now disappeared."

"Have a seat," said Mickey. "Like a beer?"

"That'd be okay as well as nice."

While Mickey went to the kitchen, Columbo looked around. The man didn't live in luxury, nor yet in poverty, either. From his living room he had a view of the highway and the beach, then the ocean beyond. The living room was cluttered, and the furniture was well worn. Seeing that the ashtrays were overflowing, Columbo lit a cigar. Dog, lying against Columbo's leg, was already asleep.

"Uh, Mr. Newcastle, did Johnny Corleone tell you I asked for a blood sample?"

"Yes, he did," Mickey answered from the kitchen. "He and I are going to the medical examiner's office in the morning. Johnny's picking me up. You know what he's going to find in *my* blood."

"I'm not gonna worry about that."

Mickey came back into the living room, carrying two bottles of beer and two glasses.

"The old man . . ." Columbo said.

Mickey shook his head. "He was always around. From the first time I met her, he was around."

"What do you mean by 'around'?"

"I was working a show in Las Vegas, and I got a call from Joe Fletcher. He didn't have to introduce himself to me; I knew who he was. He told me he'd taken on a client, a girl who'd opened a show in Reno and needed help. What did he mean by 'help'? He said she didn't know what she was doing and needed somebody to fix her show. I asked him how she could be doing a show if she didn't know how to do a show, and he said never mind, just come up here and listen to a proposition. He said it would be worth a lot of money."

Mickey paused to drink beer. Then he went on. "To tell you the truth, Lieutenant Columbo, I was past my prime. I'd been big, a superstar, but I was in decline. My style was in decline. So I went up to Reno, and that was how and when I met Regina."

"And the old man was with her then?"

"Oh, yes. He was there. I don't know exactly how to say this. Let's put it this way. He was *a presence*. He was always around, quiet but always sort of brooding. She had a hotel suite with two bedrooms. When I'd come to the suite, he'd duck into one of the bedrooms and close the door. She said he didn't speak English and didn't want to meet people. I saw him, but only for a moment each time."

"Did she say he was her grandfather?"·

"That's what she said. But Lieutenant—*she slept with him!* It was perfectly obvious she did. I mean, she did nothing much to hide the fact. Calling the old man her grandfather was some kind of a joke for her."

"And you went to work for her?"

"Joe Fletcher offered me a first-class deal. I took it. Her show in Reno was bad, bad, bad! It was loud and vulgar. That's all it was. I designed a different show for her. She wasn't easy to work with. Regina couldn't read music, she didn't know flat from sharp, she had no sense of rhythm . . . She had no talent at all. But somebody paid me a handsome bit of money to build a show for her. I gave up performing on my own and went to work to make her what she became. In all modesty, Lieutenant, I *made* Regina. I was Professor Higgins, and she was my Liza Doolittle."

"Uh . . . you say 'somebody' paid you? Don't you know who paid you?"

"At first my checks came from Joe Fletcher. But I knew perfectly well he wasn't paying me, not that kind of money. He was passing it through. Later I was paid by Regina, Incorporated."

"You say Fletcher was 'passing it through,'" Columbo said reflectively. "Can you explain that?"

"The show we did in Reno didn't earn enough money on its contract with the saloon to pay the expenses of producing it. Actually, Fletcher paid me as much as the hotel-casino could possibly have been paying for the show. The money was coming from some other source. It had to be."

"And you think maybe the old man was the source." Mickey shrugged. "Who else?"

"So who was he? And where did he get the money?"

"I didn't ask." Mickey shook his head. "I didn't think it would be a good idea to ask."

"Whatta ya mean by that?"

"I don't know. The old man gave me the impression he wasn't anybody to mess with. Anyway . . . Regina was the center of a vortex, and before long she sucked me into it." Mickey grinned and shook his head. "I should have put that in other terms. The point was, I didn't *want* to know anything negative about her. Lieutenant . . . I was in love with her."

"Seems like a lot of people were," said Columbo. "Mostly people who didn't know her."

"Lieutenant . . . We don't need to go into details. It's been six months since the last time. But she was . . . something extraordinary. At first I was naíve enough to suppose she couldn't have done what she did if she didn't love me."

"You knew her about six years?"

"A little less than that. It wasn't always a pleasant relationship. You'll find out when you go over the books of Regina, Incorporated—if you haven't already—that she reduced my compensation three times. She didn't need me as much anymore. Or so she thought."

"She humiliated people," Columbo suggested.

Mickey nodded. "She did that. She was like a vampire. She sucked people dry and cast them aside. I think she would have cast *me* aside sooner or later."

Dog rolled over on his back, thrust all four feet in the air, and yawned.

"He's got no manners at all." Columbo shook his head. "Never could teach him anything. I guess he learned everything he figured he needed to know before I got him."

"He's alright," said Mickey wanly. "I wish I had a dog like him."

Columbo tipped his glass and swallowed the last of his

beer. "Well, I won't need to bother you any longer. Thanks for the beer. Ya play pool?"

"No, I'm afraid not."

"I know where you can get the best chili in Los Angeles, have a beer or two, and play pool. Over the lunch hour."

"Chili, I'm afraid, is an American taste," said Mickey. "And I used to try my hand at snooker back in London, but I was never really very good at it."

"Sn— Oh. You English fellows call it 'snuke-er.' We call it snooker. Never played it. Big tables with rounded corners on the pockets, right?"

"It's the English pool-type game," said Mickey. "Our people love it. You know, pool and billiards go back a long way with us. At Knoll House, down in Kent, there's a pool table King Charles II is said to have played on. With square cues that had flat handles."

"Imagine that!" Columbo stood. "Well, sir. I'll take Dog home." He stepped to the window and looked down for a moment at the highway and the beach. "Y' got a nice view here."

"I've lived better places," said Mickey.

"Right. Well . . . thank ya again."

Mickey Newcastle opened the door.

"Oh, say. There's one little thing that bothers me. Maybe you can clear it up, so I'll sleep comfortable all night and won't have to think about it."

"Sure. What is it?"

"Well, ya see, on Friday morning you said you got up in the middle of the night to go to the bathroom and you heard a scream. You went to the window, you said, and you pulled back the drapes. Right?"

"Yes . . ."

"And you saw a light-haired man in a red jacket. He broke out running and ran into the diving board and fell down. Right?"

"Right."

"I'm curious how you did that, because from the window in the room you had that night, you couldn't have seen the diving board. There's a real healthy palm tree there in the corner between the wing and the main house, and the palm fronds block the view of the diving board. They block the view of all that end of the pool."

"Oh . . ." said Mickey. "I can explain that without any problem. I said I looked out the window. I did. But when I saw the man, I opened the sliding glass door and went out on the balcony. That's how I saw the man bang into the diving board."

Columbo nodded. "I'm glad I asked, and I'm glad you explained it," he said. "Little things like that, little details, bug me. That's the way I figure out cases, y'see: by noticing little discrepancies and— It's not the way real clever detectives solve cases, but it's the way I have to do, since I'm not as smart as some of them."

"That's how it was, Lieutenant. I went out on the balcony."

"But you didn't see Regina in the pool?"

"No. Maybe that's because I was staring at the man. Maybe it was because she'd sunk and was under a reflection on the water. I don't know. I saw him, but I didn't see her."

Columbo nodded. "Good. I won't have to worry about that."

NINE

1

Johnny Corleone drove skillfully. That didn't make much difference in Los Angeles, where the traffic cops had no appreciation of fine cars and fine drivers. Only on rare occasions did he have the opportunity to demonstrate what he could do with his Ferrari; and this Monday morning, returning from the medical examiner's office, did not offer one of those opportunities. Mickey was just as happy. Johnny could be scary when he decided to put the car through its paces.

Mickey Newcastle had never owned a Ferrari, but he had owned two Jaguars and an Austin-Healey, and he knew what fine cars were. Sitting in the beautiful red machine, his thoughts turned to what might have been if he had not become hooked on substances. He could still be driving a car like this, except for what he had smoked and sniffed and shot up.

Drugs hadn't ruined him as a performer. He could go out on the stage right now and do what he had done in the seventies. What he'd said to Lieutenant Columbo was right: he'd simply gone out of style. And he'd smoked, shot, and sniffed everything he'd made and saved. Oh, it had been glorious! He had wedded himself to all the delightful things chemistry could do. And he had to meet his bride's demands. Right now, he was beginning to feel the pangs of need.

"We've got a problem, Mick," said Johnny. "We might as well face up to it."

"I can think of more than one problem," said Mickey unhappily, "starting with the fact that I've got to have some money to cop. I'll be shaking before the day is over."

"Where you need to go, Pershing Square?"

"Around there."

Johnny pulled out his billfold and handed Mickey two fifty-dollar bills. "That handle you for a day or so?"

Mickey nodded. "For a day or so."

"Now let's talk about something more important. Excuse me, I guess nothing is more important than copping some speedball when you need speedball. But listen to me. Somebody saw us Thursday night. There's a witness."

"Jesus *Christ*!"

"Well . . . This is Monday, and that was Thursday. Our witness has kept clammed so far."

"Who was it?"

"I don't know for sure. But let's do some figuring. I looked up and saw the old man in his window. Okay. But somebody else was standing at the sliding door in the cross hall. I only got a glimpse. Whoever saw me look up ducked back into the dark."

"Who?"

"Think about it. Who'd it have to be?"

"Who the hell did it have to be?"

"It had to be Bob or Christie. Why would the Gwynnes be in the hall? They could look down from the sliders in their room. If Bob or Christie heard the screaming, that was where they'd have to come to look: from the door between the hall and the balcony. There was nobody else in the house. It had to be one of them."

"Why haven't they said anything?"

"Could be one of two reasons." Johnny turned the car onto Broadway. "If it was Christie, she didn't have her lenses in—which is what she told Columbo—and couldn't see enough at that distance to identify anybody. So why didn't she tell Columbo she went to the window and looked but couldn't see anything? At least she could have said that much. That wouldn't have hurt her, would it?"

"Good question," Mickey said. "That she hasn't said anything probably means she wasn't the one."

"That leaves Bob. He knew I was never just a house-boy, and I'd guess he's not talking because he's afraid to be the guy that fingers Johnny Corleone. Or maybe he figures he's got us between a rock and a hard place and can hit us up for something. He's got nothing to gain by squealing to Columbo, but maybe he figures he's got something to gain by showing me he's a good guy who wants to be on the right side of things."

"Besides," said Mickey, "maybe he didn't give a damn that Regina was dead. She'd given him a hard enough time."

"I figure we'll hear from brother Bob pretty soon."

"Next subject," said Mickey. "We just gave blood. To match bloodstains on her robe. There weren't any blood-stains on her robe!"

"Right. But the guy who refuses to give that blood is in deep you-know-what. I don't understand this Columbo character. He acts dumb. But he isn't, is he?"

Mickey shook his head. "I should be so stupid."

"Anyway, we got an eyewitness. One of the two, or maybe both. What are we gonna do about it?"

"Are you telling me we have to get rid of the two of them?" Mickey asked ominously.

"Gimme an option," Johnny said. "But don't worry about *us* getting rid of them. If anything along those lines has to be done, somebody will do it for us."

"My God, Johnny! Who are we mixed up with?"

"Don't ask. What you don't know can't hurt you. Isn't that an old saying: 'What you don't know——'?"

"Don't believe it," Mickey said bitterly.

2

Bob Douglas and Christie Monroe lived in a small, palm-shaded stucco house in Van Nuys. Columbo arrived there at mid-morning on Monday.

"I've been expecting you, Lieutenant," she said as she greeted him at the door. "You understand Bob isn't here."

"That's what ya told me on the phone, ma'am. I can talk to him some other time."

"Well, come in. I'm sitting out by the pool. Would you mind if we talked there? Can I offer you coffee? It's ready."

"That'd be nice."

She stepped into the kitchen to pick up a thermos carafe and a mug, then led Columbo out into a walled-in garden with swimming pool. After she had poured coffee for them both, she slipped out of a short flowered silk wrapper and tossed it aside. She was wearing a tiny white bikini, and as she stretched out on a towel on a wheeled wooden chaise longue, she put on a pair of dark sunglasses.

"Bob will be here late this afternoon," she said. "I'm not exactly sure where he is, or I'd call him."

"Don't bother yourself about it, ma'am."

"He's out trying to scare up a new contract. He's very good at what he does, but there aren't very many shows that can use his special talent."

"Somebody called him a genius."

"He is, but there's not much demand for geniuses."

"And what about yourself?" Columbo asked.

"I have to find a new job. I'm not a genius. There's more demand for me."

Columbo nodded. "Right. That's the way it is with me. I'm sure no genius. I just plod along, doing what I do the best I can, and some way there's always been a job for me."

Christie smiled at him. "Have a pencil today, Lieutenant?" she asked.

"As a matter of fact, I do." Columbo grinned and pulled a long yellow pencil from his inside jacket pocket. "This time I actually do."

"Then, uh . . . do you have a pencil *sharpener*?" she asked, laughing.

"Aww. Mrs. Columbo must have sharpened it too sharp." He frowned over the broken point. "Well, sometimes it doesn't pay to get up in the morning."

"Anyway, how's the investigation going? Is there anything I can do to help?"

"Right now, ma'am, I'm focusing on two things. The first thing is, I gotta have a motive. Y' see, I can't figure out why somebody'd *want* to kill her. It could be that somebody came onto the property and did it. More likely somebody in the house did it, and—"

"That makes *me* one of the prime suspects," said Christie. She pulled off her sunglasses. "Doesn't it?"

"Well . . . not necessarily."

"If you haven't found out yet, my name is not Christie Monroe. I am Christina Oleson, from Swift Falls, Minnesota. Not quite Lake Woebegon, but something like. I took the name 'Monroe,' thinking it would suggest Marilyn Monroe. Of course— Actually, I have a better figure than she did."

Columbo smiled. "I'll testify to that, ma'am."

"Oh, don't call me 'ma'am,' dammit! You're not a

movie cowboy, and I'm not a schoolmarm. Use my name, Lieutenant."

"My friends just call me Columbo . . . Christie."

"Columbo."

"Anyway. Motive. The way it looks to me, everybody in the house that night had a lot to lose by Regina's death. You had a good job—I suppose it was a good job. I've heard you fought to save it when she threatened to fire you. Mr. Douglas had a good contract with her. The Gwynnes say they'll lose a fortune from her death."

"Don't be naïve about that, Columbo."

"Meanin'?"

"Regina is worth more to the Gwynnes dead than she was alive. Stores are selling out of her discs. Joshua Records is going to be hard put to keep up with the demand. And the demand will continue. Think of the greaseball junkie. God, if only somebody'd had the gumption to murder him!"

"Grease . . . Who?"

"Ell . . . viss. Elvis Presley. If he'd lived, he'd have alienated his fans. So would Regina, sooner or later. Death is the best thing that ever happened to her, business-wise."

Columbo ran his hand through his hair, tipped his head, and frowned. "Not personal-wise," he said.

"Not personal-wise, no. She wasn't a nice person, but she didn't deserve to be murdered. I suppose somebody has told you what she did to me. I detested her. But I couldn't have killed her. I mean, emotionally I couldn't have. Physically— No. She was *strong,* Columbo! A weak person—a person without good muscle tone— couldn't have performed the way she did."

"Mr. Douglas—"

"I'm sure you've heard what she did to Bob. You've heard enough to know. He was fool enough to think that meant she loved him. Kill her? If he wanted to kill her, why'd he wait until last Thursday night? Why didn't he do it when she dropped him? That was when it hurt.

Now . . . Now he has *me,* and I can do anything for him she could do—and better, because he knows I love him."

"Johnny Corleone?"

Christie shrugged. "There's a good question. Who knows who he is? What he is?"

"Mr. Newcastle?"

"Has anyone told you that Regina caught him stealing money from her?"

By now Columbo's coffee was cool enough to drink, and he spoke into his mug as he said, "Tell me about that."

"I hope you get confirmation from somebody else, but the fact is, Regina caught Mickey stealing money from her bedroom. I don't have to tell you, he has an expensive habit. She shared stuff with him, too: grass, coke, and so on— but never heroin and never speedball. She never shot anything. How do I know? She *told* me. Regina would never shove a needle in her veins. She liked her body too well for that."

Christie used her right index finger to snap away a gnat that had landed in her navel.

"She destroyed Mickey's self-esteem, Columbo," she went on. "You know, she was what they call a 'ball buster.' She did for Mickey what she did for Bob. Hell, they ought to form a fraternity and have secret hand-shakes and rings and all that: all the guys she did her special thing for. But she made Mickey Newcastle know, over the years, that she needed him less and less, that he was a has-been and, much worse than that, a junkie. That's the worst thing in the world to have to face, Columbo: that you were something good and now you're not, not anymore. Anyway—"

"The money, Christie. He stole money from her?" Columbo prompted.

"Regina didn't like credit cards. She didn't like the paper trail they left. She carried a lot of cash. I've been with her when she paid a dinner check for eight or ten people, and she'd pull hundred-dollar bills from her billfold; and you could see there were still plenty of them in there. I was told she kept money in the house—tens of thousands."

"Now—"

"I didn't see Mickey steal from her, Columbo. I can't testify that he did. I can only tell you what I heard her say."

Columbo nodded. He reached in his pocket and pulled out half a cigar. "Do ya mind?" he asked. "It bein' outdoors—"

"Be my guest," she said dryly, clearly telling him she wished he wouldn't but wouldn't ask him not to.

He did not light the cigar. He fumbled in his pockets for a match, didn't find one, and put the cigar back in his pocket rather than ask her to go in the house and bring him a light.

"She loved to raise hell," said Christie. "I don't know. I think she got a sadistic pleasure out of it. One night in her dressing room, about four months ago, she was giving me hell. She hated the way I danced because she knew I could dance much better than she could. So she was in an angry mood. Mickey came in. He always liked me and always defended me against her rages. That night she turned on him and shrieked at him that he was a thief. I don't remember the exact words, but she told him to stay out of her bedroom. I supposed she meant, you know, sexually. But that wasn't it. 'What'd you grab this time?' she yelled. 'Fifteen hundred? I'm taking it out of your check, you thieving hophead bastard.'"

"She had a safe in her bedroom," Columbo said.

Christie nodded. "She had it put in right after this episode. She turned on me and yelled, 'You ever speak a word of this, I'll—' She left it there, but I knew what she meant."

Columbo put his coffee mug aside on a glass-topped

table. "I'd appreciate it if you and Mr. Douglas would give us blood samples," he said. "You can stop by and let the medical examiner take them, or you can have them taken by your own doctor."

"That sounds ominous," she said. "When do I get the cuffs slapped on?"

Columbo smiled: mouth and eyes. "The blood may eliminate you as a suspect, just as much as the other way. You don't have to do it, of course."

"We'll do it. You said you were looking at two things. I guess we've been talking about motive. What's the other thing?"

"Well, ma'am . . . Christie, I'm curious to know who was the old man that lived on the second floor. He wasn't her grandfather. I guess nobody thought he was. Whatta you know about him?"

"Regina was afraid of him. I can tell you that. She used to pass up fun times, saying, 'I gotta get home to Grandpa.' I mean, we'd finish a rehearsal or something, and somebody'd suggest we get something to eat and maybe go to some fun spot, and lots of times Regina'd say, 'Not for me. Gotta get home to Grandpa.' He had some kind of hold on her."

"Yeah . . ."

"I'll tell you something else. I've seen bruises on her. I can't say he slapped her around, but somebody did."

"You say she was strong, had good muscle tone. The old man was eighty, if he was a day, and sort of feeble. I mean, could he . . . ?"

"If he did it, she let him. I don't know. I wondered if he didn't have something on her."

"Three people say she slept with him."

Christie shrugged. "Maybe. Not recently, I don't think. But when I first met her, first danced for her, maybe . . ."

"We haven't released the word yet, but the old man has disappeared. Friday night."

"That would explain a lot, wouldn't it?"

"How d' you mean?"

"*He* killed her, or had her killed. That old son of a bitch was a menacing presence behind Regina. There was something strange about her, Columbo. Things weren't what they seemed."

Columbo nodded and rose from his chair. "Well— I thank ya, Christie. I better be on my way."

She walked through the house with him, to the front door. "Shall I tell Bob to call you?" she asked.

"I'd appreciate that. My, I hope it doesn't rain. My car's got so the top leaks, and I have to put a sheet of plastic over it, and that sometimes blows off."

"Time for a new car, do you suppose?" she asked playfully. She stood in the doorway in her bikini, her head cocked to one side, grinning.

"I don't know what I'd do with this one," he said. "I couldn't just let it go to the junkyard. It's like an old friend, y'see. I couldn't let somebody crush it just 'cause it's got one or two minor problems. Anyway, it's got lots of good miles left in it."

"I can see that."

"Oh, Christie, there is one little thing I'd like to clear up." He turned away from the car and took a couple of steps back toward her. "I'm curious about the way you said you were so dead drunk that night. You explained about how you got your lenses out. But— Well, you see, you and Mr. Douglas didn't go straight to sleep like you said, I don't think."

"No?"

"No. I hate to have invaded your privacy like this, but we sent the sheets off your bed down to the forensics lab to be examined. It seems you and Mr. Douglas left something on the bed that shows you had a pretty vigorous time during the night."

Christie shook her head. "When you're around a murder, you lose your privacy, don't you?"

"I'm afraid so."

"Well, we did it in the morning, after we woke up."

"No, ma'am. I'm afraid that doesn't explain it. Y' see, your sheets were dry when Sergeant Zimmer and I looked at your bed. The lab boys say that particular fluid takes some time to dry up. Besides, you said you had an awful headache that morning. That doesn't seem consistent with—"

"So I lied," she interrupted curtly. "I was trying to make you believe I couldn't have had anything to do with the murder. No, I wasn't as drunk as I said. And Bob and I did make love before we went to sleep."

"Then why'd you crawl up the stairs?"

"I was drunk enough that it seemed funny. It was a little act. C'mon, Columbo."

"Well, miss . . . Christie, I suggest you don't lie to the police during a murder investigation. You might make somebody draw a bad conclusion."

"I'll be a good girl from now on, Columbo. I didn't kill Regina. And I didn't have anything to do with it."

3

Columbo's next visit was to First Central Bank, where he was ushered into the office of William O'Casey, vice president. A small, precise-looking man who wore rimless eyeglasses, O'Casey shook hands warmly enough but was unable to conceal his astonishment that this unkempt man in a stained and rumpled raincoat was the police detective he had talked to on the telephone on Friday.

"Well, Lieutenant, the deputy district attorney had the order served on us this morning, so I have your information ready. I hope you understand I could not release it except on a court order."

"Oh, of course not, sir," Columbo said. "I understand

entirely. And I'm sorry to have to put you to so much trouble."

"You did say you could accept the information on a computer disk?"

"Yes, sir. Me, I don't know how to manipulate those machines. Mrs. Columbo tells me I could if I'd just set my mind to it, but electronic gadgets just sort of defy me. I guess I don't have the mindset for them. Anyway, we have experts at headquarters who can make computers stand on their heads . . . figuratively speaking."

"Well, then. This disk contains the bank's complete record of Miss Savona's personal account from 1990 to date. It records every deposit and every check. *These* six disks contain the same information for Regina, Incorporated."

"Oh, I appreciate this, sir," said Columbo. "This is gonna be very helpful."

"I made a preliminary search and didn't find the check you mentioned as being interesting to you. She did not write a check to Sunset Classic Cars. I checked the yellow pages for the names of other agencies that sell Ferraris, and there is no check to any of them, either from her personal or corporate account."

Columbo frowned. "Now, that's very strange, because the title for the car I'm interested in says it was transferred to the man who now owns it by Sunset Classic Cars. I guess I'm gonna have to go see Sunset."

3

Columbo stood among the shiny new cars in the showroom at Sunset Classic Cars. "One of the things I like best about new cars is that they *smell* like new cars," he said to the salesman.

"Will that be your trade-in?" the salesman asked, skeptically eyeing the Peugeot parked just outside. "I guess I could probably give you *something* for it."

"Trade-in? Oh, no, Mr. Cohen. I'm not ready to trade my car in. No, it's got lots of good miles on it. I'm here about somethin' else. I'm Lieutenant Columbo, LAPD homicide. I'm investigating the murder of Regina."

Cohen shook his head. "A hell of a tragedy," he said.

Columbo judged Cohen was of the generation that would have appreciated Regina. "I bet you enjoyed her," he said.

"I have every one of her discs."

"You ever meet her?" Columbo asked.

Cohen shook his head. "I wish I had."

"Well, I thought maybe she was in the agency here, like about a year ago."

Cohen shook his head again. "No way. If she was ever in here, I'd have known it."

"Well, let me show you the copy of an automobile title. This is a copy of the title to a red Ferrari. You see, it was transferred from this agency to a Mr. John Corleone a year ago."

"Sure," Cohen said. "I sold that car."

"You— What a lucky coincidence for me! Do you remember Johnny Corleone?"

"Absolutely. You don't sell a $78,000 Ferrari very often. I remember him very well."

"Can you describe him?"

Cohen paused for a moment, then said, "He was a young man. I remember thinking how lucky he was to have enough money to buy a Ferrari at his age. He was a handsome fella. Actually, his face was more like pretty than handsome. Dark hair . . ."

"How did he pay for the car?"

"I don't know. We can ask the cashier."

Standing behind the glass window of her office, Mildred Barnes pulled a manila folder from a file cabinet. "Here we are," she said. "The car was paid for by a cashier's check on Erie National Bank, in Cleveland."

"A check on whose account?" Columbo asked.

"It's a *cashier's* check, Lieutenant. It's a check on the

bank itself. Someone paid for it, obviously, but it's not a check on any individual account."

"The bank in Cleveland can tell me—"

"Probably," she interrupted. "Not necessarily. I remember the transaction. The young man handed over the cashier's check for the price of the car, then paid the tax and title fee in cash."

Columbo nodded. "I thank ya. Thank ya very much."

TEN

Carlo Lucchese drew his right hand back over his left shoulder and swung, slapping Johnny Corleone hard across the right cheek with the back of his hand. *"Buffone! Idiota!"* he yelled. "You're lucky the old man went to the bottom of the ocean! He'd have— He'd have seen to it you got a serious headache."

They were in the warehouse where they had stuffed the body of the old man into a drum and poured concrete over it.

"Carlo, it wasn't my fault!" Johnny pleaded, wiping blood from his lips. "I did what the old man said! I did it when he said and where he said, and—"

Carlo glowered. "There's one thing you're supposed to know if you don't know anything else," he said darkly. "Don't make excuses! You a man, you not a man? You a wiseguy, you not a wiseguy? You was made, you wasn't made? If I decide you get a headache, what you gonna do, Johnny? Beg? You gonna get down on your knees and beg?"

"Carlo . . . I was made. I'm a man!"

"Yeah. You came recommended. Johnny Visconti. Johnny Discount. Cleveland said we could depend on you."

"My mistake was doing what the old man said."

"Your mistake was doing it *bad!* First, that stupid Englishman put a cut on her. Then you didn't get the fixed powder into the Englishman's veins, so he's still walking around. Now you tell me there was an witness! You got one chance, Johnny. You got twenty-four hours to come back here and tell me there ain't no witness. An' you wanta know why? 'Cause we don't trust you anymore, Johnny. You get busted, you'll talk. That's not gonna happen. You're not going to get busted. You understand why?"

"I understand why," Johnny said quietly. "Will you help me?"

"What do you want?"

"I need a biscuit, a clean biscuit. I can't figure any other way to do it."

"Sal," said Carlo. "We got a safe biscuit around? Get Johnny a safe biscuit."

Sal didn't have far to look. He reached inside his jacket and withdrew a .38 snub-nosed revolver. "This one is clean," he said. He handled it carefully, not letting his fingers touch the bare metal. The trigger and grip were wrapped in rough surgical tape that would not take fingerprints. "Never fired in anger, as we could say. No ballistics record of it."

"How about a car?" Johnny asked.

"How about an airplane?" Carlo asked. "Okay, we'll get you a car. I guess since it's California and not Ohio, you don't know your way around."

"And some speedball with somethin' in it," Johnny added. "Mickey's the dangerous witness. The others—"

"Get rid of all of 'em, Johnny," Carlo said. "You got a lot ridin' on it."

2

Mickey Newcastle lay in a dreamy state on his couch. He had not shaved since Saturday, and his clothes were only a sleeveless undershirt and a pair of tattered slingshot underpants. Johnny stood over him.

"You're in a hell of a nice condition," Johnny grumbled. "You aren't going to be of any help to me at all, are you?"

"I didn't know you needed any help. What ya got in mind, man?"

"Never mind. You're in no shape to do me any good. Look—I gotta use the bathroom."

Mickey tossed a lazy arm toward the door. "Be my guest," he said. "Want a beer?"

Johnny shook his head as he went to the bathroom door. Inside, he closed the door and shot the little bolt.

He found what he expected: a needle, a vial of white powder, and a bottle of what had to be distilled water. He poured the contents of the vial into the toilet, then poured the contents of a vial of his own into Mickey's vial. He wiped off his fingerprints and replaced the little bottle precisely where he had found it. Finally, he flushed the toilet.

"See ya, Mick," he said airily as he left the flat. "You figure on coming down off the ceiling anytime soon? You do, gimme a call."

3

Bob Douglas's studio filled a one-time radio studio in Culver City, a facility where famous quiz and comedy shows of the 1940s had originated. The building was ideal for him. It had been built to keep street sounds from intruding on the radio broadcasts, and it was equally good at keeping Bob Douglas's electronic sounds from escaping to the street. Almost the entire space was filled with electronic equipment, the whole completely mysterious to Columbo. The officious young woman who had made him show identification before she would believe he was a police detective had told him emphatically he could not smoke a cigar in the presence of these sophisticated electronic devices.

"Sort of like a shrine here, hmm?" he asked her. "Have to behave ourselves in its presence?"

"The voltages inside the cabinet attract any kind of dust or fumes, Lieutenant," she said. "Tobacco smoke collects in the form of a sticky grease, on thousands of components."

"Like in the lungs, huh?"

She smiled faintly. "Just like that. Anyway, have a chair. Mr. Douglas will be with you in a moment. Would you like me to hang up your raincoat?"

"Oh, no. No, thank ya. It's my office, ya might say. I mean, I carry a lot of stuff in my pockets."

"Mr. Douglas will be with you in a few minutes," she said again.

Columbo stared at a board that must have included a thousand small switches and wondered whatever they were for. Two keyboards were less enigmatic; they made music. But—

"Lieutenant! What can I do for you?"

Columbo's first reflection on seeing Douglas again was that he and Christie Monroe were just possibly the best-looking couple he had ever seen. Bob Douglas was an exceptionally handsome man, conspicuously intelligent and personable. If he had a flaw, maybe it was the pride that kept a replica of his Olympic gold medal always visible on his chest—this afternoon under a green shirt unbuttoned just enough to show it.

"Well, sir," said Columbo, "I don't like to take your time, but you're the only one of the people who were in the house that I haven't yet interviewed privately. I will appreciate your goin' over with Miss Monroe and giving the blood sample, incidentally."

"Have a chair," Douglas said amiably. "Like a cup of coffee? Pepsi?"

"A Pepsi would be nice," said Columbo.

Douglas picked up a telephone and ordered two Pepsis. "So," he said. "Do you know who killed her yet?"

"Sir, if I knew I wouldn't be here botherin' you."

"No bother. Can I be of any help?"

"Well, sir, I'm the sort of fella that, when he gets some idea in his mind, he can't get it out." Columbo slumped in his chair and grinned and shrugged. "You know how it can be sometimes. Right now, I've got two ideas. One is, who was that old man that lived upstairs? I don't suppose you can shed any light on that?"

"Probably not. He wasn't her grandfather, I can tell you that. Or if he was, they had an odd, incestuous relationship."

"How d'ya know?"

Douglas sighed. "You know, I'm sure, that for a while *I* slept with her. There in the house sometimes. In her bedroom. Sometimes she'd tell me to come after midnight. She'd let me in at the front door, and we'd go up the stairs quietly. She said she didn't want to wake her grandfather. Well, one night we were in bed, three or four in the morning, and he came banging on her door. With his cane. He yelled there had better not be a man in there with her. He'd kill him."

"He said this in English?" Columbo frowned.

"Oh, yes. Without even an accent. If there was an accent, it was a Midwestern accent."

"So what happened?"

"She sent me out on the balcony. She let him in. And she . . . she settled him down. I remember what she said.

Vividly. She said, 'Hey, Gran'dad, don't I always take care of you? Nobody but Regina knows how.' She spoke very softly, but I could hear. 'Gran'dad, you were snoring and tossing in bed. I couldn't sleep. I gotta work tomorrow. Now, take it easy. Getting in a hot temper is not good for you.' Speaking of accents, *she* had one: Italian."

"Italian." Columbo turned down the corners of his mouth. "Well . . . figures. Of course, that the old man didn't—"

Douglas grinned. "Dumb situation, huh? At least, I wasn't under the bed."

"So, did he go back to his own rooms?" Columbo asked.

"After another minute or so. He said something more to her. I've been thinking about it. It may be significant. I didn't think of it as particularly significant at the time, but maybe it was. He said, 'You been cheatin' me, Regina. You've got somebody cookin' the books.'"

"What'd it mean?" Columbo asked.

Douglas shrugged. "Sounds like it could be a motive, though, doesn't it?"

"So. Did you come back in?"

"Oh, yes. She locked the door, and we picked up where we'd left off. I didn't think I could, but— Lieutenant . . . I don't know how to describe it. Regina was— I don't know how many guys would have given up everything for an exclusive and permanent relationship with her." He shook his head. "She was incapable of it."

Columbo ran his right hand through his hair and down the side of his face. "I said I have *two* problems. The other one is motive. You may have hit on something there, tellin' me what the old man said about cookin' the books. Still— That suggests he claimed a part of her earnings. But once she was dead there weren't going to *be* any more earnings. What about you? More than one person has called you a genius. More than one person has said you made more money workin' for Regina than you could make anywhere else. She was a goose that laid golden eggs for a lot of people, wasn't she?"

"Somebody must have hated her more than he loved the money."

An assistant brought in the Pepsis.

"Miss Monroe says you're looking for a new job," said Columbo.

"I *got* a new job—that is, a new contract."

"My, that's fine! So quick. Must make you feel a lot better. It must make Miss Monroe happy, too, that you—"

"Christie and I are going to be married," said Douglas. "Next week."

"Well, congratulations!"

"Thank you."

Columbo drank thirstily from his Pepsi. "I've really taken more of your time than I ought to. I shouldn't have to bother you anymore."

Douglas glanced at his watch. "I'll leave the building with you. I want to get home to Christie. She doesn't know about the new contract yet."

"Fine. My car's in the lot."

"Oh, say, Lieutenant. Somebody told me you've never seen a Regina show. Let me give you a tape."

"Oh, sir, it's against department policy for me to—"

"It's worth twenty dollars, Lieutenant. I could hardly bribe an LAPD homicide detective for twenty dollars, now could I?"

Columbo grinned. "Well . . . offer me *fifty,* and I'd have to think about it."

"You mean fifty thousand."

Columbo's grin widened. "As a matter of fact, somebody offered me fifty thousand once."

"You didn't take it?"

"If I had, would I be here asking dumb questions? I'd have taken early retirement."

Douglas shook his head. "I have a feeling, Lieutenant, you never ask a dumb question."

4

Johnny knew a lot about Bob Douglas. He knew, for example, that Bob favored big cars and drove a four-door silver Mercedes. It was parked, as it would be most days, in the lot beside the building that housed the Douglas studio. Getting into it was nothing. He'd grown up on the east side of Cleveland, and he'd stolen fifty cars before he became a made man. Most cars Johnny could get into and start with his tools in no more time than it took the owner to do with his key.

He lay on the floor in the rear seat. He could have started the engine and run the air conditioner, but he didn't dare. He was drenched with sweat and wondered if he stank so bad he would alert Douglas when he opened the door.

He checked the biscuit again. Foolishly. To keep checking the biscuit was nothing but a sign of nervousness. It was perfect: a deadly little revolver, probably stolen, traceable to nobody but its one-time legitimate owner. Even so— He *was* nervous. He was a made man, but he'd never whacked out a guy.

People walked past the car. He saw their heads and shoulders as they walked by. Fortunately for him, Douglas was tall and liked to drive with his seat leaned back. Johnny pressed his body to the floor and was all but out of sight.

Then— Key in lock! The driver's-side door opened.

"I agree, it's a really nice car, Lieutenant. I bought it before I could afford it. But I'm glad I did."

"Oh, yeah. It's a *great* car. I see you're like me; you favor foreign cars. My car's a French car. Of course, it was never anything like this; but, I tell ya, if you take the right kind of care of one of these foreign babies, it'll take care of you. My! Smell that leather!"

It was Columbo! My God, was *he* going to get in the car?

"The way I look at it," said Douglas, "I don't like to tie up too much capital in a car. But this one's an investment. I'll be driving this car ten years from now."

"Yeah, that's the way my car is," said Columbo. "What miles have I got? I think I'm runnin' up on two hundred thousand miles."

Johnny pressed himself as hard as he could into the angle between the floor and the tilted-back seat. He shoved the biscuit under the seat. If one of them spotted him, at least he'd be clean. Of course— What good was being clean going to do him?

"Well, sir, I appreciate the tape. I'll run it tonight. This is Mrs. Columbo's bowling night, and while she goes bowling with her league ladies, I'll just watch a Regina performance. Oughta know what she looked like on stage."

"Okay, Lieutenant. Best to you. Let me know if there's anything I can do for you."

Douglas swung himself into the car and slammed the door. In a moment he had the engine running and the air conditioner spewing cool air into the car.

Johnny had intended to shoot him here, in the parking lot. He would show the biscuit to any onlookers and walk out of the lot and down the street, to the gray Plymouth. Nobody would trouble him so long as he had the gun, and nobody would make any real fix on the gray Plymouth. Once he drove a block or three, he'd toss the biscuit out the window. Then he'd abandon the Plymouth.

Now everything was changed. He couldn't shoot Douglas here, with Lieutenant Columbo in the parking lot. The biscuit wouldn't intimidate the lieutenant. He'd pull his sidearm and blast. He'd be on the radio in a minute, calling for backup. Johnny had no choice but to crouch and wait.

Douglas pulled out of the parking lot.

Johnny reached under the seat and retrieved the biscuit.

He waited. He couldn't tell where Douglas was going. He supposed he was going home to Van Nuys, but from the floor of the backseat he couldn't tell.

He had rehearsed what he would do. He didn't have to change his plan much. Just a little.

Douglas stopped for a traffic light. Johnny pressed the muzzle of the biscuit against the back of the driver's seat. He didn't want to take so much time that the light would change again. He fired twice. Twice should be enough. Douglas slumped forward.

Johnny opened the door and stepped out into the street. The light changed, and drivers honked at him: a pedestrian in the middle of a busy street. Johnny trotted for the curb.

The Mercedes drifted across the centerline into the path of oncoming traffic and struck a Federal Express van.

5

Columbo arrived at Cedars–Sinai Medical Center a few minutes before two uniformed women officers led in a distraught and staggering Christie Monroe.

"Christie!" Columbo walked toward her. "He's not killed. He's gonna make it."

She fainted. An intern and a nurse helped the police-women to stretch her out on a gurney, and they set to work reviving her.

Sergeant Wendy Brittigan resumed making her report to Columbo. "Like I said, Lieutenant, he's gotta be the luckiest man alive."

"Lucky to have a woman care for him that much,"

said Columbo, whose attention was still fixed on Christie.

"Yeah, I— Jeez, she's *somethin'*, isn't she?"

Columbo nodded. Sergeant Brittigan was something, too, in a very different way, and he wasn't sure which he admired more: the exquisite, fluffy dancer or the husky professional policewoman. The sergeant's blond hair was cut short, and her complexion was ruddy and a little rough. What he liked most about her was that she was a woman and remained a woman in spite of her uniform and the Beretta and handcuffs hanging from her belt.

He took the cold cigar from his mouth. It was producing tense stares from people in white uniforms, who seemed to fear he might light it. He dropped it in the pocket of his raincoat.

"Anyway," Sergeant Brittigan went on, "two .38 slugs hit metal braces in the seat. That deflected one of them so much it caught him only under the bottom rib on the right, made a flesh wound, and banged into the dashboard. The other one went through another piece of steel, which took so much steam out of it that it only penetrated a couple of inches. Otherwise— Gangbusters."

"Y' got any line on the guy that shot him?"

She shook her head. "Witnesses say the guy got out of the backseat. Some say he was carrying a gun. Some don't think so. Anyway, he trotted across the street and walked away along the sidewalk. Descriptions vary, of course. Oh— Here's Dr. Gonzalez."

"We've met before," the doctor said to Columbo.

"We sure have. Hiya, Doc. We're gonna make it with this one, huh?"

"Unless he dies of frustration. He's madder'n hell. A little shock. Apart from that—"

"Tell the young lady, will you?" Columbo pointed at Christie. "She's the one in shock. We got the slugs?" he asked Sergeant Brittigan.

"Badly deformed," she said. "Enough for ballistics to make a comparison, though."

"Compared to what? If we haven't got a gun, we got nothing to compare to."

"The thing has some of the marks of a professional hit," said Sergeant Brittigan.

"Except for one little thing," said Columbo.

"What's that?"

"The guy's not dead."

6

Columbo and Brittigan sat over cups of coffee, receiving reports from officers working on the case. The best news was that a hot-dog vendor had found the gun lying in the gutter a block away from the intersection where the shooting occurred. It was a .38, and two shots had been fired.

"Tell me it's not a professional hit," said Brittigan, looking at the revolver through a clear plastic bag. "Look at the tape."

"Yeah. Have ballistics check it out. There'll be no fingerprints on it, but have it checked. I—"

"Lieutenant Columbo?" A nurse approached. He looked up and nodded. "Mr. Douglas would like to see you."

"He's in condition to see me?"

"He's in condition to fight bulls, Lieutenant."

Christie was in the room with Bob Douglas. She was crying, despite the fact that the man she loved was obviously going to survive and survive without major damage.

"How ya doin'?" Columbo asked.

"It fuckin' *hurts*!"

"Yeah, well, you should be grateful for that. Somebody had it in mind that you shouldn't feel anything anymore."

"Lieutenant . . . The guy was in the backseat on the floor when you and I were standing there by the car talking. He was waiting for me. He couldn't have got in any other time."

"I don't suppose you got a look at him?"

"Are you kidding? No, I didn't get a look at him."

"And you got no idea who?"

Bob glanced at Christie. "We have some kind of idea. Christie has something to tell you, Lieutenant."

She was sitting in a chair by the window, and now she got up, came to the bedside, and dabbed at her eyes with a tissue from the box on the bedside stand. She took deep breaths and composed herself.

"Lieutenant . . ." she whispered. "I saw the murder. I was an eyewitness."

Columbo frowned and shook his head. "Well, Christie, you could have saved everybody a whole lot of trouble, probably includin' this—" He waved a hand toward Bob—"if you'd told the truth from the beginning."

"I know that. But, you see—"

"Alright, who did it?" Columbo demanded. For once, he was annoyed.

"That's the point. I don't know. We've talked about how I didn't have my contact lenses in. Well— Without them I couldn't see well enough to identify the two men."

"*Two* men . . . Why don't you start from the beginning?"

Christie returned to the chair. "You figured out that Bob and I made love before we went to sleep. I woke up. I had to go to the bathroom. While I was in the bathroom, I heard screaming. Regina sometimes yelled and screamed when she was drunk, and at first I didn't pay any attention. Then I decided this sounded different. So I grabbed on a pair of panties and pulled Bob's white shirt over my head. That was quicker than trying to get into my dress. I went out of our room and across the hall, then along the hall to the balcony door. And I saw two men murdering Regina. Well— No. They *had* murdered Regina. I could see her—I mean, I could see a sort of vague outline of her. She was under water. One of the men had his back to me. The other one"—she sighed loudly. "You can check with my ophthalmologist. At that distance, he was a blur."

"A red nylon jacket?" Columbo asked. "Either of them? You could have seen that, right?"

Christie shook her head emphatically. "Mickey was lying when he spoke of a red nylon jacket. I could have seen a red jacket."

Columbo ran his hand through his hair. "What did you do? Did you go back to bed? Why didn't you call the police?"

"It was too late to help Regina. It was perfectly obvious that she was dead. I couldn't identify the murderers. But if I came forward as an eyewitness, they wouldn't realize how blurred my vision was, and they—"

"Tell the rest of it, Christie," Bob urged.

"Well . . . Frankly, I didn't give a damn."

PART THREE

ELEVEN

1

Martha Zimmer caught up with Columbo when he stopped briefly at his desk on Tuesday morning.

"Hey, Columbo. How come I have to find out from the papers that somebody shot Bob Douglas yesterday afternoon?"

" 'Cause you didn't check in," he said. "You'd checked the status file before you signed out last night, you'd have seen it. Me, I was tired and went home. It was Mrs. Columbo's bowling night, and I watched a tape of a Regina concert. I'll lend it to ya."

"They want to fly the body back to Italy," said Martha. "You oughta get Captain Sczciegel to authorize you to go to the funeral. You speak Italian. You could learn a lot in a day or two in an Italian fishing village."

"The answer's here."

"Maybe and maybe not. We've got another fax from Milan."

She handed him the sheets, and Columbo frowned over them.

SERVIZIO INFORMATIOZIONI SICUREZZA DEMOCRATICO

I have the honor to report additional facts about Regina Celestiele Savona. You will perhaps find them suggestive.

Regina's father exploited the child, if he did not actually abuse her. As I reported before, a few families in Marino di Bardineto earn part of their living by diving for sponges. It is not a prospering trade except as a tourist attraction. The divers collect coins for diving beneath glass-bottom boats. Some throw the coins in the water and watch the divers attempt to catch them as they sink or find them on the bottom. From an early age, Regina was trained to pursue this trade. Lorenzo Savona saw to it that his daughters became strong swimmers. While they were still very young for the business, he sent them down into the water. They earned more money than most divers.

As soon as each girl developed a figure, Lorenzo sent them down nude. For a time the naked Savona sisters were an attraction that people drove to Marino di Bardineto to see. The girls went aboard his glass-bottom boat at the dock, and people came aboard to go out to see them dive. Lorenzo did not rely on coins they might throw but collected a fee as each person came aboard. When he judged he had all the tourists he would get, he steered the boat out to a place where there might or might not be sponges, and then the girls stripped off their dresses and dived in. For two or three years it was a thriving business.

The sisters, however, resented this exploitation and the accompanying humiliation—Regina especially. She seems to have looked for ways to escape from her father. For one thing, she looked for a man who might rescue her.

The story told in the town is that she established a

relationship with an American tourist, who invited her to live with him in his hotel in San Remo. She went to San Remo, where a month later her father found her living as a concubine and learning to speak English. We have no firm evidence of this, but the citizens of Marino di Bardineto are unanimous in saying that Lorenzo Savona confronted the American and demanded whatever money he was paying Regina. The American struck Lorenzo and broke his nose but then fled, fearing that Italian law might be on the side of the father.

Regina returned to Marino di Bardineto and to diving. She was sixteen years old.

Columbo looked up at Martha. "Is this about the same girl?" he asked. "Regina could hardly swim at all, we hear. This Italian girl dived for sponges?"

"Read on," said Martha.

From time to time thereafter, Lorenzo sold Regina in prostitution. She hated him. In fact, she so much hated him that when she became a millionaire in the United States, she ignored his pleas for a few dollars. It may be significant that Lorenzo Savona pleaded for money but never suggested he would do anything else, such as reveal certain facts about Regina.

Those facts are as follows. For some time a man named Angelo Capelli had lived in a mountainside villa above the town. He was elderly and was obviously wealthy. He showed the local police an Italian passport and lived placidly and without incident, receiving visitors from time to time. The villagers assumed he was a retired leader of the Honored Society, known in the States as the Mafia. He bothered no one, and no one bothered him.

In 1984, when she was nineteen years old, Regina

Celestiele Savona moved to the villa. From that time she did not dive for sponges, nor did she submit herself to prostitution.

I suggested to you before that it would be difficult to imagine where the young woman found the money to pay her passage to the United States. Our further inquiry develops that Angelo Capelli left his villa at the same time Regina Savona left. Quite obviously, she went with him.

Angelo Capelli has no criminal record in this country. I have inquired of Interpol, and it has no record of him.

I will continue our inquiries and may have something further to report.

Galeazzo Castellano

"See what I mean?" asked Martha. "A quick trip to Italy might not be a bad idea. I bet the department would authorize it."

2

LAPD did indeed authorize the travel. As Captain Sczciegel put it, "If it was anybody but Regina who was dead, no way. But the news guys are beating us around the head, and the chief wants to close this case fast. There's a goddamn *demand* for the head of whoever killed Regina. The news guys and gals are in a feeding frenzy."

So much were they that twenty reporters and cameramen accompanied the casket to Italy on an overnight flight from Los Angeles to Milan. Columbo flew on the same plane, and it proved impossible for him to avoid the attention of hungry reporters. They hounded him through his dinner, so much that his two seat companions accepted the offer of a flight attendant to move to other seats. When the flight attendants dimmed the cabin lights, the reporters left him—some of them grumbling that he was either the most cleverly cryptic man they had ever seen or was the stupidest.

The movie was in Italian, and though he could understand it, he was not interested in it. He leaned his seat back and closed his eyes.

"Lieutenant Columbo."

He opened his eyes to find a woman sitting beside him: an extraordinarily attractive woman with green eyes and red hair, wearing a spectacularly short green minidress. It was Adrienne Boswell.

"I hope you won't mind talking to me."

"I never refuse to talk with a beautiful woman. Only thing is, I never know what to say."

"Say, 'Adrienne, I'm going to Italy because—' and then finish the sentence."

Columbo smiled and tugged at his earlobe. "Adrienne, I'm goin' to Italy because I figure I might find out something useful if I have a look at Regina's hometown."

"Let me be more specific, Lieutenant," said Adrienne Boswell. "You are going to Marino di Bardineto because you hope to learn the identity of the elderly man who lived in Regina's house."

"Well, Adrienne, I really don't think I should go into details like that. You understand, police work has gotta be partly confidential. You'll probably say the public has a right to know. And I agree, they have a right to know. But not yet."

Adrienne glanced up at the Alitalia flight attendant who was coming along the aisle. "You like champagne, Columbo?" she asked.

"To be honest with ya, no."

"*Signorina! Vorrei mezza bottiglia di champagne, per piacere.* How about you, Columbo?"

"*Uno Scotch con ghiaccio, per favore.*"

"So, you speak Italian. I might have guessed."

"That's why I'm the one going to Italy," he said.

"How are you getting from Milan to Marino di Bardineto?"

"I'm renting a car."

"A waste of LAPD money. I'm renting a car. Why not ride with me?"

He knew what she had in mind: to have him alone in the car all the way from Milan to Marino di Bardineto, so she could cross-examine him all she wanted. On the other hand, back in L.A. they would sure appreciate it when they saw no automobile rent on his expense account. He accepted her offer.

It worked out just as he'd expected. On the autostrada between Milan and Genoa she began to question him. At first he only smiled at her and didn't answer much. It was difficult to talk in the open Alfa Romeo she had rented, travelling at high speed and passing just about everything on the highway. Then a spit of rain began, and she pulled off to raise the top. Inside the closed car, he could no longer pretend he did not hear her questions.

"Why did somebody try to kill Bob Douglas?" she asked.

"If I knew that, I'd know who did it."

"You *do* believe there's a connection between that shooting and the murder of Regina."

"Doesn't seem like a coincidence," he said.

He stared around him, at the Italian countryside. Though his parents had been Italian and he spoke pretty good Italian, he had never before come to Italy. It wasn't much like what he'd expected—at least it wasn't between Milan and Genoa on the A7 autostrada.

"Columbo, let me explain something to you," Adrienne said abruptly. "I'm damned successful at what I do. I never got a Pulitzer and probably won't, but I've won some other awards. I'm a good reporter. Mostly, that's because people know they can trust me. *You* can trust me."

He raised his eyebrows and shook his head. "I never figured otherwise."

"No. I know how you figure. You're a typical cop, and you figure I'm the enemy. You figure if you're not careful you'll tell me something I'll use to foul up the investigation, or something that'll embarrass you. If you give me something as background and tell me not to use it, I won't use it."

He turned and looked at her. Her spectacularly short skirt had crept up as she drove, and he'd been trying not to stare at her legs. "I really haven't got anything much I could tell you," he said.

"Yeah," she muttered skeptically. "Well, let me tell *you* something. Then maybe you'll feel like opening up a little more for me."

"Okay . . ."

"Okay. Incidentally, Columbo, if it offended me that you were looking at my legs, I'd pull down the skirt. Or I'd have worn a longer one to begin with."

"I'm kinda old-fashioned," he said.

"I've been investigating the Regina story for a long time," said Adrienne. "I was planning on writing a book about her, an 'unauthorized' biography. I had been working on it for months before she was murdered. To be brutally frank, her death is going to make my book worth a whole lot more money."

"Everybody makes money out of murder but me," he remarked. "To me it's just a job."

She looked at him thoughtfully, but did not respond. Then went on with what she had in mind. "You've probably heard the story that there was money behind her at the beginning—I mean, before she began to make any on her own. I went after that aspect of the story. I talked to a couple of men who received some of that money. I asked them how they were paid. Checks, they said: personal checks written out by Regina with a ballpoint pen. On what bank? One of them remembered.

I won't mention the name of the bank. See how I can keep people's confidences? I went to see the bank."

"They won't tell you anything without a court order," said Columbo.

Adrienne smiled. "There are ways of persuading a tight-lipped banker to tell you things in confidence. What I wanted to know was where the money came from that made it possible for Regina to write checks for tens of thousands of dollars. And you know what? The bank didn't know. She'd come into the bank herself, carrying a briefcase full of cash. She'd insist on seeing an officer of the bank—in a private office. He'd sit and count the money, then make out a deposit slip for it. All very illegal."

"How's that?"

"The law requires banks to report all cash transactions over ten thousand dollars. By the time I got to the bank, I suspected she'd been depositing cash, and I pretended I knew. I promised them I wouldn't publish the story if they'd give me the dates and amounts. Actually, all I wanted was confirmation of my suspicion that she'd been depositing cash."

"Any idea where all that cash came from?" Columbo asked.

"What generates loads of cash? Dealing in narcotics. Skimming off casinos. And when you've got a lot of cash, you've got a serious problem: how to get rid of it, how to spend it, how to keep the IRS from finding out about it."

"Maybe you can play a bank game for me," said Columbo. "There's a bank in Cleveland that won't tell us where the money came from that bought a big cashier's check."

"They're not supposed to tell," she said.

"Well . . . maybe you can find out."

Adrienne grinned. "In case you wondered, I don't persuade people the way Regina did. You've heard that story?"

"Oh, yes. Understand, I never supposed you did."

3

The fishing village was as picturesque and as beautiful as he had expected. Fishermen had drawn up a score of small fishing boats on a narrow strip of pebbly beach and had moored larger boats alongside a short stone quay. The village extended two kilometers between the sea and the mountains that loomed behind. The narrow coastal highway was the town's main street. The A10 autostrada was silent and out of sight, since behind Marino di Bardineto it ran through a tunnel. A church stood tall and dignified to the west side of the town square. The town hall was on the north side, a big but less-dignified building. In the center of the square stood the town fountain, kept full by the thin stream of water that issued from the penis of a long-haired bronze boy, reminiscent of Donatello's *David*, who for centuries had stood with his hands on his thrust-forward hips and blandly peed in public. Generations of tourists had stopped long enough to photograph the fountain.

The houses were much alike: stone or brick, most of them stuccoed, with red tile roofs. One of them was the Albergo di Golfo, the only inn the town afforded. Adrienne had booked one of its ten rooms and offered to share it with Columbo—on a Platonic basis, she insisted. She was astonished to discover that Columbo had a room of his own. That had been arranged by Galeazzo Castellano, who had used his police authority to take it from God-knew-which American reporter and assign it to the Los Angeles detective.

She sat at a table with three other reporters, looking petulant—even sullen—as Columbo sat at dinner with Castellano. The tall, slender, graying, elegantly dressed Italian made an interesting contrast with Columbo, who, she observed, seemed to know little and care less about things she cared much about.

Columbo and Castellano spoke Italian.

"In the morning we will speak with Lorenzo Savona," said Castellano. "The funeral is in the afternoon. I have arranged for him to break away from the mourners and come here."

"Maybe he'll be able to answer the question," said Columbo. "Who was Capelli?"

4

Columbo's room had a tiny balcony that overlooked a small lush garden where a dozen cats lounged in the morning sun, scratching and yawning. Although he hadn't asked for anything, a boy brought a tray to his door, so he sat on the balcony sipping strong dark coffee and nibbling on a light roll he had spread with butter. He wished he had a hard-boiled egg.

Last night Castellano had pointed out the villa where Regina had lived with the old man. Bigger than any house in the village proper, it looked comfortable but not grand: a one-story stucco house planted on a steep slope. It was within easy walking distance of the town square. Everything in Marino di Bardineto was within easy walking distance of the town square.

As Columbo was shrugging into his raincoat, he heard a rap on the door. Galeazzo Castellano had come to help him find his way around town.

"It is never like this," Castellano said as they emerged from the hotel onto the street. "This is going to be like a circus."

The town was filling with people. Some came on buses. Some had walked. Most came in cars, and the traffic overwhelmed the police force of Marino di Bardineto: three men in Napoleonic cocked plumed hats and crossed white bandoliers. Fortunately, they were reinforced by a busload of national police brought up from Genoa.

Overnight, carpenters had built a platform in front of the church, for television cameras. Tapes or discs of Regina's music blared from speakers mounted on the balcony of the town hall.

Hawkers sold Regina souvenirs, some of them discs of her performances, most of them pictures, scarves, black bras and panties embroidered with her name, Regina dolls dressed in black underwear, and even crucifixes with a tiny portrait of her mounted in the center.

"Lorenzo Savona doesn't want to see us," Castellano told Columbo as they worked their way through the crowd to the quay where Regina's father was welcoming people aboard his glass-bottom boat. "He plans on making a lot of money today and doesn't want to waste any time."

It was true. Lorenzo was still working the old game of nude sponge divers, using Regina's youngest sister and a niece; and this morning he was selling a complete assortment of souvenirs on the quay and on the boat. He told Castellano rudely that he did not have time to talk to detectives today.

"You've never been prosecuted for selling your daughters in prostitution," said Castellano. "But it's not too late."

Lorenzo shook his head. He was a squat, bald man with only four yellow teeth in the front of his mouth. He wore a dirty black suit and a dirty white shirt buttoned up to his throat, without a necktie. "I am an honest man," he said. "Regina Celestiele went away and made a fortune and never shared a lira with me. Can this American understand what I am saying?"

"*Capisco*," Columbo said.

"Today, is my chance to recover something of what she cost me."

"If you answer straight questions with straight answers," said Columbo in Italian, "we won't waste much of your valuable time."

"What could I know?" Lorenzo Savona shrugged. "She was killed in America. I hadn't seen her for six years."

"You sold her to the old man who lived in the villa," said Castellano. "Who was he?"

"Signor Capelli," Lorenzo answered. "She wanted to move to the villa and live with him. I allowed it." He shrugged. "What else could I do? She was twenty years old and rebellious."

"But he gave you money for her," said Castellano.

Lorenzo shrugged again. "He gave me a present. Now, gentlemen, I must go aboard my boat. People are waiting." He started to walk away.

"Uh, I've got one little question, sir," said Columbo. Lorenzo Savona turned impatiently.

"I can't help but wonder how your daughter came to meet Signor Capelli. Or how you came to meet him."

For a moment, Lorenzo fixed a hostile stare on Columbo. Then he shrugged once more and said, "It's a small town, signor."

The mayor was no more helpful. He didn't know who Signor Capelli was or where he came from. He knew only that it had been good for the town to have him there. He'd been a quiet citizen and spent a good deal of money. The chief of police said the same thing.

5

In a scene reminiscent of a traditional New Orleans funeral parade, the town band led the 1930s-vintage hearse containing the coffin of Regina Celestiele Savona to the church. The hearse was followed in procession by the priest and acolytes, followed by the family: Regina's mother, Maria Savona, two of her brothers, a heavily pregnant sister, and her grandfather, Vittorio Savona.

Lorenzo was not with them. He was too busy.

Columbo and Castellano stood for a moment at the gate of the villa and stared down at the spectacle in the village. They saw many genuine mourners. Apart from the family, scores of Regina wannabes were there, some of them dressed in short black teddies, fishnet stockings, and stiletto heels, wailing over the loss of their idol. Academics from Britain and America were on the platforms, solemnly explaining for the television cameras that Regina had been an underappreciated genius. The world would one day recognize her significant and lasting contribution to American music, they promised.

Castellano turned and rang the bell. After a minute or so, the gate opened. A spare woman with a hard face and stare stood looking skeptically at the two detectives. Castellano explained who they were, and she admitted them to the villa, just inside the gate, onto the lawn before the house.

Yes, she had worked there when Signor Capelli was in residence.

Columbo spoke Italian. "The question is, who was Signor Capelli?"

"I am a servant," the woman said indignantly.

"And we are policemen," said Castellano. "Regina Savona was murdered. It is our duty to find out who killed her. It is your duty to help us. Who was Signor Capelli?"

"He was not Italian," she said. "I know that much. He spoke only a few words."

"But men of honor came to see him," said Castellano.

She shook her head. "I never saw that."

"Could he have been an American?" Columbo asked. "Tell us what he looked like."

"He could have been an American. Or a German. He had the manners of an American—that is to say, he was demanding, abrupt, and loud. He was a little man, not so tall as I am. He wore his hair cut very short. He had a wide mouth, and when he smiled, he showed his teeth. He dressed like an American: checked jackets, knit shirts. I never saw a suit."

"What of Regina Savona?" asked Castellano.

"Squaldrina," the woman sneered—a squalid woman, a slut. "He was an old man. He was lonely. She did the most shameful things to entertain him."

"Signor Capelli was the kind of man who would enjoy the company of a *squaldrina,* though, wasn't he?" Columbo ventured.

The woman turned down the corners of her mouth and turned up the palms of her hands. "He was smitten with her."

"But you don't know who he was?" Castellano persisted.

"Signor. I did my work. He paid me. All my life I have been a servant. If I had shown much curiosity about who my employers were, how they earned their money, and so on, I would soon have been discharged and would have had no references. Being nonobservant is an element of my trade."

"Well, I guess we better not take any more of your time," said Columbo.

She stood in the open gate and looked down at the town and the funeral crowd as Columbo and Castellano walked down the steep street.

"She's lying," Castellano muttered.

Columbo turned around. "Signora," he said, walking back a few steps. "I did have one more little question. If you don't mind. Just a small point, nothing important. But . . . how did Signor Capelli pay you? I mean, did he give you checks, or—?"

She planted an unfriendly stare on him for a moment, then said, "Signor Capelli paid me in cash."

"Did he pay all his bills that way? I mean, for the groceries and things."

"He paid cash."

"Well, thank you, signora. You've been very helpful."

6

Galeazzo Castellano offered to drive Columbo back to Malpensa Airport on Thursday morning, but Columbo thanked him and accepted Adrienne Boswell's offer to drive him in her Alfa Romeo.

To catch their flight they had to leave very early in the morning, and she drove on highways obscured by morning fog.

"What did you find out?" she asked.

"Nothing much," said Columbo glumly.

"C'mon, Columbo, open up! I found out something, and I'll give it to you, but you've gotta share with me."

"Well . . . The old man who lived with Regina in L.A. is the same old man she lived with here. He was just as mysterious a figure here as he was in Los Angeles. He did all his business with cash. The people don't want to talk about him."

"I can understand that," said Adrienne. "I found out something about him."

"Anything interesting?"

"I think so. Marino di Bardineto has just two distinguished citizens: the priest and a Signor Ruggerio Abbatemarco. Abbatemarco owns the villa where Capelli lived. The villa, it seems, is a little too conspicuous for Abbatemarco's taste. He rents it. He's a very distinguished citizen, very weighty."

"Why? Who is he?"

"He's the local *capo,* the local godfather. I figured he'd know more than any other man in town, so I went to see him. He's an engaging, patriarchical type; he made me think of Big Daddy. Happy to meet me. Happy to talk to me. Happy to lie to me."

"So, what did ya find out?" asked Columbo.

"He said Capelli had been a distinguished business-
man in Sicily, a successful dealer in automobiles and
trucks, but was in failing health and retired. Someone in
Sicily had sent him word that Capelli was his cousin and
had reminded him how the two used to roam the hills
together as boys. So he sent Capelli an invitation to
come to Marino di Bardineto and be his guest in his
villa. When Capelli arrived, the two of them soon figured
out they were not cousins and had never met each other
before. Both of them thought it was a big joke, and
Abbatemarco offered to rent Capelli the villa on very
favorable terms. He rented it until he left for the States
in 1988. They became friends. Knowing that Capelli was
lonely, he went up to the villa to dine with him once a
week. He also arranged for girls to visit. He sent Regina
Celestiele Savona."

"You say he was lying to you?"

Adrienne smiled. "Through his teeth. I telephoned
Palermo. The police in Sicily never heard of Capelli.
Certainly he was never an automobile dealer there."

"So that makes him probably a member of the Honored Society," said Columbo.

"I figure it that way," she said. "A big drug dealer,
likely as not."

TWELVE

1

The nonstop Alitalia flight landed at Los Angeles International not long after noon.

Martha Zimmer was waiting for Columbo. "I hope you got some sleep on the plane," she said. "Things are moving fast here. Was your trip worthwhile?"

"Worthwhile? Yeah, I guess so. I gotta have something to report, so I can report that Signor Capelli was almost certainly Mafia-connected. Which would explain why he disappeared so easy. I figure he was already a 'disappeared' guy when he was living at Marino di Bardineto."

"You think he's alive, then?" she asked.

"Why not? The question is, what did he have to do with the death of Regina?"

"You were on television," she said.

"How come?"

"Because you were there, is all I can figure out. Hey, the raincoat looks good on TV. Captain Sczciegel says to tell you to get a new raincoat."

"Yeah, I gotta do that sometime. No hurry. This one's got a lot of good wear left in it."

"Like another ten years?"

"Well . . . another year or two. Who knows? Anyway, you say things have been developin' here?"

"Right. Immigration and Naturalization got back to us again. And guess what? Angelo Capelli entered the United States on August 17, 1988—"

"Aha! The very same day as Regina Celestiele Savona."

"Exactly. On an Alitalia flight from Milan. The same flight. He entered on a tourist visa and disappeared. Immigration and Naturalization never heard from or of him again."

"He wasn't Vittorio Savona, and he wasn't Angelo Capelli," said Columbo. "So who was he?"

"Unfortunately, he came into the States on an apparently legal passport and visa," said Martha. "Which means they didn't take his fingerprints."

"Which he knew they wouldn't," said Columbo. "The man had experience in movin' around the world, never getting identified. And he had money. It takes money to be on the lam like that. This guy wasn't *nobody*, Martha. This guy was somebody."

"Which is gonna make him that much more difficult to trace," said Martha.

"We don't have a picture of him, do we?"

She shook her head. "I'd guess he was careful not to get his picture taken."

Columbo sighed and scratched his head. "Maybe I can do something with a police artist. We let the narcs see a drawing. We get the newspaper and television guys to run it—"

"Also," she interrupted, "you ought to get in to see Doc Culp as soon as possible. He's got the results of the DNA tests and wants to talk to you PDQ."

"Am I allowed to call Mrs. Columbo first? I promised

to call her from the airport, to tell her I'm home safe. She's already upset with me because I went to Italy and didn't take along a camera. I gotta call her and promise her I'll tell her everything over dinner tonight. That okay with you, Martha?"

"Yeah, so long as you don't jaw too long."

2

Dr. Harold Culp sat behind his small steel desk in his office just off the autopsy room. He was eating a ham sandwich. Columbo wondered how a man could cut open a human body and then sit down in his office and eat a sandwich. Maybe you could get used to anything. At least he'd taken off his white coat. Columbo had sometimes seen those stained with blood.

Martha had come with him to the medical examiner's office. She was very much interested in the results of the DNA testing, even though Columbo had suggested maybe she'd have to listen to things she wouldn't want to hear.

"Well, Columbo, it's kind of surprising," said Dr. Culp. "Maybe it won't be to you, but it is to me."

Columbo turned to Martha. "You *sure* you wanta hear this?" he asked. "It's kind of . . . delicate, you know."

"Columbo . . . C'mon!"

Columbo shrugged and smiled at Dr. Culp.

"The easy part first," said the doctor. "The sample found on the sheet in the guest room. That came from Robert Douglas. No surprise?"

"No. They admitted it. At first they said they went to sleep right off, as soon as they got to their room; but since then they've admitted they had a high time before they went to sleep."

"Okay. The semen found in Regina's stomach—" Dr. Culp paused as if for dramatic effect. "The DNA test proves conclusively it came from Johnny Corleone, the houseboy. She'd given him oral sex within the last hour or so of her life."

Columbo squinted and shook his head. "Doesn't figure, does it?" he said to Martha.

"Why not? She was a tawdry bimbo."

"Let's don't speak ill of the dead, Martha," said Columbo. "It doesn't surprise me that she did it. Everybody says she did. What surprises me is that she did it with *him*. 'Course, I didn't really think he was a houseboy."

"Puts a little different complexion on things, doesn't it?" Martha said.

3

Mickey Newcastle was clean. He felt rotten, but he was clean. From time to time he tried it: to go cold turkey, on his own, without help. He thought that if he ever was going to make it, it had to be on his own. If he could just get over a single week without a boost, he might make it.

He wasn't out of stuff. There was some in the bathroom. For three days, almost seventy-two hours now, he'd fought off the craving. He'd thought it would begin to diminish by now, but it hadn't; if anything it was worse.

He'd thought maybe eating would help. Digestion demanded much of the body, he reasoned, and it filled the body with nutrients that might substitute for stuff. He'd eaten sandwiches hourly, washing them down with beer. It didn't help. He'd tried to sleep, thinking he could get past some of the hours by sleeping through them. He couldn't sleep. He woke constantly, sweating, hungering.

And now . . . now the worst was coming: nausea and

chills and hallucinations—and the vivid sense that creatures were crawling on his skin. He recognized this stage of withdrawal. He'd reached it before. He knew there was no point in fighting on. He couldn't make it. He'd tried before.

Still, he lay on the couch in the living room and held out as long as he could. Maybe he could get over a hump. Maybe in another hour—

No! *No!* He couldn't make it! He couldn't . . .

He tried to stand and fell back on the couch. He vomited. He trembled. He crawled to the bathroom, where he pulled himself up and with shaking hands opened the one vial of stuff he had left. He picked up his needle, pulled it open, and poured it full of distilled water. The next step was to—

Christ! He dropped everything. The needle fell to the floor. The bottle of water hit the vial where it sat on the edge of the basin and knocked it into the toilet. It sank and filled with water. All the stuff he had in this world dissolved in the toilet.

He didn't have enough money to cop. Mickey sank to the bathroom floor and sobbed.

4

Johnny Visconti was sobbing at the same hour. He was in the warehouse where they had packed the body of the old man in a steel drum. Johnny was stark naked, and his hands were handcuffed behind his back. Sal and Frank fixed lazy smiles on him and watched him rush around the warehouse after Carlo, who was constantly on the move, going here for a tool, there for something else, always a few paces ahead.

"Carlo! Please! Man, you can't blame me for everything! I'm a soldier. I do what I'm told."

"You don't do anything *right*, Johnny," Carlo snarled

over his shoulder. "Nothing at all. Douglas is out of the hospital and walking around. Shit, man! You can't even shoot a guy in the back. Not even with the clean biscuit we gave you."

"Carlo, I shot him point-blank!" Johnny sniveled.

"Through a car seat. And a Mercedes at that. What you think a car seat is made of, dummy? Vinyl and kapok?"

Carlo strode off through the garage, toward the back where the fifty-five-gallon drums stood in a rough line.

Johnny ran after him. "Carlo, man . . . You gotta give me another chance! I'll get Douglas. I swear I'll get him."

"Whatta you think with, Johnny? Not with your brains, for sure. Douglas wasn't the witness you saw in the doorway. Neither was Christie Monroe."

"It *had* to be?" Johnny protested.

"*Think,* you stupid bastard! You shoot Douglas in the back. The detective comes to the hospital. The broad comes to the hospital. If either of them had anything to spill to the homicide dick, they'd have spilled it then and there. Neither one of them was your eyewitness. You didn't even have that right. You shot the wrong guy."

"Then it had to be the Gwynnes. One of them," said Johnny. "There was nobody else in the house."

"Yeah? Then why are *they* holding out on the homicide dick? Face it, Johnny. You imagined your eyewitness."

Johnny didn't respond. He knew he hadn't imagined the eyewitness, but he knew also it would be better for him if Carlo thought he had.

"How about the Englisher?" Carlo asked. "He's more important. He knows way too much. Did you at least take care of him?"

"He's dead. I gave him the stuff Monday. If he was alive he'd be calling me, asking for money to cop another fix."

"You haven't seen the body?"

"I can't go near that place! The cops are going to find a stinking corpse in there!"

Carlo gave one of the drums a hard shove, to hear if it was empty or if oil sloshed around inside. "You remember how we broke the old man's back so's he'd fit in one of these?" he asked Johnny. "You remember that, Johnny. You keep that in mind."

Johnny whimpered.

"I'm gonna tell you one thing that you'd better get damned straight. If that goddamned detective finds out who the old man was, you're a dead man—and you're not gonna die fast and easy like he did."

"Carlo— *Nobody* knew who he was. Nobody but Regina and you and me. I don't know about Sal and Frank. If you told them, that's your business. But nobody else knew."

"You see the homicide dick on television?" Carlo asked. He strode back toward the front of the warehouse, and Johnny scurried after him. "He was in Italy. What's he trying to do?"

"Hey, he'll never trace the old man down that way," said Johnny, trying to inject confidence and optimism into his voice.

"Yeah? Well, Don Abbatemarco called me. A newspaper broad went to see him, askin' all the wrong questions."

"And the don gave her all the right answers, I bet," said Johnny.

"Yeah, but she's no dummy. She figured it out, probably. The don's a Mustache Pete. He probably figured she couldn't possibly be any threat, bein' a woman. Johnny—The secret's too damned important for any of us to take any risks with it. You go see if Newcastle's really dead."

Sal unlocked Johnny's handcuffs and stood smirking while he dressed. After he was gone, Carlo shook his head.

"The guy's gotta go," Sal said.

"I'll have to ask," Carlo said grimly. "We can't do it on our own say-so."

5

Mickey's whole body shook as he waited just outside the red neon light from the beer sign in the window of a bar called Teddy's. He pulled from his pocket an old and corroded .32 caliber revolver, not a good enough gun for a biscuit, rather what some people would call a Saturday–night special. About a year ago a guitarist had begged him for some rocks of crack and had shown him the pistol, saying he'd have to use it to mug someone if Mickey couldn't lend him the price of a fix.

He knew little about firearms, but he knew enough to know he'd be lucky if it didn't explode in his hand if he had to fire it. He had no intention of firing it. He had thought about unloading it. The trouble with that was, a person looking at it closely could see there were no bullets in the chambers.

Drunks came out of Teddy's. He'd been waiting half an hour for the right one, and he was not sure he could wait much longer. Chills racked his body.

Now— There they were. Two Hispanics, a young man and a young woman. They staggered as they reached the street, then laughed and walked west. They laughed again as the man fumbled with his keys and had difficulty unlocking his car.

Mickey came up behind them. "All right," he muttered, trying to conceal his English accent. "I don't want any trouble. Just empty your pockets on the ground. You"—he said to the young woman—"drop the purse."

The young man turned, grinned, and shook his head. "Hey, man, you crazy?"

Mickey brandished the gun.

"Geef heem wha' he wants!" the young woman shrieked at the young man.

"I'll give him what he wants."

The young man stepped back to set himself to throw a punch. He staggered as he jabbed at Mickey and caught him only with a glancing blow along his left ear. Mickey pulled the trigger. The revolver exploded as he had feared it would, but the explosion drilled a bullet into the young man's right leg.

The young woman tore money from her purse and tossed it at Mickey's feet. She did not see that Mickey's hand was burned and bleeding and did not understand that the gun was now useless. She knelt sobbing beside the young man and pulled money from his pockets. She tossed that on top of hers.

"Leef us 'lone now!" she begged. "Leef us 'lone. Look what you done!"

Mickey was horrified. Even so, he stooped and gathered up the money. He thrust the wreckage of the gun into his pants pocket and hurried away.

Two blocks away, he stopped to count the money. He'd got $116—enough for two fixes and cab fare downtown and back.

6

Johnny hated Carlo Lucchese! He would kill him. Sooner or later he would kill Carlo, if it was the last thing he ever did. Carlo had *humiliated* him! Him, Johnny Visconti, Johnny Discount! The image of himself, naked and begging that arrogant bastard, burned in Johnny's mind. He'd shoot him in the balls.

And how would he explain that back in Cleveland? Well, he'd say that Carlo knew who the old man was and that Carlo wasn't a guy you could trust with an important secret. The don would buy that. Or would he?

No, he wouldn't. He'd want to know why Johnny had taken it on himself to whack out a made man without getting permission first. The Regina hit was one thing. He could do that on the old man's say-so. But a made man, a member? The don would say, "What you tryin' to do, start a war?" Of course, he didn't have to say he did it. He could go home and say, "Jeez, somebody knocked off poor Carlo!"

Yeah. Sure. That's what he'd do. He lit a cigarette. Yeah, that's what he'd do. Only he wouldn't. If there was anything he hated more than Carlo Lucchese it was himself. He'd *begged*. They'd laughed at him, and they were still laughing at him.

One thing. He had one thing over all of them. He knew the whole story. Carlo knew who the old man was, but that was all he knew. Johnny had been around a long time, and he knew the whole history.

7

Johnny had gone home and picked up his Ferrari. While he was there he picked up also his .25 caliber Baby Browning automatic.

He parked the Ferrari a block from Mickey's flat and armed the security system.

At Mickey's door he knocked gently at first, then harder. No response. He wanted to get in without damaging anything. When the cops found the body, they shouldn't see a busted lock. So he worked patiently on the lock.

He was good with locks. He'd done a lot of locks in Cleveland, when he was working his way into the organization. The lock yielded, and he entered the darkened rooms.

Where would he be? In the bathroom? He wasn't there, and he wasn't on the bed, and he wasn't on the couch.

A sudden stab of fear stiffened Johnny. If they'd found him and taken him out already, they might very well be watching this place! He opened a bedroom window and dropped to the ground. He went through a couple of backyards, then out on the street.

And here came Mickey, ambling along, shaking.

8

After he'd taken his fix he didn't make much sense. He'd used tapwater, not distilled, and Johnny wondered how that would play.

"You're telling me you shot a guy?"

Mickey nodded. "I couldn't help it. Shot him in the leg. Didn' kill 'im."

"What'd you do to your hand?"

"Gun blew up."

"Where is it?"

"In my pocket," Mickey mumbled. He pulled it out and dropped it on the floor. The cracked cylinder fell out of the pistol as it struck the floor.

"We've gotta get rid of this," said Johnny. "Could the guy identify you?"

"Maybe. Also his girl."

"Girl!"

"Johnny. I had to have the stuff. I tried to make it without it. Well . . . I can't. I've just got to have it. You ought to understand that."

"Why didn't you call me?"

"I—I don't know. Why didn't I?"

"Listen, man. You and I are in deep. Deep. Somebody saw us, and whoever that is, they're playin' games. You gonna help me, or are you not? You wind up in the slammer, you'll go cold turkey for sure, climbin' the bars."

"Yeah, Johnny. Jesus, I never thought I'd get so low I'd use a gun."

"Well, you did. So what's next?"

"I'm good for a day or two. I can handle a day or two."

"Then we got a day or two for what we gotta do."

"You already tried, Johnny. I saw it on TV. You must be the guy who tried to take out Bob Douglas."

"You think you can do better?"

"Christ— Do we have to do things like this?"

"If you don't wanta climb the bars, Mickey. If you don't want to climb the bars."

Mickey drifted off.

Johnny sighed. With a partner like this . . . Jeez, with a partner like this. He found a beer in Mickey's fridge and sat down to ponder how he could best take advantage of his one asset: that he knew the whole story of the old man, the way nobody else did.

THIRTEEN

1

Columbo trudged along the corridor toward the squad room and his desk, dreading the chore he would have to perform when he sat down: filling out the forms to account for his travel money. He carried a rolled, tattered white bath towel.

"Hey, Columbo," said a detective sergeant known to Columbo as something of a smart-mouth. He was the picture of neatness: creased slacks, a white shirt, necktie properly knotted, Beretta hanging in a holster under his left arm. "What ya got there, a new raincoat?"

Columbo smiled wanly. "Naa. It's my gun."

"Your gun? How come you're carrying it rolled up in a towel?"

"It's a long story."

"I'm interested."

"Well . . . y' see, I flew in from Italy yesterday, so I went to bed early. I got what ya call jet lag. Like, I got up at six o'clock in Marino di Bardineto, to drive to the airport in Milan in time for my flight. Now, six o'clock in the morning in Italy is ten o'clock the night before in California. So, it was like I'd been up since ten o'clock and got no sleep at all a whole night."

"Columbo—"

"You asked. So, when Captain Sczciegel called, I was sound asleep, and my wife took the call. The message was, be sure to bring in your gun this morning. So here I am, with my gun. Y' satisfied?"

"You never cease to amaze us around here, Lieutenant."

"Yeah, well— Y 'gotta match?"

2

Inside the closed door of the captain's office, Columbo stood awkwardly, without his raincoat—in fact, without his jacket, his head tipped, looking with pronounced skepticism at the harness of nylon webbing wrapped around his body. A canvas holster hung in his left armpit.

And now Captain Sczciegel ceremoniously shoved a new 9mm Beretta automatic into the holster. "There!" he said. "Now you look like an LAPD homicide man."

Columbo grimaced at the deadly looking pistol. "Hey, is that thing *loaded*?"

"No, but it's gonna be in a minute." The captain turned toward Martha, who was standing there grinning. "Show Lieutenant Columbo how to load his Beretta and how to set the safety on it."

"Y'know, I ought not to carry it loaded until after I qualify with it," Columbo suggested.

"Martha . . ."

She began to shove 9mm cartridges into the clip. "Y' see, Columbo," she said. "Easy as pie. Then you shove the clip in like this, cock the gun, which puts a round in the chamber, and set the safety to *on*, like . . . this. Here y'are."

Columbo accepted the automatic and shoved it into his holster. He shook his head. "Well, I . . ." He shook his head again and cast a glance at the revolver lying on the white towel on the captain's desk. "Y'know, I really hate to give up that gun. I mean, you know how it is. Y'got something that does a good job for you year after year, you kinda develop a sort of *affection* for it. I kinda feel that way about that gun."

"It served you well by lying under hats and scarves on a closet shelf for all those years, Columbo," Captain Sczciegel said severely.

"Yeah, but I always knew if I needed it, it was there. Y' know?"

"What good would it have done you? You didn't have any ammunition."

"I coulda got some. It's just that— Well, that gun there is *trusty*. Like I know how it works. This one—"

"That's your regulation sidearm, Lieutenant, and I expect you to carry it."

"Yes, sir."

3

Betty D'Angelo sat in a small office crowded with three desktop computers.

"Sorry I didn't get to ya sooner, Betty," said Columbo. "After telling you what a big hurry I was in, I took off for Italy."

"No problem, Lieutenant. Have a seat."

She was an exceptionally pretty young woman, in an appealing, innocent way, and men around headquarters found excuses for dropping by her office to see her. People said there was nothing she couldn't make one of her small computers do.

"Did you find anything?"

She shook her head. "No. Not a check written to anyone named Corleone. No checks to Johnny, none to

Giovanni. I haven't found anything in her checking account that looks like wages paid to a houseboy. A maid, Rita Plata, yes."

"Did you look for checks that came up every week or every month, the same amount?"

"Right. And found what she paid the maid. Also, she paid in withholding and Social Security for Rita—none for anyone else."

"Corporate account and personal account?"

"Corporate account and personal account," Betty D'Angelo agreed. "The corporation had a payroll, of course. But no one named Corleone was on it."

"Well, I thank ya. That's every interesting, and very helpful."

"Anytime, Lieutenant Columbo. Anytime. Always glad to be able to help."

4

As soon as he was a block or so from headquarters, Columbo pulled over to the curb. He took off his raincoat and jacket and removed the shoulder holster. He wrapped the straps around the holster and pistol and shoved that tight little package under the front seat of the Peugeot.

He drove to Beverly Hills, to the mansion where Regina had lived and died. A car belonging to a private security company blocked the driveway. He parked and got out.

"Hiya," he said to the uniformed man in the car. "Columbo, LAPD homicide. Anybody home?"

"Corleone is in there," said the guard in the pale-blue uniform.

Columbo nodded. "Good. That's who I want to see. You gettin' any business?"

"Yes, sir. If we didn't guard this place, guys'd break in and strip the place clean. It's more than just the fans now. Anything that was hers is valuable. Would you believe a guy offered me a thousand bucks just to let him go in there and pick up some of her underwear?"

"That's the way it goes," said Columbo. "I was at her funeral. You wouldn't believe."

The guard grinned. "To tell you the truth, I've give a hundred bucks myself for something she'd worn: a pair of her shoes, even a bra or a pair of panties, I guess. Hell, my wife'd buy a little glass or lucite showcase and seal it in there."

Columbo waved and walked on up toward the house. He rang the doorbell, and Johnny appeared shortly.

"Hey, Lieutenant! Glad to see you. Anything I can do for you?"

"Let's go out to the pool and sit down, where I can smoke a cigar," said Columbo.

"Sure. Can I get you anything: coffee, a drink?"

"Not this morning, thanks."

Johnny opened the folded umbrella over a glass-topped table, and they sat down.

"I figured out somethin'," Columbo said as he fumbled through his pockets, looking for a match. This time he found one and lighted his cigar. "I, uh—" He paused as he puffed to get his cigar going. "I figured out you were not really Regina's houseboy."

Johnny smiled. "I knew I couldn't fool you with that one. How'd you figure it out?"

"Well, you gave us some blood for a DNA test—"

"Saying there were bloodstains on her robe," Johnny interrupted. "I knew better than that."

"I knew I couldn't fool you with that one," said Columbo. "But it wasn't bloodstains I wanted to match. Y'see, we found something else. That is to say, the medical examiner found it during the autopsy. There was somethin' in her stomach. Something from you."

Johnny frowned. "Uh . . ."

"You know what I mean?"

Johnny drew a deep breath and lifted his chin. "She swallowed it," he said.

Columbo nodded. "That means that within an hour or so before her death, you and Regina were, uh, intimate."

"I don't think many people—people who knew us well, that is—bought the houseboy bit. I bet people you've talked to have told you I was no houseboy."

"I guess there's a little skepticism about it," Columbo said.

"Okay. So you know. We were lovers. What she did for me that night . . . she was an artiste. Do you remember what Marilyn Monroe is supposed to have said—that now she was a big success, she'd never have to do that again? Well, Regina didn't feel that way. She was a big success, and she still did it. For any man she liked—or a man she wanted to influence."

Columbo turned down the corners of his mouth and scratched his right ear. "Y' know," he said, "I think I will have a drink. Say a Scotch. Just a shot, with maybe a glass of water for a chaser."

"Sure, Lieutenant, sure. This kind of talk does give a man a thirst. I'll be right back."

While Johnny went into the house, Columbo walked around the pool, staring up at the house, at the windows, the balconies. He walked to the diving board. The palm at the corner where the wing joined the main house did block the view of the diving board from Mickey Newhouse's room. But it blocked more than that.

Johnny returned with what Columbo had asked for: Scotch in a shot glass with a tumbler of water for a chaser. He brought what looked like a gin and tonic for himself.

"All this explains a little thing that's been botherin' me," said Columbo. "Y'see, a look through Regina's checking account shows that she paid the maid regular wages, but she wrote no checks to you. But then, you wouldn't get wages, would you?"

"No. She gave me money. But it was always cash."

Columbo tossed back his Scotch and chased it with water. "She must have given you a lot of money," he said.

"Yes, it came to a good deal. I was a kept man, if that's what you're driving at."

"Gonna have to find a new deal."

"Yes. I'll have to move out of here before long. I thought I'd stay until you solve the case."

"Uhmm . . . Well . . . Shouldn't be too long."

"I'm glad to hear it."

"What time is it? I got a lunch appointment."

"About eleven-thirty." Johnny checked the Vacheron Constantin watch.

"Oh, yeah. Gotta be on my way."

"Well, it's been real nice to see you again, Lieutenant. If there's anything I can do—"

"I'll call on you," Columbo finished the sentence. "I'll sure do that."

Wrapping his raincoat around him, against a stiff breeze that had begun to blow, Columbo strode off toward the gate that opened on the front of the house and the driveway.

Suddenly he stopped. "Oh, say, Johnny. There's a dumb little idea I got. Maybe you wouldn't mind—"

"Anything you say, Lieutenant."

"Well . . . This is a little thing and kinda embarrassin', but you notice the guy that's guardin' the premises, the guy from the security company?"

"Sure. Nice guy."

"Well, I was talkin' with him, and he told me his wife would be grateful for any little memento she could have of Regina. I mean, you figure you could come up with a handkerchief or something?"

Johnny grinned. "No problem. Hang on a minute and let me run inside and pick up something."

Johnny strode off toward the house. Columbo walked back to the table. He pulled a handkerchief from his pocket, picked up the shot glass from which he'd drunk

Scotch, and wrapped the glass in the handkerchief. He
dropped the glass and handkerchief in a raincoat pocket
and walked back toward the gate.

5

From a window, Johnny watched Columbo give the
security guard a half-used bar of *Savon Fin, Gardenia
Passion, aux sucs de laitue 2%*. It was from his own
bathroom, and Regina had never touched it; but the man
and his wife would never guess that and would—the
fools!—cherish it as a bar of soap with which Regina had
washed herself.

He picked up a phone and punched in a number. The
number answered. "Marty? Johnny. I can make a deal.
You say twenty thou? You've gotta do better. Sure, I
know, but you have to understand I can't remove so
much stuff it's obvious and causes an inquiry. Look—
Here's what I got. Here's what I can do. Eight pairs of
panties she'd worn and never had laundered. Got the
girl's smell on 'em. Six pantyhose, the same. Four bras,
likewise. Okay? Stuff that's been laundered's not worth
as much, but I can do about the same numbers, laundered. Shoes, I can do six pairs, all worn. I got two
combs with her hair in it. I got a razor with itty-bitty bits
of hair on the blade. Don't ask *me* what she shaved. I got
a couple bars of soap, used. Listen, I gotta have fifty. No
way twenty-five. No way thirty. Thirty-five is robbery
but I can use the money. Cash. This afternoon. Deal."

Laughing to himself, Johnny went in his bedroom and
gathered women's underwear off his bed. For three
nights he'd slept on these items from Victoria's Secret
so they did stink of sweat. He took the collection into her
suite, dripped Gardenia Passion into a wad of toilet
tissue, and rubbed the tissue on the garments until each
faintly exuded the distinctive scent. The odor was

unique: the combination of his own perspiration and a whiff of the priceless perfume.

Ha! Thirty-five fuckin' thousand!

6

Adrienne Boswell waited in a booth in the paneled dining room of the Press Club. Today she wore tight and nicely faded jeans, with a white golf shirt. This time she denied Columbo a view of her spectacular legs displayed in spectacularly short skirts. The knit shirt displayed something else interesting. Columbo tossed his raincoat in a corner of the booth and bent down to bestow the kiss on the cheek she very conspicuously extended. He did not recognize the scent she favored, but it was as distinctive as the one Regina had worn.

"I appreciate your hospitality," he said. "Seems like I'm always accepting it. My, this is an elegant place."

"In my line of work, I live for lunch," she said. "I write mostly for morning papers, and lunch is when I pick people's brains to get material I use in the afternoon. Don't worry about the hospitality. The car was paid for, whether you rode with me or not, and so is this lunch."

"I'm afraid I can't tell you much," he said. "Anything I said, y' understand would have to have come from me, and it'd be obvious I'd told you what I hadn't told anybody else."

"We'll call it a backgrounder, Columbo. Nothing for attribution. Anyway, I've got something for you. What'll you have from the bar?"

"Technically I'm on duty."

"Let's not live by technicalities, ol' buddy. Technically, I should be grabbing a bite in the office canteen— or at least I should most days. I can't think of anything so sterile or counterproductive."

"I like to get out for lunch," said Columbo. "There's a place where I shoot pool and eat chili. It's great."

"I'll join you sometime," she said. "You shoot a mean stick, Columbo?"

"That's what some people tell me."

"So do I, I'm told. It'll be fun."

"Burt's chili is so hot it'll melt the wax in your ears and burn the lint out of your belly button," Columbo said with a broad grin.

"Anyway—" She nodded toward the waiter.

"Scotch," he said. "And soda."

"So. You want my news first?"

"Sure. What ya got for me?"

"Erie National Bank in Cleveland. I have a friend there who pressed the question of who bought the cashier's check you asked me about. She had to tell the vice president it was an unofficial police inquiry involving the Regina murder. That opened him up."

"So—?"

"The cashier's check was bought with another cashier's check, this one drawn on a bank in Detroit. I haven't got to the bank in Detroit yet. I'm not sure I can. That bank has a reputation for keeping its clients' confidences." She shook her head. "We may have come to a dead end."

"Yeah, but somebody went to a lot of trouble to conceal the source of the money that bought Johnny Corleone's Ferrari. I've been interested in the question of who Vittorio Savona—or Angelo Capelli—really was. Now I'm beginnin' to wonder who Johnny Corleone really is."

"Let me make a suggestion," Adrienne said. "You ought to talk to Maude Ahern. She's written several articles about Regina and knows more about her entourage than anyone besides Regina herself."

"Maude Ahern . . ." Columbo pondered. "Oh, yeah. She was at the party. Her name was on the list."

"I haven't given up on finding out who Angelo Capelli

was, or is," said Adrienne. "He showed the police in Marino di Bardineto an Italian passport. They didn't check on its validity. They had no reason to. But it was not a valid passport. It was a forgery. What is more, the Italian government never issued a passport to Vittorio Savona."

"Which means," said Columbo, "the man was somebody and not nobody. You have to know your way around to know how to get a forged passport."

"The common term for that is that he was 'connected,'" said Adrienne. "As was apparent in Marino di Bardineto."

"The whole deal makes sense. All that cash. The big money from very early on, when she hadn't made any yet. The connection. No wonder she was a success, considerin' what she had behind her."

"What you got to tell me, Columbo?"

He ran his hand through his hair and tipped his head to one side. "Well, that's gonna be tough. I could tell you one or two things, but it's obvious nobody knows but me—or at least LAPD—and it'd be obvious I'd given you the information. I don't hardly need tell ya how much pressure we're under. If the idea got around that I was feedin' you information the other media guys can't get—"

"I protect my sources, Columbo," Adrienne said forcefully.

"Well . . . I guess I can tell you some things. But this is— How they say? 'Strictly in background.'"

7

"Hiya, Dave," Columbo said as he walked into the office of Sergeant David Gould. "Glad to find ya in. I got something I'd like for you to look at."

For this shift, Sergeant Gould was in charge of the fingerprint unit. A veteran officer, with maybe thirty years on the force, Gould was a chain-smoker. A yellow nicotine stain streaked his right eyebrow and his hair where a constant stream of cigarette smoke rose through them.

"Columbo," he said. "When you going to put the cuffs on the guy that drowned Regina?"

Columbo shrugged and did not tell him he didn't have any handcuffs.

"Watch out the FBI doesn't jump in, make a collar, and nab all the credit."

"Whoever makes the arrest, it's okay with me," said Columbo. "Look what I got for you."

He fished the handkerchief and shot glass from his raincoat pocket.

"Have you brought me a souvenir of Italy, or has it got prints on it?"

"Let's hope it's got prints on it," said Columbo.

"Prob'ly yours," Gould muttered as he accepted the glass and peered at it critically.

"Yeah, mine," said Columbo. "I had to take a drink from it. But some others, I hope."

"Let's see." Gould dusted the glass. Because his hands were busy, he spoke with his cigarette wobbling up and down in the corner of his mouth. "Oh, yeah. Yeah— Here." He handed Columbo a glass slide. "Put your middle finger, right hand, on that."

"Can you lift anything good enough to send to the FBI?"

"Yeah. I want to get yours off the slide, so I don't send *them* to the FBI. We'd prob'ly find out you're wanted in seven states back East."

"Eight," said Columbo.

"Oh, yeah. I got a good impression or two. Where you want 'em sent?"

"Local check," said Columbo. "But FBI for sure. If nothin' from that, then Interpol."

"Interpol? Say!"

"Just a hunch. How soon can I know?"

Gould glanced at his watch. "Tomorrow," he said.

8

Martha Zimmer came in to sign out for the day. Columbo was waiting for her.

"Got a question," he said to her. "When you got to the house, had they pulled the body out of the pool already?"

Martha nodded. "And covered it."

"Covered with what?"

"Covered with an officer's jacket. Also, they'd put a handkerchief over her face."

"Where was the terry-cloth robe?"

"Lying on the deck beside the chaise longue."

"What happened to that robe?"

"I had it picked up and put in a plastic bag. Forensics checked it for strands of hair and so on. It's in the property room, tagged as evidence, but I guess it's got no particular significance."

"What about the people in the house at that point? Where were they?"

"In bed. They'd had a big night. I went upstairs and knocked on their doors to wake them up."

"They couldn't have seen the terry-cloth robe, then."

"By the time I woke them up, it was gone. On its way to be examined by forensics."

"Besides which," said Columbo, "if one of them had got up early and looked down and seen the robe lying there, they'd have also seen the body in the pool, wouldn't ya think?"

"Absolutely. How could they have missed her?"

Columbo nodded. "Thank ya, Martha. That's interestin'. That's very interestin'."

FOURTEEN

1

Maude Ahern favored pink, apparently, as she also favored wearing tight clothes over her ample figure. As she received Columbo in her pink living room, she was wearing pink silk pajamas that impressed Columbo as being a couple of sizes too small. She had been taking coffee off a white wicker tray that sat on a glass-top coffee table. Without asking if he wanted any, she poured Columbo a cup and pushed it across the table toward him.

"Frankly, I'd begun to doubt you would ever call on me," she said. "I gather it means you're desperate, that the usual techniques have not turned up the murderer."

"Well now, I wouldn't put it quite that way, ma'am."

"No. You wouldn't. Have you by any chance read my articles on Regina?"

"Afraid not."

Maude Ahern softened and showed a faint smile. "I imagine you don't often read *Rolling Stone* and *Vanity Fair*," she said, her smile widening.

"As a matter of fact, I don't. Mrs. Columbo brings home *Vanity Fair* once in a while, but I have to admit I don't find much in it that interests me."

"Immaterial," she shrugged. "Wouldn't you like to take off your raincoat?"

"Well . . . I guess. Indoors—"

"Yes. Do you smoke?"

"As a matter of fact, I do favor a cigar now and then."

"Well, I'm going to light a cigarette, so you light a cigar if you want to. We have a few things to talk about, and we may as well be comfortable."

"Yes, ma'am. I don't want to take too much of your time. Y' see, I'm no genius. The only way I know to figure out who killed somebody is just to get all the information I can, then work at trying to put it together."

"I can't think of a better way, Lieutenant. And don't apologize for not being a genius. I'm not sure there are any. I've been around a long time, to a lot of places, and I haven't found a genius yet. I sure as hell didn't expect to find one in the Los Angeles Police Department."

Columbo accepted her lighter, offered as soon as she saw he didn't have one of his own. "Well," he said as he held the flame to his cigar, "we do have a lot of very bright people in the department. They get what you might call insights and can skip steps I gotta take. I gotta figure things out by sweat."

"I've heard better of you."

"I thank ya, ma'am, but I—"

"You want to know what was going on in that house," she interrupted. "Okay, I can tell you a few things. Regina's home was a strange ménage. Nothing was what t seemed. Have you figured that out?"

"Well, I've figured out a few things," said Columbo. "I mean, like—"

"That the old man was not her grandfather and that Johnny was not her houseboy." Maude smoked her cigarette in the European manner, holding it between her thumb and index finger instead of between her index and middle finger, and she sucked hard on it, burning a great deal of it at once.

"Right. He was not her grandfather. For sure. And the houseboy was somethin' besides a houseboy."

"That was obvious. It was also obvious that Johnny was her lover. What I could never understand is, why? I always took him for something of an oily character, more egomaniacal than any household servant should have been. Anyway, Regina could have any man she wanted—and did. She distributed her favors democratically and ecumenically. So why should she have been keeping Johnny and giving him money and presents? There was more to the situation than met the eye."

Columbo nodded. He sipped his coffee. "This is very good coffee, ma'am," he said. "Exceptional. How do you manage to make it so good?"

"My companion does that. She's out doing grocery shopping right now. She does the cooking. She's a real treasure."

"Well . . . getting back to the old man. Who was he? Do you know? You got any ideas?"

"Ha! Try and find out. When I interviewed Regina for my articles, she was open about everything. She told me more about her sex life than I could publish. But when I asked about her 'grandfather,' she clammed up."

"She lived with him in his villa in Marina di Bardineto."

"So I read in this morning's paper. Have you seen the piece by Adrienne Boswell?"

"I did see that. She and I were together part of the time, in Italy. She found out more than I did."

"The second time I asked Regina about her grandfather, she got quite huffy. She stalked off and came back in a couple of minutes with his passport. Sure enough, i was an Italian passport in the name of Vittorio Savona her grandfather. Yet, Adrienne Boswell says she met and spoke with Vittorio Savona in Marina di Bardineto and that he told her he had never been outside Italy in his life."

"The passport was a forgery," said Columbo. "The Italian government never issued a passport in the name Vittorio Savona."

"Well, I can tell you something about that forged passport," Maude said. "I flipped through it, looking at the visas stamped in it. There was one in it indicating that Savona had entered the States through Kennedy Airport in 1988. There was another one. In 1992 he paid a visit to Brazil."

"The stamp showing when he entered the States had to be part of the forgery," said Columbo. "Maybe the Brazilian visa was, too. Even so, I sure would like to know what date it indicated."

Maude Ahern grinned. "I'm a journalist, my man. I take notes." She reached for a little steno pad lying on the coffee table. "I didn't write these dates down while Regina was looking, but Savona entered Brazil on February 18. His visa was stamped in his passport at Galeao Airport, Rio di Janeiro. He returned to the States through Miami on February 21."

"Doesn't sound like a winter vacation," said Columbo. "More like a business trip."

Showing her lacquered pink fingernails to advantage, Maude smiled and closed the notebook. "You see? You should have come to me sooner."

"Yes, ma'am. I guess I should have."

2

FBI agent Robert Brady shook hands with Columbo and pointed at a chair. "I'd say you've got a real tough one on your hands. Wouldn't you?"

Columbo nodded. LAPD and the FBI were friendly and worked cooperatively; still, there was a reluctance on both their parts to draw each other into investigations. Columbo had taken the precaution of calling Captain Sczciegel and asking for permission to ask for FBI assistance in anything more than checking fingerprints against their vast Washington file. Even so, he had known Bob Brady many years and knew him well.

Brady was of the old FBI, when J. Edgar Hoover was still in charge and required every agent to wear a felt hat in winter, a straw hat in summer, dark suits, white shirts, conservative neckties, and well-shined lace-up shoes; and Brady had never changed styles. He had a pistol hanging in a holster inside his jacket, but he'd had his suit cut so the weapon could never be noticed— particularly in view of the fact that he always kept his jacket buttoned. Bob Brady was a buttoned-up guy, Columbo had once remarked at Burt's and had gotten a laugh.

There could hardly have been greater contrast between two men.

"The news media aren't making things easier," said Brady. "I saw the Adrienne Boswell story this morning."

"Actually, Adrienne's been helpful. She gave me some information that's been useful."

"I wouldn't think of telling you how to do your business, Columbo, but beware of red-haired news gals offering to exchange confidences—or more."

"Nothin' like that, Bob. Nothin' like that."

"Okay. What can I do for you?"

"One Vittorio Savona entered Brazil on an Italian passport on February 18, 1992. I figure he'd flown to Rio di Janeiro from L.A., though maybe from somewhere else. Anyway, he returned to the States through Miami on February 21. Some quick trip for a man in his eighties. I was wonderin' if Brazil could give us a list of other Americans who landed at Rio on February 18 and if the FBI could run the names to see who they were."

"A minor diplomatic problem, but it shouldn't be too difficult if Brazil cooperates."

"It could answer a whole lot of questions."

"You got it," Brady said crisply. "Since this is Saturday, it will take a little time."

3

At noon Columbo went to Burt's for a game of pool, a bowl of chili, and a Dr Pepper. The crowd that played on Saturdays was tougher than the weekday crowd, and he lost two dollars.

Annoyed—not at having lost but because he felt he hadn't played well—he decided to go home. Maybe he and Mrs. Columbo would take in a movie this evening. Maybe he'd take Dog to the beach. He wondered if there was anything good on television tonight. He wondered if there was stuff in the house to make fettucine carbonara, for which he suddenly had a hankering. Maybe he'd call and ask, and if there wasn't, he could pick up the necessaries on the way home. Plus a nice bottle of Chianti.

First he'd call headquarters and tell them he was going off duty for the rest of the day.

Yeah. The best-laid plans.

"Columbo? Glad you called in. Listen, you ought to pop down here. We've got a couple of people in custody that ought to interest you. The maid. Rita Plata. And her husband."

Rita sat in a small conference room, with a uniformed woman officer.

"What?" Columbo asked.

"She took a knife to her husband," said the officer. "You can see why."

"Yeah."

Rita's left eye was swollen almost shut. Her nose was bloody, maybe broken. Blood had dripped on her white T-shirt and on her white knit shorts.

"Domestic disturbance," said the officer. "The husband's gonna be short an ear but otherwise will survive

intact. Captain recognized the name as the name of the
maid at Regina's house and thought you'd want to see
her."

"Thank ya. Lemme talk to her alone, okay."

The officer left, and Columbo sat down across the table from the teary Rita.

"We've only seen each other once," Columbo reminded her. "I meant to get to you, to ask you some
questions, but—"

"I know nothing."

"That's what I figured. What happened at home?"

"He beat me. Too much. I take the knife and—"

"Why'd he beat you, Rita?"

"None you business."

"Afraid it is my business. Police business, anyway.
You don't want us to have to lock you up, do you? Now,
tell me why your husband beat you."

"He calls me *una puta*. He think I have done *el
adulterio* with Hohnny."

"With who?"

"With Hohnny. Hohnny Corleone. I have *not* done
this thing. I let him kiss, kiss— He touch *tetas* one time.
But no more. I make big mistake. I am honest woman,
and I told Julio these things."

"Julio's your husband?"

"*Si.* I told him, and he decide I have done more."

Columbo put his hand in his hair and shook his head.
"He thinks you—"

"I tell him. I am *not* done this thing. I do not go in bed
with Hohnny. I am honest woman. I say, kiss, kiss, touch
tetas maybe, just for fun. With laugh. But Julio go crazy.
He say he kill Hohnny." She stopped and shook her
head. "He *get* killed."

"What makes ya say that?"

"Hohnny has gun."

"Tell me about it."

"I clean house. Sometime I see gun, *una pistola,* in

Hohnny's room. Little gun. Very little. Hohnny is a bad man. Bad men come to house to see him. They think I don't know. I had left house but had to go back to get keys I had left in kitchen. I saw. Three men. Not nice men. They had come to house before, to see the old man."

"When was this, Rita?" Columbo asked.

"Day after murder."

"Like a Coke?"

"Yes."

Columbo went to the door, opened it, and asked the waiting officer if she would mind bringing a couple of Cokes.

He sat down again with Rita. "Whatta ya know about the old man?" he asked.

Rita shook her head. *"Muy malo!"* she snapped. "He was . . . He was wicked old man." She shook her head again, almost convulsively. "He was Miss Regina's grandfather, but he make her do dirty things . . . *her grandfather!*"

"Do what things?" Columbo asked.

"She go to bed with him! I smell her perfume when I make his bed. On sheets. Bad old man."

"These men who came to see him," said Columbo. "Could they have taken him away?"

"Maybe."

"Did he have other visitors?"

Rita nodded solemnly. "Sometime. He have friends. Old men some. Like him. One of them speaks *español* to me. He sees me, he speaks *español*. Mexican."

"Are you sure he was Mexican?" Columbo asked. "How could you tell?"

"He speak like me. Mexican. He see Hohnny, he say, *'Este mozo me cae gordo.'* It mean he no like Hohnny, but only Mexican say it that way."

"Did he come to the house once or more than once?"

"He come again. Sometimes. Old man come down.

They sit by pool. Old man swim. He swim every day, much. When old man come out of pool, they sit and smoke cigars and drink whisky. Friends."

"But you don't know who he was?"

Rita shook her head.

"Okay, Rita," said Columbo. "Domestic Relations will work out your problems for you and your husband. You listen to what they tell ya."

4

Johnny sat in a blue Chevy, parked across the street and a little up the block from the house in Van Nuys where Bob Douglas lived with Christie Monroe. He'd stolen the car an hour ago. He hadn't grown up a Cleveland wannabe wiseguy for nothin', and there weren't many cars he couldn't lift if he wanted to.

. He was worried. No, he was worse than worried—he was terrified. He'd told Carlo that Mickey was dead, and Mickey wasn't dead. How long before Carlo found out? What was more important, getting rid of Mickey or getting rid of Bob?

Carlo would never accept his own share of responsibility for what went wrong. Mickey'd shot the stuff Carlo'd sent. Hadn't he? Was Mickey so far gone that he could take the toxic chemicals in the stuff and survive? Or hadn't he shot it? Or had Carlo provided weak stuff?

And what about the biscuit? If it had been tough enough, the slugs would have gone where they were supposed to. A stupid .38! If it'd been a .357 magnum or a .44 magnum, forget the steel in the back of a car seat; the slug would have gone through.

But— Carlo would lay it all on him. Everybody would lay it on him. He didn't have time to think out something smart. He had to *do* it!

Everything was fouled up. It was all fouled up! They'd

given him a tough job, but he'd taken it on and done it right till the old boy lost his temper.

This time, no biscuit. The gun he carried tonight was a goddamned *cannon*: a .44 magnum Desert Eagle automatic, capable of cracking an engine block and stopping a car, capable of throwing a man on his back, as dead as if he'd been hit by a cannonball. Marty, who'd bought the underwear, had provided it. Marty would hear on TV what it had been used for, and he'd be too scared ever to talk.

There wasn't going to be anything subtle about this hit. He was going to take both of them out if he could. Then he'd finish off Mickey. Then he'd disappear.

Friends would take care of him after all that. The way they'd taken care of the old man for twenty years. Guys took care of guys who had taken risks to do something right. With Bob and Christie out, Mickey out, and himself disappeared, guys would take care of him. It was a shame it had to be so messy. Nobody liked that. But it would be *done*—that was the point—and he'd have been a sharp guy, who'd done what was necessary.

The only thing he was sorry for was that he couldn't take out Carlo while he was at it.

He wasn't good at waiting. Sitting in the car was too suspicious. Some citizen might come along and wondered why a guy was sitting in a car at night. Some citizen might even call the cops. Johnny got out and walked. He did not amble; he walked briskly, as if he knew exactly where he was going. He rounded the block and returned. Three times. The house remained dark.

Dammit! He wanted to catch them as they came in, not have to bang on their door.

Then the car came. He was still driving the Mercedes, even if it did have bullet holes in the seat. Actually, *she* was driving it. She turned off the street and into the driveway.

The garage door went up. *Damn!* A radio-controlled

garage door. Christie drove into the garage, and the doo
closed.

Johnny hurried across the street. He ran to the fron
door. The lock was not simple. He rang the doorbell and
knocked. They didn't answer. But the lights came on
over the door and on the front lawn. A moment later a
siren began to scream.

Johnny ran. He left the stolen car sitting on the stree
and walked out of the block. A black-and-white came
The cops inside didn't see him. He was just far enough
away. He walked six blocks and caught a bus.

5

He recovered the Ferrari from a parking lot where the
attendant knew how to appreciate a car like that. He
drove home. His night wasn't over. His telephone was
ringing when he entered his room. He let it ring and
didn't answer. He sat down to watch television. Fifteen
minutes later the phone rang again.

"Johnny? Carlo. I wanta talk to you. Be here in fifteen
minutes."

So. Summoned. They didn't even come for him
weren't waiting in the dark outside the garage. The
called him, confident that he would come, like a
obedient dog, to take whatever punishment they had for
him.

So, okay, Carlo. Johnny Discount is no dog. Live or
die, by God, Johnny Discount is no dog.

He fortified himself with half a tumbler of whisky
then drove downtown, jump-started a Dodge van, and
drove to the warehouse. He pulled up to the door and
honked the horn.

The doors swung back, and he drove inside.

Frank was waiting.

"Where's the man?" Johnny asked.

Frank smirked. He pulled a pair of handcuffs from his pocket. "Strip down, Johnny," he said.

As Johnny stepped down from the van he shoved the muzzle of the Desert Eagle toward Frank and pulled the trigger. The huge gun roared and spat twelve inches of flame as muzzle flash. The enormous slug blasted Frank's torso wide open. Shock energy lifted him from the floor and threw him backward.

Johnny turned the gun toward the office. He fired three times. The big slugs tore through the wall and through whatever was inside.

Sal ran out of the bathroom, pistol thrust forward. Johnny fired and missed, fired and missed, but caught him in the leg with his third shot. With his leg all but torn off, Sal writhed and screamed on the floor. Johnny stepped closer and finished him with a shot in the back.

He opened the door of the office. Carlo lay in a spreading pool of blood.

Johnny Visconti—Johnny Discount—smiled. So. "Greetings from Cleveland," he muttered.

He backed the van out of the warehouse and drove back toward another lot where he had left the Ferrari. Cleveland didn't need to know what happened to Carlo. No one would guess that Johnny'd whacked him out.

FIFTEEN

1

The next day was Sunday, and Columbo decided to take a day off. A man needed time to think, to try to match things together. He couldn't be on the run all the time.

Anyway, he wanted to work on his car. He'd bough another can of the plastic stuff that was supposed to be good for patching up a car body. You took a file and wen around the rusty edges of a hole, then put tape over it then smeared the plastic on with a putty knife. When i set, you could sand it smooth and match it in with the steel, so when you painted over it, it would look smooth so that you really couldn't tell where the patch was Anyway, that was the theory, what the instructions said Of course, he'd never had the car painted, so the patche remained gray. What was more, the plastic stuff devel oped pits, making the patches look something like gol balls.

He decided to wash the car first. Also he wanted to patch a hole in the canvas top, where rainwater had bee leaking in.

Mrs. Columbo had gone to church, and afterward she was going to stop by a market and pick up a few items. That was fine. He'd have time to do all this work before she suggested they go to the beach or for a drive.

Casual in a pair of wash slacks and a shirt that had gotten so scruffy he guessed he couldn't wear it to work anymore, he puffed on a cigar as he taped the rent in the top and sang quietly to himself:

> This old man, he played one.
> He played nick-nack on my thumb.
> With a nick-nack patty-whack,
> Give a dog a bone.
> This old man came rolling home.

Well . . . nothin' ever went the way you expected. He'd got the tape on the canvas and had just dragged out the hose to wash the car when Martha Zimmer pulled into his driveway.

"Hey, Columbo, why don't you answer the phone?"

"Day off. Besides, most of the calls are for Mrs. Columbo. People'd expect me to remember whatever they said and tell her when she comes home, or write it all down, which is a nuisance. Anyway, out here I can't hear it ring."

"What you doing?"

"Takin' care of my car. You know my idea: if you take good care of a car it'll take care of you. There was a hole in the top. Can't have rainwater drippin' on the seats. Also, after I wash it, I'm goin' to patch that hole in the fender."

"Why don't you have it painted, Columbo?"

"I oughta. I really oughta."

"I've got something for you."

"You on duty today, Martha?"

"Oh, no. I always drive a department car and carry a gun, like to the grocery store. Passing by your desk, I saw you had an envelope from Dave Gould. I figured you'd want it toot dee sweet."

"Right," said Columbo. "Even on my day off."

She handed him the manila envelope. Inside was the FBI report on the fingerprints lifted from the shot glass handled by Johnny Corleone.

FEDERAL BUREAU OF INVESTIGATION

Fingerprints Records Division

Notice: This confidential report is offered to the requesting law-enforcement agency for its exclusive use.

Requesting agency: Los Angeles Police Department

The fingerprints submitted with your request, wire-photoed to this office, are those of one Giovanni Visconti, aka Johnny Visconti, aka Johnny Discount.

The subject was born in Cleveland, Ohio, on June 1, 1966. He completed eight years of public schooling, one year of which he completed at the Fairfield County Industrial School, an institution for juvenile offenders.

He has a criminal record as follows:

Arrested Cleveland, Ohio, August 8, 1985, aggravated assault. Pleaded guilty to simple assault and was incarcerated in the Cuyahoga County jail from August 8 to September 7, 1985.

Arrested Cleveland, Ohio, December 10, 1985, grand larceny. Charge dropped.

Arrested Cleveland, Ohio, February 11, 1986, aggravated assault. Convicted May 3, 1986, entered Mansfield Reformatory May 12, 1986, paroled January 21, 1988. Granted final release from parole, May 5, 1989.

No subsequent arrests.

The subject is regarded by the Cleveland Police Department as a "made" member of the local crime family, allegedly headed by one Don Antonio Samenza.

The subject holds a United States passport and visited Italy in 1987 and 1988.

Columbo handed the report to Martha, and she scanned it. He began to run water on his car.

"Tell ya what, Martha. As long as you're on duty, why don't ya wire this report to Castellano in Milan? Also, don't we have a photo of Johnny? If we don't, ask Cleveland to wire us a mug shot. Wire that along to Castellano, too."

Martha smiled over the report. "Interesting," she said.

"We're bein' beat up in the papers, for not comin' up with Regina's murderer. You see this morning?"

She nodded. "Hey. Be glad we don't have that triple homicide that came down last night. Be glad we're tied up with the Regina case, or we might have got that Lucchese shooting."

"I'm glad I don't have to look at those bodies," said Columbo. "Kinda thing that happens when people carry guns."

Martha grinned. "Speaking of which, where's your Beretta?"

"It's in the house. Am I supposed to have it on me while I'm washin' my car?"

"Just so you haven't lost it."

"I haven't lost it. I know exactly where it is."

2

Adrienne Boswell had driven all the usual players away from the pool tables. The Monday-noon customers at Burt's had decided they would rather sit and watch her play. Their interest was not subtle. When she leaned over the table to make a shot, she presented a rounded bottom to them—covered only with well-stretched white slacks.

Besides, she was a good player. She chose shots they would not have attempted and was giving the skilled Columbo a challenge.

"You were right about the chili," she said. "I'll never forget it. Not within the next seventy-two hours anyway."

"Not everybody appreciates it," Columbo said.

"Anything interesting happening?"

"Well, one thing. You bein' a journalist and all, what do the dates February 18 to February 21, 1992 mean, i anything? I mean, if we're talkin' about something that happened in Brazil."

"My God! Don't tell me something connects the meeting in Brazil with—"

"What meeting in Brazil?" he asked.

"Maybe no meeting in Brazil. It may not be anything at all. It may be a rumor. But the story is—Well, you've heard of the Appalachian meet in 1957. I mean the time the godfathers of Costra Nostra all got together and the cops descended on them. Okay. They never risked that again. But the rumor is that they do meet from time to time. The last time is supposed to have been in Brazil in February of 1992."

"That's interestin'," said Columbo. "Looks like that nine-ball shot is pretty near impossible, stuck on that rail like it is—unless I can kiss the cue ball off the eigh when I shoot the seven and . . ." He squinted at the layout of balls and shook his head.

"Five dollars says you can't."

"Well, now . . . Five dollars is a lot of money."

"Five dollars to your two," she said.

"Ma'am—I mean, Adrienne. You tempt me. I guess have to try it."

He chalked his cue, letting blue chalk dust drift down on his raincoat. He bent close to the table, sighting his shot down the length of his cue. He shot, gently, sending the cue ball slowly toward the seven. It struck the seven, then took its English, struck the eight lightly, caromed toward the nine, hit it, and drove the nine off its impossible position frozen on the bottom rail.

"Brr-inging in the sheaves, brr-inging in the sheaves," Columbo sang happily as he sank the eight and nine easily. "Here we go rejoicing, brr-inging in the sheaves."

"You bastard!" Adrienne laughed. As she handed him a five-dollar bill, she bumped her hip against his. "I should know better than to play a hustler."

"I cheat," said Columbo. "I practice."

Burt and his regulars laughed.

3

When they emerged from Burt's, into the midday sunlight, Adrienne reached impulsively for Columbo's hand. She drew him closer to her and planted a quick but firm kiss on his mouth.

"Columbo . . . Why don't you come to my place to-night? For dinner. I cook meaner than I shoot pool. We ought to have got to know each other better when we were in Italy. But— Tonight? Say about seven?"

He ran his right hand through his hair, as if to smooth the unruly mop. "Jeez, I'd sure like to, Adrienne," he said regretfully. "But, y' see, Mrs. C. has asked her brother to come over to dinner tonight, bringin' his wife, of course, and she drinks too much, and it'd just be awful awkward if I wasn't there. Besides, he's makin' her special lasagna, with a lot of Greek olives in it, which is her particular way of makin' it. And—"

"Sure," said Adrienne. "*Hasta la vista,* baby. Another time maybe."

"Hey! Listen, I can call and ask her to add another person to the party."

Adrienne smiled. "Columbo, you're something else again. We'll keep in touch, huh?"

"Oh, absolutely. Wouldn't think of doin' anything else."

4

Mickey Newcastle walked on the beach at Santa Monica. He'd asked Joe Fletcher, the agent, to meet him there because he didn't want Joe to see his shabby flat. For the moment his step was springy, and he walked happily in the sand. My God! Some young people still recognized him! Two even asked for his autograph.

"You see? Not everybody has forgotten me," he said to Fletcher.

"Nobody said you were a has-been," said Fletcher.

The wind off the ocean lifted Fletcher's fine white hair, so that it undulated like a field of grain in a summer breeze. That annoyed him. He didn't like the beach.

"What do you think of my proposition?" Mickey asked.

"I talked to four possible publishers. I'm a little surprised, but they'll buy. *Regina: The Inside Story!*"

"'By the man who knew her best,'" Mickey added.

"Did you really know her best?" Fletcher asked skeptically.

"I knew her in every possible way."

"Did you know who her 'grandfather' was?" Fletcher asked, putting an inflection on the word that was not quite a sneer but conveyed his meaning clearly: that the old man in the house was not Regina's grandfather.

"I knew he wasn't her grandfather," said Mickey. "The old boy had money, I mean a *lot* of money. He—"

"Are you going to tell who he was in the book?"

"I don't *know* who he was. I know he was the boss man. At first, anyway. Regina *belonged* to him."

"Are you going to make a guess about who he was?"

"Why do we say 'was'? The old man's gone, not dead. And, yes, I'll make a guess about who he was. I think he was a Mafia don, retired. I'll say that. I'll say she slept with him. That ought to titillate the readers."

Fletcher nodded. "I haven't suggested you to any television people. There might be a better offer for a TV appearance than for an article or a book."

"We're talking about big money, right?"

"We're talking about a quarter of a million."

"With that I can get started again. You know, I can really get started. The latest thing is the nostalgia kick. I mean, Peter, Paul and Mary came back. The Beatles— what's left of them—are back. I—"

"You got a problem they don't have," said Fletcher.

"I can lick it. If I've got money, I can go into a clinic."

"Well— Okay, Mick. You're serious about this thing. When you're going to see somebody, you gotta be clean."

"What am I now?"

"Between hits," Fletcher said dryly.

"Give me twelve hours' notice, and I'll be like I am now. Man, I was functioning for Regina. The night when— I was working on plans to improve the show. I can function."

"I'll be in touch, then. In a day or three."

"Great! Uh . . . look, Joe. I need a little money."

"You always need money."

"Everybody needs money. Don't you? Look, I lost my meal ticket. Regina gave me— Anyway, you're talking about a quarter of a million. Give me a thousand advance. That's all I need. You'll get it back. Plus your commission on a quarter of a million. That's real money."

Fletcher sighed loudly. "All right. You'll have to come

to the bank with me. I don't carry a thousand around.
My car's up there."

They walked toward the highway.

"Identifying the old man would be a real coup,"
Fletcher said. "If I could assure people that you will
make a reasonable ID on him, we could maybe double
the price. Somebody else is working on it, you know.
Why don't you talk to Lieutenant Columbo? Putting
what he knows together with your observations, the two
of you might come up with something. If we could bill
you as the man who identified Regina's 'grandfather' for
the police, the sky's the limit on what we might make out
of the deal."

5

His life was a series of fine adjustments. For a while
after he shot up, he was good for nothing much. He
didn't deceive himself. When he was afloat in euphoria,
he did not function. After he came down, he could have
a good day. Until— Until the craving began, until the
shakes began. He knew the good times were getting
shorter. The shakes came sooner. And before they came
this time he had to talk with Lieutenant Columbo.

He was lucky. The lieutenant had returned his call
promptly. He had told Columbo about his talk with
Fletcher, and the lieutenant said he would stop by
Mickey's flat later in the afternoon. He could hold out
that long. This evening he'd have to shoot what he had
left of what he'd copped after he mugged the Hispanics.
Tomorrow, in his good time, he'd have to go downtown
and cop.

He showered and shaved. He made a sandwich and
ate. He drank a can of beer.

He heard the knock on the door. Okay. He was ready.
He opened the door.

"Hi, Mick." It was Johnny.

"Uh . . . Come in, Johnny. Come on in."

"You're looking prosperous. Inherit something? Or did you pull off another mugging?"

"A man has to clean up sometime."

"Right. Clean up. You could mean that two ways."

"What can I do for you, Johnny?" Mickey did not want Johnny here when Lieutenant Columbo arrived.

"I been thinking about our eyewitness. Never came out of the woodwork. I figured we'd get a blackmail demand, since obviously whoever it was didn't talk to the cops."

"How could anybody blackmail us?" Mickey asked. "We don't have any money. The old man walked away and left us high and dry."

"Right. Well . . . I tell ya what I'm thinking of doing. I'm thinking it might be a good idea if I left town. Y'know? They're gonna close the house, then lease it to somebody else. So— You gonna be okay, Mick?"

Mickey understood the implication behind the question. He grimaced. "I don't know. What am I going to do for money?"

"You wanta go with me?"

"Where you going?"

Johnny shrugged. "Say, Mexico."

Mickey shook his head. "I've got to start making a living again. I can't just be a parasite on you."

Johnny nodded. "Well . . . I tell ya what, Mick. I said I'd do what I could for ya. So here's some stuff. It'll keep ya for a while. And here's five hundred bucks. It's the best I can do."

"I appreciate it," Mickey said quietly.

"Okay. If anybody asks about me, don't tell them I said anything about Mexico. Uh— Somebody at the door."

Mickey opened the door. Columbo.

"Mr. Newcastle. And, ha, Mr. Corleone, too." He had a lighted cigar in his mouth. He took it out. "I remember you don't mind my smokin' in your apartment. Okay?"

"Okay. Come in."

Johnny was on his feet. "I was just leaving," he said. "Is there anything I can do for you, Lieutenant?"

"No, sir. You've been very helpful already. I hope I'm not runnin' you off."

"Not at all. I'd just stopped by to see how Mickey's doin'."

"Well—"

Johnny stepped outside. His red Ferrari was parked just ahead of Columbo's Peugeot.

"That's a nice car," Columbo said.

"Right."

"Oh, say. There is one little thing I'd like to ask. I keep comparing things, y' know, and trying to match fact with fact, tryin' to make some kind of sense out of everything. There's one point that bothers me, and maybe you can help me out."

"I hope I can, Lieutenant."

"Well, y' see, you told me you didn't go to bed until maybe half-past two. You also said that the last guests didn't leave until about that time. But the medical examiner says that Regina drowned between one and one-thirty. If that's so, she'd have been lying at the bottom of the pool for an hour or an hour and a half, while you were still up and there were still guests in the house. How can you explain that?"

Johnny turned up the palms of his hands and shook his head. "When we wanted a party to end, wanted to suggest people leave, we started turning off lights. Usually the first ones turned off were the underwater lights in the pool. I went to the switch panel and turned them off. I don't know what time that was, but after that the pool would have been dark. She could have been in the water, and nobody would have seen her—not unless somebody went out and looked down in the water."

"Ah. Well, I thank you very much," said Columbo. "Ya see how I have to try to resolve certain anxieties."

Johnny nodded. "If you need anything more, give me a call," he said as he unlocked the Ferrari.

6

Columbo sat down in Mickey's living room, and Mickey explained why he had called him.

"Even if I knew the answer, I couldn't tell ya," Columbo said.

"If we put together what you know and what I know, we might come up with something," Mickey suggested.

"I know he was not Vittorio Savona and he was not Angelo Capelli," Columbo began. "I know he had passports in both those names. I know he came to live in the Italian village of Marino di Bardineto, about 1986. That was Regina's hometown. He bought her, so to speak, and eventually brought her to the States. I got a suspicion he was a drug dealer."

"I don't think so," Mickey said.

"Why not?"

"You know I'm a user. So was Regina, on a much smaller scale. There was always stuff in the house. If the old man was a dealer, why'd she have to send Johnny and me downtown to cop for her? You always take a chance on stuff you get downtown. If he had a source, why didn't we get it from him?"

"He was retired."

"He'd never lose all his contacts. He could have got us stuff if he'd been able. I don't think he was in that business."

"Then what?"

Mickey shook his head. "He was not a lonely old man. Apart from what he had with Regina, he had friends. They came to see him."

"Who?"

"I don't know. Men his age. Men younger. I wasn't

supposed to see them. But I did. They treated him with a certain deference. The old man was *somebody*."

Columbo nodded. "D'ya mind if I use your bathroom?"

"Uh— Go ahead. You'll find some stuff in there. You already know about it, so what the hell?".

Columbo went in the bathroom. Sure enough, lined up at the edge of the basin were—he counted—twenty-one vials. He picked one up and dropped it in his raincoat pocket.

"Change the subject," Columbo said when he returned to the living room. "When did you first meet Johnny?"

"He was always around. When I met Regina, he was there. He was always where she and the old man were, never away from them. I never knew him to take a vacation."

"Was he always the houseboy?"

"Lieutenant! He was never a houseboy. I don't know what he was, exactly, but he was never a houseboy."

"What you gonna say about him when you do this article or television show?" Columbo asked.

Mickey shook his head. "Nothing."

"Why not? Isn't the relationship between him and Regina interesting?"

"Why do you figure?" Mickey asked.

"You tell me."

"I'm afraid of him."

PART FOUR

Rugguet

Rueguetton

Reguetton

SIXTEEN

1

"Good news, Columbo." Captain Sczciegel encountered Columbo between the parking garage and his desk on Tuesday morning. "You can close the Regina case. We've got the murderer in custody."

"Who is it?"

"Ever hear of a fellow named Edgar Bell? He went to jail for ninety days last year under the stalker law. He'd stalked Regina for months, until we finally caught up with him. Last night he turned himself in. About four this morning he signed a confession. The chief calls the case closed."

"Has he released the story to the news guys and gals?" Columbo asked.

"The chief's calling a news conference for ten o'clock."

"Don't y' think it would have been polite to call me?"

"Oh, I would have, but it came in on the midnight-to-eight watch, and they didn't even call me. I found out about it when I came in. You got the information as fast as I could get it to you."

"Have you talked to the guy?"

"Not yet. Waiting for you."

Columbo stared for a moment at the cigar in his hand. It had gone out, and he dropped it in his raincoat pocket. "If I were you, I'd call the chief and advise him to hold up that announcement for a little while. I mean, we wouldn't want the chief to look bad, would we?"

"Hope you're right, Columbo. If we don't close this case pretty damned soon, the chief may bounce us off it and put a new team on. But I'll call."

2

Edgar Bell sat quiet and disconsolate in an interrogation room. He wore a handcuff on his left wrist; the other cuff was locked to a steel ring set in the table.

"Sure doesn't look like a murderer, does he?" Captain Sczciegel said to Columbo as they looked at Bell through a window before they went in.

"They never do. You been in this business as long as I have. You ever see one that looked like a murderer? Our job would be easy if murderers looked like murderers. All we'd have to do is go out on the street and pick up the guys that looked the part."

Edgar Bell was a slight man of late middle age. He'd been crying, and his eyes were damp and red.

Sczciegel entered the room first. "Mr. Bell, I'm Captain Sczciegel of the homicide squad. This is Lieutenant Columbo, the detective in charge of the investigation into the death of Regina Savona."

Bell's head was down. He stared at the handcuffs that bound him to the table, and he did not look up. "When I read that Lieutenant Columbo was on the case, I knew I might as well turn myself in," he said. He looked up at Columbo. "I've heard of you, Lieutenant."

"That's flatterin', I guess," said Columbo.

Sczciegel sat down. "Why don't you just tell us the story? You've been read your rights, and you've signed a confession, so you can't hurt yourself by telling us exactly what happened."

"The thing of it is, I loved her," said Bell. "She knew I did. She loved me a little, too. I know she did. I saw her every time I could. I went to every concert I could get a ticket for. I was there that night at the Hollywood Bowl. She was *so beautiful,* so marvelous. I loved her so much. She could sense it and kept looking for me in the audience. Finally she found me, and I caught her eye, and she winked at me! I could tell she—"

"She didn't want you following her," said Captain Sczciegel. "You went to jail for that."

"I wasn't a stalker!" Bell said indignantly. "I never meant to harm her."

"Go on, then."

"She didn't invite me to her party. She never invited me to her any of her parties. But I went. I waited until late, when maybe most of the others would be gone. I came in over the fence. And there she was! She was sitting by the pool. And she was *naked!* She was a vision of loveliness."

"So how'd the lady get dead?" Columbo asked.

"I walked toward her, smiling in a loving way. But she was afraid of me. She jumped up and backed away. I'm afraid she'd had more than a little to drink. She backed off the edge of the pool and fell in. She couldn't swim! I couldn't swim. She sank."

"Why didn't you call for help?" Sczciegel asked.

"I wasn't supposed to be there. I was afraid somebody would think I'd pushed her in, or something. I . . . After all, I'd gone to jail for—" He shook his head and began to weep. "I didn't hurt her! I couldn't have. But I am the cause of her death. I'd rather it had been me."

"There's somethin' wrong with your story, Mr. Bell," said Columbo. "What about the bloody robe? How'd all that blood get on her robe if you just stood and watched her sink?"

"It was already bloody," he sobbed. "I don't know where the blood came from. Maybe it wasn't hers."

"And she just drowned, and never even screamed, huh?"

Bell shook his head. "No. She didn't scream. It was like I told you."

Columbo looked at Sczciegel. "Good thing the chief didn't announce a news conference."

"What's that mean?" asked Bell. "What are you going to do to me?"

"If it was up to me, you'd go to a psycho ward," said Columbo. "What you confessed to is the way you got it out of the newspapers and off television, not the way it happened."

"What's wrong with the way I told it?"

"In the first place, there was no bloody robe," Columbo said.

"Well . . . well, maybe I didn't remember that part of it right. Robe? No. In fact, I never said there was a bloody robe. *You* said it! You sucked me into saying that!"

"I could suck you into sayin' half a dozen other things that wouldn't be right. You weren't there, Mr. Bell. You just weren't there."

3

Lieutenant Billy Low was at his desk in the narcotics squadroom. He was a compact, balding man with a reputation for being humorless and unbending. "Where'd you get this stuff, Columbo?" he asked. "I'm not going to give you our analysis till you tell me."

"Gimme a break, Billy. That stuff's got to do with the Regina murder. If you arrest the guy I got it from, it could foul up the investigation."

"Has the guy got any more of it, do you know?"

"I wouldn't be surprised," said Columbo.

"If he does, the first time he shoots up this stuff, he's a dead man. What we've got here is speedball. You know: a mixture of cocaine and heroin. That's heavy stuff. But it's got worse in it. This stuff is laced with digitalis. Not just a little, either. Tell me he's not a dealer. Tell me this mixture isn't getting loose all over town."

"He's a user. And excuse me, Billy, but I gotta get to him before he shoots the stuff—if he hasn't already."

Columbo bolted into the hall. "Sarge!" he yelled at the first uniformed man he saw. "Got a black-and-white handy? Gotta make an emergency run, siren and blinky lights!"

"What's the deal, Lieutenant?"

"I'll tell ya when we're movin'. Let's go! We may be too late already."

4

The sergeant didn't drive Columbo but sent him with two officers in a black-and-white, screaming across the Santa Monica Freeway. This was the kind of police work Columbo did not like. It was too dramatic, too nerve-racking. He sat in the backseat behind the prisoner screen, gnawing on an unlighted cigar.

They came to a screeching halt on the street in front of the building housing Mickey Newcastle's flat. An emergency squad wagon coming from the other direction arrived within half a minute. It pulled out, and the paramedics jumped out and followed Columbo to the door, carrying cases of equipment.

Columbo puffed as he mounted the wooden steps to Newcastle's door. "I'm gonna knock once. If he doesn't answer, break down the door. Got it?"

"Your responsibility, Lieutenant," said the older of the two officers. "We got no warrant."

"Whose responsibility if the guy's dead?"

Mickey Newcastle wasn't dead. He opened the door and stood blinking at the sunlight. "Wha'? Wha'? Lieutenant Columbo! What's going on?"

"That stuff in your bathroom. You know what I mean. You shot any of it?"

"Lieutenant! You said—"

"I said I wouldn't bust ya for possession. And I'm not. I took the evidence yesterday, without a warrant. But I had what I took analyzed by the narcotics lab. Mr. Newcastle . . . that little vial of powder, supposed to be speedball, had enough digitalis in it to stop the heart of a horse."

Mickey staggered backward. "No!"

"Where'd you get it, Mr. Newcastle?"

Mickey turned and threw himself on his couch. He shook his head. "How do I know where I got it? You get it from guys. Who are they? I don't have any regular supplier."

"Whoever supplied you this came close to killing you, Mr. Newcastle. Now, either someplace downtown there's a guy you don't know who's sellin' deadly poison speedball, or you got a special source of this who's got some reason for wantin' you dead. My idea is, it's got somethin' to do with the murder of Regina Savona. You got any idea it might have somethin' to do with that?"

"You mean to say somebody is trying to murder me?" asked Mickey.

Columbo turned down the corners of his mouth. "How you figure? Guys cut dope with all kinds of stuff— sugar, soda, flour, plaster, even rat poison. But why would a dealer cut speedball with digitalis? It doesn't save him any money, and it's gonna kill his buyer, for sure. Hmm?"

Mickey Newcastle covered his face with his hands. "What will you do for me, Lieutenant?" he asked.

"What ya got in mind?"

"Well, right now— If you'd gotten here ten minutes

later, I'd have shot some of that stuff. I need it. I need it bad. Right now. I need one clean shot, Lieutenant. Then I can tell you things. I know things I can tell you, things you want to know. But why should I? I'm on the verge of going into convulsions."

Columbo sighed and shook his head. "No matter what you're goin' into, Mr. Newcastle, I can't supply you with a fix. I haven't got the stuff, and if I did, I couldn't give it to you."

Mickey stared at Columbo and smiled sadly. "Do you remember the old Wolfman movies, Lieutenant? Lawrence Talbot was the werewolf, bitten by a werewolf and turned into one."

"Yeah, I remember," said Columbo.

Mickey went on, his breath shortening. "Larry Talbot would beg the doctor—'But doctor, you don't understand. When the moon is full, I turn into a *wolf*!' And of course the doctor never understood and would just pat him on the shoulder and say, 'Now, now, Mr. Talbot.' Nobody understood but the old gypsy woman, played by Maria Ouspenskaya. *She* understood."

"Mr. Newcastle—"

"Nobody who hasn't been to the gates of hell like I have can understand it. In a few hours, I'll turn into an animal. Maybe you can't give me a fix, just one safe fix. But you can put me in a detox program. If you just lock me up, in hours I'll be climbing the walls! You've got no idea what it's like to go cold turkey."

Two paramedics and two police officers had stood just inside the door and heard all this.

"One of you guys get on the radio and call Lieutenant Billy Low. Tell him I need him here, fast!"

5

"Columbo, you've gotta be out of your mind! I can't give this guy a fix!"

"Billy— Just one. Just one time, so he doesn't go into withdrawal before I get some answers out of him."

Lieutenant Billy Low stood outside Mickey Newcastle's flat, staring through the door at the woebegone man sitting on the tattered couch. "The best I can do is get him on a methadone maintenance program."

"Which'll take time," Columbo protested. "By the time we get him to a doc and get that started, he'll be writhing around thinkin' things are crawling on him."

Billy Low shook his head emphatically. "You can't ask me to take something out of the evidence lockers and let him shoot it. Be reasonable, Columbo."

"Yeah. Well . . . No harm in asking, was there? Look. I'm gonna arrest him on a serious charge. I want him to cooperate, and I think he will, providin' we promise him he won't just be locked up and left to go cold turkey. Can you promise he'll be taken care of? I mean, put in detox."

Low nodded. "I can do that."

"Then let's talk to him."

Columbo led Billy Low into the flat. Mickey stood.

"Mr. Newcastle, this is Lieutenant Billy Low of the narcotics squad. I asked him to come talk to you."

Wide-eyed and alarmed, Mickey shook hands with Billy Low.

"Mr. Newcastle," said Columbo, "I'm gonna have one of the officers place you under arrest. The charge will be interfering in the investigation of the murder of Regina Savona. They'll give you your rights and so on, so don't say anything now. Right now, the point is, you're goin' to jail. Billy Low has promised me, and he'll promise you, that you'll go to a hospital ward and be treated for addiction, not just locked up."

Tears flooded Mickey's eyes. He began to tremble.

Billy Low frowned hard. "I promise what Lieutenant Columbo said. We'll put you in a detox program, so you won't have to go cold turkey. Now— I want something from you. That stuff you've got is deadly poison. You have any more of it?"

Mickey nodded. "I'll give it to you."

"Where'd you get it?"

"Where I got it, there's no more. Somebody mixed it especially for me."

"You mean somebody tried to kill you?" Billy Low asked.

Mickey's voice broke. "Yes," he whispered. "No doubt about it."

6

Mickey went into the bathroom to get the vials of speedball—leaving the door open. He'd noticed that one vial was missing, and he'd suspected Columbo had taken it. Damned good thing he did, too.

Twenty vials. His stash. It would have taken care of him for more than a month—except that the stuff in nineteen of the twenty would have taken care of him permanently. Johnny had brought twenty. Just one vial was left from Mickey's own supply. It was lucky that when Columbo grabbed one, he'd grabbed one of Johnny's.

Mickey picked up the one that was his own and stuck it in his pants pocket. He gathered up a double handful of the rest and took them out to hand over to the narc. "There's more," he muttered and went back to get another double handful.

"I'll make the necessary arrangements," Billy Low said.

Mickey nodded. He spoke then to Columbo. "Before I . . . have to go, I have to go. You know what I mean? I don't think I could get downtown without having an accident."

"Uh . . . you wouldn't have it in mind to harm yourself or somethin', would you?"

Mickey managed a faint smile. "I don't think you could cut your wrists, or your throat, with a Gillette Sensor razor. Anyhow . . . no way."

"Okay, Mr. Newcastle. I trust ya. Don't be too long."

Mickey closed the bathroom door this time. He took the vial from his pocket and quickly mixed it with water. He needed one final shot. He needed to be sharp when they interrogated him.

7

"He put one over on you, Columbo," said Billy Low. They had returned to headquarters in Billy's car. Mickey had come in with the uniformed officers. By the time they met again, Mickey was dreamy, floating on his fix. "He had to go to the bathroom, alright, but not to use the toilet."

"It may be okay," said Columbo. "By the time he needs another one, you'll have him established in a detox program, methadone or whatever. I need to talk to the guy. He wouldn't have been much good to me if he was shakin' with D.T.'s."

"Well— After you get his mug shots and fingerprints, you can have him delivered to the hospital." Billy shook his head. "It's disgusting how damned happy they get."

"He'll be coherent enough so I can talk to him by this evening, I figure," said Columbo. "Anyway, I thank ya, Billy."

Captain Sczciegel stopped Columbo in the hall between the narcotics squad room and homicide. "Hey, Columbo. Martha's looking for you."

"That woman can find out anything," said Columbo. "Gonna have to promote her."

"Right. Look, uh— Explain to me this charge you've placed against Mickey Newcastle."

"Preliminary charge," Columbo corrected. "I'm prob'ly gonna charge him with the murder of Regina."

"You can make that stick?"

"Good enough to make him talk."

"Did he really do it?" Sczciegel asked skeptically.

"He had somethin' to do with it."

"I'd like to be there when you question him."

"You got it."

"Columbo— Where's your Beretta?"

"I didn't bring it this morning. I don't figure I should carry it around till I have a chance to get some bullets and get out to the range and shoot it a few times."

"Is it wrapped in a bath towel and stuck on the hat shelf in your hall closet?"

"Right. That's where it is, temporarily."

"Columbo . . . Dammit!"

8

As Captain Sczciegel had said, Martha was waiting to see him. She pulled a chair to his desk and sat watching him, bemused, as he scanned a stack of memoranda and bulletins and casually tossed them one by one into the trash. She was not impatient. She knew Columbo would need no more than half a minute to dispose of departmental paperwork.

"Poop from the group," he said as he glanced at papers and tossed them.

"I've got poop from the FBI, from Bob Brady," she said.

Columbo scooped up half a dozen more sheets and tossed them without scanning them. "What's Brady got for us?"

"The boys from Brazil."

"Already?"

"Columbo, there's something you and I have gotta understand. In Rio they never heard of you or me, or of the Los Angeles Police Department either—and what's more couldn't give a damn. But about Regina— About *that* they give a damn. People are stumbling all over themselves to help us find out who killed her."

"I never been so important," said Columbo.

"Brady called. You were out trying to save Newcastle. So he sent this over by messenger." She handed Columbo a memorandum from Brady. "A list of guys who flew into Rio from the States on February 18, 1992. Recognize the names? Get the drift?"

Columbo ran his finger down the memorandum, reading the names. Each was followed by a sentence or two identifying the subject, but Columbo didn't need the explanations; he knew most of the names.

Of the notorious Five Families of New York, four of their chiefs had entered Brazil on February 18, 1992. *"Capi di tutti capi,"* Columbo muttered. "New York, New Jersey, Philadelphia, Boston, Cleveland, Detroit, Chicago, L.A. . . . And look at this: even Albanese from Palermo."

"Bigger than the Appalachin meet," said Martha.

"And our old man, supposed to be Vittorio Savona, was there. It's no coincidence, Martha. The old man was at the meet. I been sayin' he was *somebody*. Well, he was."

"Keep reading, Columbo. You haven't come to the most important name."

"Who could be more important than—? Uh-oh! Giovanni Visconti!"

"Johnny," said Martha.

SEVENTEEN

1

As promised, Mickey Newcastle was in a hospital, not in jail. For all the difference it made. He might as well have been in jail. The four-bed ward had barred windows and a barred door. What was worse, on his right ankle he wore a steel shackle attached to a chain that was bolted to the bed frame. He wore a rough white hospital gown stenciled with the word PRISONER. It was open in back, and he could not possibly have walked out wearing it.

He was one of four men chained to their beds in that ward. One was recovering from a gunshot wound. The others were like him: jailed addicts going through detoxification and in varying stages of discomfort. He watched them closely. They were going through what he would be going through shortly.

"Better than cold turkey," a big black man said to him.

"Anything's better than that," said Mickey.

He was not surprised when Lieutenant Columbo ap-

peared at the barred door and the attendants admitted
him to the ward. A taller man accompanied the lieutenant, a man distinguished by a head as bald as a cue ball,
as the Americans liked to express it.

Two ward attendants came in. Unceremoniously, they
wheeled the other men's beds to the front wall and
Mickey's bed to the window. Then they surrounded the
bed with screens and pulled in two chairs.

"Mr. Newcastle, I'd like you to meet Captain
Sczciegel," said Columbo as he sat down. "He's my
boss."

Mickey nodded. It didn't seem appropriate to say he
was glad to meet the captain.

"How're they treatin' ya?" Columbo asked.

"Alright. I had that fix you know about. When I start
coming down, that's when we'll see how they'll treat
me."

"You've been told your rights, haven't you? Okay.
Then you know you don't have to talk to us. You have a
right to a lawyer, too—at public expense if you can't
afford one. But if you're willing to talk, then I'd like to
run this little recorder here and make a record of what
you say."

Mickey shrugged. "It's alright with me."

"Okay. But before you consent, let me tell you one
more thing: I'm chargin' you with murder."

2

For a long moment Mickey Newcastle covered his face
with both hands.

"I think you killed Regina," Columbo went on. "I
don't think you did it all by yourself. I think somebody
else was in on it. In fact, I suspect you were just a helper.
I also got a pretty good idea who you were helping."

Mickey shook his head. "Why me?" he asked hoarsely.
"What makes you think *I* did it?"

"To start with, you're an addict. You've got a very expensive habit. You'll do just about anything to get the money to support your habit. Right?"

"Exactly what do you have in mind?" Mickey asked apprehensively.

"You stole from Regina," said Columbo. "She put a safe in her bedroom because you'd been stealin' money. You told me she reduced what she was payin' you. That was because she was taking back what you'd stolen from her."

"Stealing is one thing. Murder is quite another."

"Right. That's certainly true," said Columbo. "And lying isn't the same thing as murder, either; but the lie you told me and persisted in made me suspicious of you from the beginning."

"What lie?"

"About the man in the red nylon jacket."

"Why is that a lie?"

"For two reasons. You told me you had to go 'way down the balcony to get a view of the diving board. And that's right; you couldn't have seen a man bang into the diving board just by looking out your window. What you also would have had to do was walk more than halfway to the end of that balcony—which you didn't do."

"What makes you believe I didn't?"

"Because to get far enough out on the balcony to see the diving board, you'd have had to go past the door to the little crosshall that makes it possible for people in the front guest rooms to get out on the balcony. And you didn't. There was an eyewitness to the murder standing at that door, staring."

"Bob . . . or Christie?"

Columbo smiled faintly and nodded. "Christie. She's terribly nearsighted without her contact lenses, but she'd have seen you go by. She's so nearsighted that she couldn't identify you down by the pool. But she's not so nearsighted she couldn't have seen a red jacket—and she didn't see any red jacket."

"It's her word against mine." Mickey didn't sound very confident.

"True."

"I don't think you've got much of a case against me, Lieutenant, now that I think of it."

"Maybe. But there is one more thing I need to ask you."

"What?"

"Who's been tryin' to kill you?"

3

Mickey shuddered.

Captain Sczciegel, who had kept silent and solemnly listened all this time, spoke now. "You'd better answer that one, Newcastle."

"I got a pretty firm idea who," said Columbo. "But suppose you tell me."

Mickey Newcastle closed his eyes and seemed to be exerting great effort to control himself and stop shuddering. He shook his head convulsively. Then he drew a deep breath and muttered, "I don't know."

"C'mon, Mr. Newcastle. Of course you know. Okay, let's come at it another way. Why would anybody want to kill a nice fellow like you? Why would somebody serve you a cocktail of speedball and digitalis?"

"Why do you think?" Mickey asked weakly.

Columbo turned up the palms of his hands, lowered his chin, and looked up at Mickey from under his eyebrows. He smiled. "The only reason I can think of is, to shut you up. And what is it you could talk about that would be so harmful to somebody that he'd kill you to prevent your tellin'? Pretty simple, I think. It took two people to drown Regina, because she was a strong swimmer. You and somebody else. That somebody else tried to kill you. And he'll try again if you get outta here."

"Lieutenant Columbo's the best friend you've got, Newcastle," said Captain Sczciegel. "You're *alive* because of him. I wouldn't forget that if I were you."

"We've got enough on Johnny to pick him up," Columbo said. "You think he's gonna protect you?"

"What you're asking me to do is confess to murder," Mickey whispered tearfully.

"Well . . . only if you did it," said Columbo.

Mickey pressed fingers to his eyes and squeezed out tears. "It was Johnny," he sobbed. "And me. The two of us."

"Why did Johnny want Regina dead?"

"He didn't. It was the old man that wanted her killed, and I don't know why."

"Which raises the big question again," said Columbo. "Who was the old man?"

"If I knew, I'd know where to find him. He promised Johnny and me a million dollars to kill her. Then he cut out and disappeared, and we didn't get our money. My share was to be $250,000. I had plans. I was going to check into a private detox clinic, then rebuild something of my career."

"You were *had,* Newcastle," said Captain Sczciegel. "You couldn't trust either one of your partners."

4

"Gotta grab a quick lunch," said Columbo as they left the hospital. "I know a place that serves great chili. Why don't ya join me, Captain?"

"I've heard of the place," said Sczciegel. "Which is why I think I'll just grab a sandwich and take it to my desk. You go on. I'll get a warrant for Johnny Visconti. Once we get him in and booked, you can take over the questioning."

"Well, I—"

"Go on, Columbo. Have your chili. You can't go out

and make the collar. You don't have your sidearm with you."

Columbo grinned. "I'll make a point of—"

"Sure you will. I'll see you a little later."

He drove to Burt's and pulled into the little parking lot. And there she was: Adrienne Boswell, coming across the lot, handsome and elegant in a miniskirted iridescent blue dress, smiling broadly as her heels click-clicked on the asphalt.

"Columbo!"

"What a coincidence."

"Coincidence, hell. I've been waiting in this parking lot for half an hour, on the chance you'd show up for your noontime chili and pool. You're late."

"Uh, a little. I had some business."

"I need to talk with you. How about letting me drive us to a place where we can have a better lunch than this? I know nothing can match Burt's chili, but I'd like a few minutes' privacy."

"Well, I don't have an awful lot of time to spare."

"I'll bring you back within forty-five minutes."

Once in her BMW, she told him something she considered nauseating. "You know what's going on? There's a market for anything that belonged to Regina, especially clothes, especially underwear, especially things she'd worn and had not yet had laundered. A pair of panties that smells of her sweat is worth five or six thousand dollars."

"If anything like that's bein' sold, Johnny's found himself a profitable little sideline," said Columbo. "Or maybe Rita. That is . . . supposin' the stuff is authentic."

"Humanity never ceases to amaze me," said Adrienne. "I guess that's why I like my job."

"It's one of the reasons I like mine," Columbo agreed.

The place with a better lunch was a dimly lighted private club, where customers sat with a considerable degree of privacy in heavy oaken booths served by topless waitresses. Adrienne smiled slyly and said, "I sort of thought maybe you'd relax better in a place like this."

Their waitress knew him. "Hey, Columbo," she said. "Fancy seeing you here." She was a tall, well-built young woman with red hair obviously made redder with dye.

"Hiya, Aggie," he said. "It's been a long time."

"You told me I'd learn a trade. How's this for a trade?"

"It isn't what I had in mind. But—"

Aggie grinned at Adrienne. "The lieutenant and I are old friends," she explained. "He had me sent to Fontera. I did thirteen months." She grinned at Columbo. "Good behavior."

"You keep it that way, Aggie."

"Right."

When she had gone off to the bar for their drinks, Columbo shook his head. "In my line of work, you meet just about every kind."

"Mine, too," said Adrienne. "I recommend the hamburgers here. Big, thick, and juicy."

"Sounds good."

"I understand you've arrested Mickey Newcastle. Fact?"

"Who says?"

She smiled. "I'm a *journalist,* Columbo. I have sources, and I can't disclose my sources."

"I'd like it kept quiet until we get another guy in jail," said Columbo.

"Johnny Visconti."

"You know too much."

"I'm like you, Columbo. The only way I can do my job is to scurry around, getting a fact here and a fact there, until it works into some kind of pattern."

"I talk too much," he said.

"Au contraire, mon ami," she said. "You don't talk enough. Off the record, why did Johnny Discount kill Regina?"

"It comes back to the old man we tried to identify in Marino di Bardineto. Mickey says the old man wanted her killed and offered a lot of money to the guys who undertook to do it."

"I have a suggestion for you," said Adrienne. "There's a lot of excitement in town, because of the Carlo Lucchese murders. That was a mob hit, pure and simple. Talk is, there'll be a retaliatory hit. Or maybe that *was* a retaliatory hit. The old man disappeared. He was almost certainly connected. Maybe—"

"I get ya," said Columbo. "As if this case wasn't complicated enough. If we could just figure out who the old man *was*—"

"I've got a present for you," said Adrienne. She took a manila envelope from her shoulder bag and handed it to him.

Inside he found two photographs. One was of Regina getting off a small private jet. Behind her, scowling at the camera, was the old man. The second was an enlargement, blowing up the face of the old man as much as could be done from a small negative.

"Newspaper morgue files," she said. "An AP photographer took that four years ago. Don't ask me who the old man is, because I don't know. But it's picture enough to put up in post offices."

"Yeah, right."

"Notice how small he was. He wasn't nearly as tall as Regina. But look how he carries himself. Cock of the walk."

"He swam every day," said Columbo. "Even when he was eighty years old, or whatever he was."

"Short hair. Square face. Damn, he looks like *somebody!* I can't place that face, but when this picture runs in fifty newspapers, I bet you somebody identifies him."

"I wanta circulate it on the wire, to police departments," said Columbo.

"Okay."

"I thank ya for this, Adrienne."

She nodded. "You see? I'm not such a bad type. You and I work well together, Columbo."

He grinned. "Maybe I could get you a job with the police department."

5

Johnny's telephone rang. The caller was Marty, the guy who'd bought what he thought was Regina's underwear.

"Hey, Johnny! You got any more of that stuff? I can sell as much as you can supply."

Johnny pondered. He had decided to lam. When they found Mickey—and this time they'd *for sure* find Mickey—they'd suspect him immediately. Well . . . If he was going to beat it out of town, he might as well sell Marty her real stuff.

"There's no more of the soiled stuff, Marty. I can bring you some that's been laundered."

"Not worth near as much."

"Okay. I'll see what I can find. We'll figure a price when you get a look at it. Wanta meet me in front of Grauman's Chinese at four?"

"Right. Sure. Oh, say, Johnny. Uh . . . I don't know how to ask this exactly, but Saturday night somebody blew away three guys with a .44 magnum. I don't wanta know if— Well, you know what I don't want to know. But I'd like to be sure you don't have that cannon anymore."

"You think I'm stupid?"

"No. No, I don't. Deep-sixed, I bet. I needed the assurance. See ya at four."

Johnny put down the telephone. Stupid. Yes, he'd been stupid. No, he hadn't deep-sixed it. That Desert Eagle was the finest gun he'd ever seen. It was damned effective. Nobody would come looking for it. He wasn't a suspect in the killing of Carlo and his flunkies. He didn't have a motive—not one that the cops could find. Or the boys, either. Hell, even Dirty Harry hadn't had a gun like this. And there was something about it that just wouldn't let him get rid of it, even if that would have been the smart thing to do. When a man had something as good as that, he just couldn't toss it off a pier.

He packed. He didn't have much to take. The money He had a nice hunk of money. Some clothes. And he stuffed two pillowcases with Regina's underwear. His stuff fit in a two-suiter bag and an overnight case Everything fit in the Ferrari.

He backed out of the garage and started down the driveway, without a twinge of nostalgia for leaving the house. If he'd ever felt anything for the place, he'd los those feelings long before the night he killed Regina.

The private guard sat in his car. Johnny blinked hi lights at him. The guard waved and grinned.

Then— Two black-and-whites, lights flashing, screeched into the driveway. Four cops with guns drawn trotte toward the Ferrari.

EIGHTEEN

1

Dressed in loose blue coveralls, wearing handcuffs attached to a belly chain, plus leg irons, Johnny sat dejected on a steel folding chair. He was not frightened by the trappings of arrest and imprisonment. He'd been strip-searched and shackled before, and it wasn't so scary once you knew what to expect. He was not frightened, but he was worried. He had much to think through and no time to think. Lieutenant Columbo was coming to interrogate him, and he knew now that the lieutenant was no easy man to fool. He needed time to straighten some things out in his mind, and he wasn't going to have time.

The big thing was, they were charging him with the murder of Regina. They couldn't make that stick, he was confident. Their case had to do with discrepancies about the time when this happened and that happened and what he'd said. They couldn't hang a murder charge on that.

Which was what worried him. They wouldn't have

charged him if that was all they had. They must have something else.

Like, why had they arrested him as Giovanni Visconti? How'd they know? How'd they found out? What did they think the significance of it was?

Another thing. They'd found the Desert Eagle when they searched the Ferrari. But would they relate it to the deaths of Carlo and his two thugs? There was no reason for them to identify that .44 magnum as the gun that killed Carlo and Frank and Sal. Of course, if they did—

So here they were. His tormentors.

Lieutenant Columbo was not as dumb as he looked. He'd shed that stupid-looking raincoat for once, and seeing his suit sort of explained why he always wore the raincoat. The gray suit didn't fit him very well, and it needed pressing. And, his necktie. The narrow end hung out below the wide end. My God, how old did a man get before he learned to tie a necktie? Actually . . . Yeah. Suddenly Johnny understood. Columbo didn't care. Or— His mind was fixed on other things.

The fat broad. Detective Martha Zimmer. She was still in the process of proving herself, Johnny judged. So she was thorough—methodical and thorough. She knew the book and went by it.

"This is Captain Sczciegel." Columbo nodded at the tall, bald man in shirtsleeves. "He's my boss."

The fourth person was the stenographer. Johnny had agreed to talk with the detectives and let them make a record of what he said. The stenographer was pretty: a luscious little blond with beautiful hair. She looked at him thoughtfully, and Johnny sensed the electricity. He didn't much care about the chains, which were only temporary anyway; but he sure wished *she* didn't have to see him that way. He tried to return her signal, but she turned her eyes away . . . because of the handcuffs, for sure, because of the handcuffs and belly chain and leg irons. *Damn,* he wished she didn't have to see them!

"We'll go on the record, miss," said Sczciegel, nodding at the girl.

She began to work her Stenotype.

"You've been given your rights, Visconti, so you know you don't have to talk with us. I looked over the inventory of what you were carrying when you were arrested, and obviously you're not without money to hire a lawyer. You don't have to talk with us until your lawyer arrives."

Johnny smiled. "Captain Sczciegel," he said in his best calm, rational voice, "I've got no problem about talking with you. This is all a mistake, and I know you'll make it right as soon as you figure it out."

He knew this was the way to handle the situation. If he were smooth and cooperative, they'd get the idea they had to act civilized, and civilized cops weakened their cases.

The stenographer was looking at him, putting his words on her tape. Johnny gave her a warm smile.

"Alright," said Sczciegel. "This is Lieutenant Columbo's case, so he'll ask you the questions."

2

Columbo sat on a steel chair like the one Johnny sat on, and he leaned forward, put an elbow on his knee, and cupped his chin in his hand. For a long moment he stared at Johnny with a look of half-amused skepticism.

Captain Sczciegel and Martha Zimmer sat on wooden chairs with writing arms. The stenographer sat on a folding chair. Her Stenotype machine stood on its own sturdy tripod.

"Mr. Visconti—"

"Can I ask one question?"

"Sure."

"What makes you think I'm Giovanni Visconti?"

Columbo smiled. "Well, are you?"

"What makes you *think* I am?"

"Only that your fingerprints match the fingerprints of Giovanni Visconti, also known as Johnny Discount. The FBI made the match for us. The Ohio Bureau of Criminal Identification made it also."

"So, okay. That's my real name. Visconti. Regina knew it. I called myself Corleone because—" He smiled and shrugged. "You know. The book, the movie. Anyway, Corleone is the name of a town in Sicily. I could use it if I wanted to. Legally."

"You're not charged with illegal use of a name," Sczciegel said dryly.

"Incidentally," said Martha, "I think we ought to inform you that some other charges will be filed. Specifically, grand larceny. You were carrying about a quarter of a million dollars in cash, and—"

"That's mine," Johnny interrupted curtly. "I didn't steal a penny of it." He turned and spoke to Columbo. "We've already gone over the fact that Regina gave me cash. I lived in her house and didn't spend much. That's what I saved over six years."

"Well, you were carrying something else you didn't save and was definitely not yours." Martha picked up her statement. "A collection of women's underwear and some other items of clothing. Ordinarily, a bunch of used clothes wouldn't make grand larceny, but it seems there's a market for Regina memorabilia, which makes that property worth a lot of money."

"I took some souvenirs," Johnny confessed weakly.

"I think you stole something else." Columbo shifted and sat erect. "Off the old man. That wristwatch, the Vacheron Constantin watch. When I met the old man, he was wearin' a watch. I couldn't say it was that one. But *you* weren't wearing one. Shortly after, you are wearing that valuable watch."

"I've had it for years."

"Yeah? Well, let me look at your wrists. And I'm

gonna ask Captain Sczciegel to push his watch back a little and let us look at his wrist. See? His arm's tanned. But he's got a white stripe around his left wrist, where the sun doesn't reach because the watch blocks it. If you'd been wearing that watch for years, you'd have a white stripe."

"Except for one little thing, Lieutenant. When I went swimming in the pool or went to the beach, I didn't wear the watch."

Columbo shrugged. "Got a point," he conceded. "But it won't wash. Vacheron Constantin is a very expensive and very unusual watch. When we check the serial numbers with the company, we can probably trace it."

3

A uniformed officer rapped on the door of the interrogation room and signaled to Columbo through the glass. Columbo got up and went out.

"Lieutenant McCloskey would like to see you, sir."

"Where is he?"

"Just down the hall. He thought you wouldn't want your suspect to see him."

"Sharp thinkin'," said Columbo. He walked down the hall a few paces. McCloskey was waiting in another interrogation room. "Hiya, Bert."

"Hey, Columbo! Whatcha doin'? Closing up the Regina case?"

"Maybe. And maybe you can help me. And maybe I can help you."

"There you go," said McCloskey.

"Okay. When we arrested Giovanni Visconti, also known as Johnny Discount, also known as Johnny Corleone, he had in his car a .44 magnum Desert Eagle automatic. I understand the Lucchese murders were done with that kind of a gun. It's a long shot, but I'd appreciate it if you'd pick up that .44 and do a ballistics test. It sure would be interestin' if my guy killed Lucchese."

"You got it."

"Quick as possible, okay?"

"I'll do it right now," said Bert McCloskey.

4

"Sorry about that," said Columbo as he sat down again facing Johnny Visconti.

Johnny was feeling aggressive. "You got no murder case against me," he said.

"I wouldn't say that, Mr. Visconti. You see, I got a surprise for you. In spite of your best efforts, you didn't manage to get rid of Mickey Newcastle. He's alive, he's in a detox program, and he's signed a confession."

Johnny failed to conceal his surprise, but quickly he recovered his equanimity and smiled. "Okay, I figured you thought you had something." He grinned and shook his head. "But tell me something, Lieutenant . . . Captain. Do you guys really think a jury will convict a man of murder on the word of a down-the-drain *junkie*? Hell! Mickey Newcastle would confess he killed his grandmother, for a fix. Let me see. You picked him up because he was in possession of a big stash. Instead of sending him straight to jail, where you'd send any other junkie with a big supply, you put him in detox. You did him a favor. He did you one. C'mon!"

"He confessed to details he couldn't have known if—" Sczciegel began to say, until he was interrupted.

"I tell you what," Johnny interrupted. "Go back and check your hospital and police records for Thursday night. You'll find a guy was shot in the leg during a mugging. His girlfriend was with him. Put Mickey in a lineup and let those two see him. How good a witness is he gonna be, fellas?"

"Maybe good enough," said Columbo. "Maybe he doesn't have to be so good. We got other stuff. You've been pretty good about explaining the time when this and that happened. But you can't have been off as much as you say. A neighbor heard Regina screaming at 1:23. He's a neighbor who sometimes got annoyed at the noisy parties she had. He says that night it was awful, but it got quiet by half-past twelve or something like that. Then at 1:23 he heard her screaming. You've said you were working in the house at that time. How could you *not* have heard her screaming, if a neighbor heard her?"

"Maybe I'd gone to my room, to go to the bathroom or something."

Columbo glanced around at the others in the room. "Okay, Mr. Visconti. The maid found the body and called the police. Right?"

"Right."

"Where were you?"

"I was in bed. I'd been up late. I didn't wake up till a cop banged on my door. As a matter of fact, it was Sergeant Zimmer. She went around and knocked on all the doors."

"Then what'd you do?"

"I used the bathroom, got dressed, and went downstairs."

"Did you go out by the pool?"

"No. But I looked out the window."

"Okay." Columbo used a hand to flip his hair back off his forehead. "You've had an easy answer for everything so far. Let's see what your answer is for this. You said you knew I was pullin' some kind of funny on you when I asked you for a blood sample to match some blood found on Regina's terry-cloth robe. You told me you knew there was no blood on that robe. How did you know that?"

"I looked out there and saw it."

"No, Mr. Visconti," said Columbo with an air of

wounded patience. "No, you didn't. Before Sergeant Zimmer came into the house and started waking people up, she'd already had the terry-cloth robe packed in a plastic bag and taken away as evidence."

Johnny closed his eyes for a moment. Then he said, "I don't have a very good memory for little details. Maybe actually I woke up earlier and looked out."

"Sure. You went down the hall, then through the cross-hall, and went out on the balcony so you could see past the palm tree. And got a good look at the robe, while you overlooked the body lying at the bottom of the pool. You tell a jury that," said Columbo.

Johnny lowered his eyes and stared for a moment at his handcuffs. "I guess I'll have to take my chances," he said.

Columbo nodded. "Yeah, I guess you will. I guess we'll just have to put you in jail and let the D.A. develop his case." He stood. "So. Anything you wanta ask, Captain? Martha?"

The two shook their heads solemnly.

"I'll get somebody to take him." Columbo opened the door and looked up and down the hallway. He closed the door. "Oh, there is one more little thing I meant to ask you, Mr. Visconti. One of those things, you know, that kinda sticks in a man's mind and bothers him."

Johnny stared at Columbo, abruptly apprehensive.

"How well did you know a fella named, uh"— Columbo reached into his pocket and pulled out a small note—"named Carlo Lucchese?"

Johnny shook his head quickly. "I never heard the name."

Columbo nodded. "You got that big, powerful gun. They're doin' some ballistics tests on it right now. The slugs fired from your .44 magnum won't match the slugs that killed Carlo Lucchese and a couple other fellas, right?"

"Lieutenant Columbo, what the hell do you want from me?" Johnny screamed.

5

Columbo suggested a short break while someone brought Cokes. Johnny could manage his by tugging his belly chain up and bending forward. He could drink from a can, or scratch his nose if he needed to. Then he needed to go to the bathroom, and two uniformed officers took him to a men's room and unhooked him while he urinated. Back on his chair, he was no longer the confident young man he had been when he had first come in.

While he was out of the room, Captain Sczciegel had grinned at Columbo and said, "Guess the chief can call his news conference, huh?"

Columbo shook his head. "I wouldn't. We know who killed Regina, I think. But we don't know why. And that's what everybody's gonna want to know."

"And the key to that, I suppose, is the identity of the old man who lived upstairs."

Columbo nodded.

"Do you think he knows? I mean Johnny. Does he know?"

"Maybe not. But maybe he thinks he can cut a deal."

Which was exactly what Johnny thought. "What do I get out of it if I give you complete cooperation?" he asked as soon as he was seated again.

"Same thing anybody gets that cooperates," said Columbo. "I'll give the word to the D.A. and the court that you cooperated."

"Meaning nothing," Johnny said bitterly.

"Well, there's the difference between concurrent and consecutive sentences," said Columbo. "And there are different slammers we can send you to. I'm not gonna tell you any of them are fun, but—"

"Ask your questions." Johnny bent forward and raised his hands far enough to rub his eyes.

"You know what the big questions are. Who was the old man? And *where* is he?"

"He wasn't her grandfather," Johnny said.

"Never figured he was," said Columbo.

"He was a big man," said Johnny. "A powerful man. A rich man."

"A drug dealer," said Sczciegel.

"Nothin' like," Johnny sneered. "You always look for the easy answers."

"What was his name?" Columbo asked.

"What'll you do for me if I tell you? Hey! Be real, man! If I tell you and they found out I told you, they'll get me, even inside. I gotta have a better deal. I don't figure on ever gettin' out. But I don't want to die in the joint, maybe beaten to death. Send me where guys that do that kind of thing don't go. Send me to a country-club joint."

"Don't forget, Johnny, we do have the death penalty in California," Sczciegel said.

"You never do it."

"We will. We've got more than three hundred people on death row. You don't have to worry about getting beaten to death there, 'cause you never get out of your cell."

Johnny glanced at the stenographer. "What are you tryin' to do to me? She's takin' this down! There'll be a record of what you said to me."

"Just suggesting you face reality, Visconti," said Sczciegel.

"Well . . . that's up to Johnny," said Columbo. "Isn't it? You want some time to think it over?"

"Yeah," said Johnny. "Yeah. And I guess I better talk to a lawyer."

Columbo nodded. "When you say that, the interrogation is over. I'll have them take you— Wait a minute."

6

Bert McCloskey was at the door. Columbo got up and stepped outside.

"Bingo!" McCloskey laughed. "You've closed my case. Does it close yours?"

"C'mon in and let's see."

McCloskey was a tall white-haired man with a long, jolly face. He was a career man with LAPD, who had started as a patrolman riding in a black-and-white and worked his way up. There wasn't a chair for him, and he stood.

"Mr. Visconti," said Columbo, "I wanta introduce you to Lieutenant Bert McCloskey, a man you may be seeing a lot of. He's in charge of the investigation into the death of that fella I mentioned a while ago: Carlo Lucchese. It seems the bullets fired from your .44 magnum automatic match the ones taken from the body of Lucchese and one of the other men found dead in a warehouse on Washington Boulevard. You'll have your chance to explain to him why that is."

Johnny bent forward and shook with sobs.

"I can't imagine why a man would keep a murder weapon," said Martha. "Wouldn't you think getting rid of it would be the first thing he'd do?"

"There's no understanding it," McCloskey said. "But it happens. You go back through the files, you'll find that in twenty or twenty-five percent of murders with a gun, the murderer still has the gun when we nab him."

"That's because he thinks we won't be able to nab him," said Columbo.

NINETEEN

The way the case had developed suggested to Captain Sczciegel that they should move the questioning of Johnny Visconti to a larger room and bring in a bigger cast of characters. When the interrogation resumed after about an hour, Robert Brady of the FBI was in the room, as was Paul Trevor, resplendent in the gold-trimmed uniform of a deputy chief, LAPD.

Also, they had brought in Mickey Newcastle. Dressed and chained the same way Johnny was, he sat beside Johnny at the conference table. He seemed not entirely to understand where he was and why.

During the hour, Johnny Visconti had given Bert McCloskey a written statement, confessing to the murders of Carlo Lucchese and his two henchmen. By now he seemed totally defeated. He shuffled in his leg irons and seemed to have diminished inside his blue coveralls.

"There's just one thing left in this case," Columbo said when they were all seated around the table and the stenographer was working at her Stenotype. "Who was

the old man, Mr. Visconti? If there's any way at all that
you can help yourself, it would be by telling us who he
was and where he is."

"He's dead," Johnny muttered.

"Are you confessing to a *fifth* murder?" Sczciegel
asked incredulously.

"Carlo killed him."

"Who *was* he?" Columbo persisted.

"He was Jimmy Hoffa."

2

Johnny sat hunched, the corners of his mouth turned
down, and watched them express their skepticism, vo-
cally or with frowns and shaking heads.

"What good does it do me to tell you that, if it isn't
true?" he asked.

"Jimmy Hoffa died twenty years ago," said the rotund
Chief Trevor.

"Really?" asked Johnny. "Where's the body?"

"You tell us," said Columbo.

"It's at the bottom of the San Pedro Channel. In an oil
drum filled with concrete."

"Where of course we can't find it, so what you're
saying can't be proved," said Chief Trevor with a gesture
of contempt and dismissal.

"It makes no difference to me if it can be proved or if
you believe it," said Johnny. "It doesn't lay anything
more on me—or take anything away."

"Why did he want Regina dead?" Columbo asked.

"That's the one thing I don't understand exactly,"
said Johnny. "It was stupid. He insisted he was gonna
get rid of her, even when we told him it was a bad idea.
He told us when to do it and how to do it, and he was
gonna pay us very well. Hey— If Mick and I hadn't
taken the job on, he'd have gotten somebody else. He'd
made up his mind. How could I have stopped him?"

"You must have some idea why," said the deputy chief.

"Yeah. He made her what she was, with his money and influence. She owed him everything. Face it, Regina had no great talent—except for bamboozling him and a hell of a lot of other people. Jimmy *paid* for her buildup. He called in favors to get her bookings. Without him she wouldn't have been anything, and he didn't think she was grateful enough."

"Pygmalion—" Martha suggested.

"What about jealousy?" Columbo asked. "She, uh, distributed her favors pretty widely."

Johnny nodded. "Yeah. He was jealous. Not so much if she was gettin' something out of it—I mean, advancing her career, getting herself something he didn't have to pay for. But . . . other guys—" Johnny shook his head. "He didn't know about Regina and me. Can you believe it? She slept with that old man every night, almost—a lot of times after she'd already been with me. When I first knew them, he was still very able, I think. She could make any man able. Lately . . . I don't know."

"Threatened in his manhood," said Sczciegel. "What'd he expect at his age?"

"She didn't make things any better by the way she got to treating him. It was one thing for him to pretend to be her grandfather, but it was something else entirely for her to call him 'gran'pa,' which she did.

"What about a money angle?" Columbo asked.

Johnny nodded. "He was supposed to get a percentage of everything she made. I don't know what percentage, but I heard him talk to her about it. He got in his head the idea she was cheating on him, cookin' the books. It preyed on his mind. He got so he actually hated her. Hey, he got so he hated everybody. He got bitter, very bitter, toward the end."

"I think," said Columbo, "that what we better do is start at the beginning. I think you better tell us everything you know about that old man. Maybe there are things we can check out. And after a while we'll be able to tell if he was Jimmy Hoffa or he wasn't. I guess you could be wrong about it, couldn't you?"

"I suppose I could. I knew him for more than six years. I was told he was Jimmy Hoffa, and I always believed it. Anyway, it won't do me any harm—or any good—to tell you what I know."

3

"Start with this," said Johnny. "The old story is that Jimmy Hoffa was murdered in the parking lot of the Red Fox Inn in Detroit on July 30, 1975. Over the years a lot of guys have said that was bullshit. Why would anybody have wanted to kill him? They just didn't want him taking control of the Teamsters Union again. Hey. Jimmy was a great man for his members. They loved him. They had better wages, better safety, better perks; and if Jimmy had made himself a millionaire, that was strictly okay with them."

"He didn't live like a millionaire," said Brady.

"He had enough brains not to," said Johnny. "Anyway, while he was in the slammer, some other guys had taken over the Teamsters and were skimming off the dough, and they didn't want Jimmy comin' back.

"One of the guys who didn't want him back was Anthony Provenzano—Tony Pro. He was a connected guy, ya know, and the head of a big local in New Jersey. He had soldiers. He sent some to Detroit. They didn't kill Jimmy. They snatched him."

"And hid him out for twenty years?" asked Chief Trevor. "C'mon!"

"So don't believe it! Makes no difference to me."

"Go on with the story," Columbo urged.

Johnny smiled wanly at the rumpled but solemnly listening Columbo. "The one smart guy in the room. He wants to hear the story. Okay. Tony Pro was waiting in a

house in Grosse Pointe. The guys took Jimmy there, and
Jimmy and Tony sat down for a talk. Tony Pro explained
to Jimmy that there was no way he was going to get loose
and stand for election again. No way. To the bottom of
the lake first. On the other hand, Jimmy could have
an honorable retirement. Well, they talked. And they
talked. I heard they talked all night."

"Where were you when this was going on?" Brady
asked.

"Man, when this was goin' on, I was nine years old! I
was *told* about all this. By others, but some of it by
Jimmy himself. Anyway, they made a deal. Jimmy was
to turn over to Tony Pro all the money he'd skimmed off
the union, in return for which Tony Pro would support
him in style for the rest of his life. Jimmy gave over the
names and numbers, and what I hear Tony Pro collected
from Jimmy's accounts was $12,000,000. A week or so
later, he had Jimmy flown to Acapulco, where he would
have the whole top floor of a luxury hotel.

"This upset Jimmy's calculations. He'd figured Tony
Pro would put him in Vegas and he'd live like Howard
Hughes—until he figured out a way to get loose. Acapul-
co was somethin' else. Jimmy didn't speak Spanish.
Most of the guys that guarded him spoke nothin' but. So
there he was."

"How'd he get from Acapulco to Marino di Bardineto?" Sczciegel asked.

Johnny jerked on his chains, frustrated in an effort to
make a scornful gesture. "I'm comin' to that," he said.
"Jimmy'd handed over $12 million, but he had a lot of
other money that Tony Pro didn't know about—some of
it overseas. Also, he had friends. He had friends that
would have whacked out Tony Pro in a minute if they'd
even *suspected* he was holding Jimmy Hoffa prisoner. You
see, Tony Pro was a captain in the Genovese Family. The
Gambino Family—later the Gotti Family—was one of
the families that wouldn't have liked it a bit. Sam

Giancana wouldn't have liked it either. And so on. I don't know how Jimmy got his hands on some of his money, but he did. He bribed Tony Pro's guards, and they looked the other way while he got the word out.

"It took a while. Meantime, something else happened. In 1979 Tony Pro went to the slammer in California. He died there in 1988. From 1979 on, Jimmy could do whatever he wanted to."

"Like come back," Brady suggested.

Johnny shook his head. "By then he didn't want to. His wife was sick and didn't have long to live. He told me he loved her, but he figured it would do her more harm than good to have him rise from the dead. Besides, it was very convenient to be 'dead.' Nixon had pardoned him for some crimes; but if he hadn't been 'dead,' he'd have been asked to explain where some millions of dollars went. Anyway, he'd acquired some new tastes. All his life he'd lived—what's the word?"

"Abstemiously," said Brady.

"That's the word. But when Tony Pro set him up in Acapulco, he gave orders that Jimmy was to have the best of food and wine and liquor—and lots of nice young broads. Hotel living bored Jimmy. He indulged. He found out there were things in this world besides living with one wife and fighting your way up in a union. He decided to stay 'dead.'"

"He had forged passports," said Columbo.

"Right. He had friends and money. He left Mexico and flew to Palermo, with a Brazilian passport. In Sicily he lived in a villa: a guest of the Honored Society. He called in his IOUs—and he had a lot of them; he'd used his political clout to help guys, better'n he was ever able to use it for himself. Guys came to visit him, from all over. He knew an awful lot about a lot of people. He still knew what strings to pull. He did important favors for some powerful guys, and they did important favors for him. He lived very well in Sicily. He enjoyed it.

"But it's not wise for a guy like him to stay too long in one place. He wears out his welcome. Things get more expensive. So in 1986 he moved to Marino di Bardineto. And that's where he met Regina."

"So how do you get into the story?" Columbo asked.

"Regina . . . Jimmy was in his seventies by then, and she was a gift of the gods. The guy fell for her. What she wanted more than anything else was to come to the States. It wasn't wise for Jimmy to come back here, but she talked him into it. I think she could have talked him into anything. He contacted friends in the States and told them what he wanted to do."

"Was he already thinking about making her a star, or just about coming to the States?" asked Columbo.

"She was the only reason he was coming. She firmly believed there was nothing Madonna did that she couldn't do better, and Jimmy believed her. He was no better judge of talent than she was."

"She didn't need talent," mumbled Mickey Newcastle. "We built a great show for her."

"Let's get back to the question of how you got into the act, Mr. Visconti," said Columbo.

"I was Jimmy's bodyguard," said Johnny. "More than that, I was supposed to keep track of everything he did and report it to the right people. Wherever he went, somebody was watching him and watching out for him. I was the inside man."

"Why you?"

"They didn't want anybody from Detroit. That raised a possibility—not a big possibility but a possibility—that somebody might make the connection, make the identification. I'm from Cleveland, of the Samenza Family. Don Antonio Samenza assigned me to Jimmy. Jimmy paid me. After Regina and I got close, she gave me money, too."

"So you went to Italy and met him."

"I took him his new passport. He entered the States as

Angelo Capelli. Capelli 'disappeared,' and Jimmy became Vittorio Savona."

"You went to Brazil with him," Columbo said. "What was that for?"

"If you know we went, you have to know why. A big meet. Jimmy was still an important man."

"You say Carlo Lucchese killed him," said Columbo. "Why?"

"In every town where he went, I had to get in touch with a contact man, and he kept in touch with the dons. When we came to L.A., the new contact man was Carlo. Carlo was a stone killer, and he strangled Jimmy. It was because he'd done something so stupid in having Regina killed that the dons didn't trust him anymore. They must have been afraid of what he'd do next. Besides, he wasn't useful anymore. He was out of touch. He'd got to be a . . . What's the word?"

"An anachronism," said Martha.

"What could he have done next that would have been so bad?" Columbo asked.

"Got himself identified," said Johnny. "He'd been a big asset to some families and not to others. Some important guys went behind bars because of information Jimmy supplied—information that some way got in the hands of district attorneys. In fact, there's a rumor Jimmy had his revenge on Tony Pro by handing tips to the Gambinos. If the wrong people got the word that Jimmy had been alive all those years, talking up a storm, it might have broken the peace."

"So," said Columbo. "You got four life sentences comin'."

"The rest of my life, for damned sure," said Johnny. He lowered his head and tugged his hands up to his face. "And I'm not yet thirty," he whispered. "But— Hey! You guys gotta protect me inside! They'll get me! They'll kill me. Not an easy way, either. You gotta take care of me."

"Sure. We'll do our best," sneered Chief Trevor.

4

Adrienne Boswell caught him as he was unlocking the Peugeot—a cumbersome process involving working the key in and out to just the right depth in the lock, then jiggling it back and forth until it caught the tumblers and made them move.

"Hey, Columbo! How 'bout a game or three of nine-ball before you go home? You gotta let a girl get even."

She was wearing tight stonewashed blue jeans, and her red hair fell over a white golf shirt.

As they shot pool at Burt's, the local evening news appeared on the television set high on the wall. The sound was turned off, but the picture was on, and the first picture was of Mickey Newhouse and Johnny Visconti in chains.

"Okay, Columbo," said Adrienne. "Who was the old man?"

He told her. A confirming picture appeared on the screen.

"How long have you known?" she asked.

"About an hour."

Adrienne stared at him for a protracted moment, frowning, shaking her head. "There was *no way* you could have given me a scoop on that, was there?"

"No. Sorry. No way."

She sighed. "You s— Okay. Five bucks says I can sink the nine-ball on this shot."

"Five says you can't."

She flipped back her hair so it would not interfere with her aim. The next ball in the rotation was the two-ball, and four balls sat between it and the nine-ball. She shot the two-ball hard against the right rail about a third of the way between the end pocket and the middle pocket, it bounced to the bottom rail and off it to the left rail, which it struck just below the middle pocket, then rolled toward the upper right corner pocket, where it knocked the nine-ball in and won the game for her.

"Brr-inging in the sheaves," she sang as she collected Columbo's five one-dollar bills.

"Adrienne, I think you've played this game before," Columbo said ruefully.

She threw her arms around him and kissed him firmly on the mouth.

"A-humm," said Burt.

Columbo grinned. "When constabulary duty's to be done, to be done," he chanted. "A policeman's lot can be a happy one."

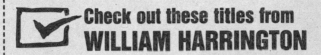